THE PENGUIN CLASSICS

FOUNDER EDITOR (1944–64): E. V. RIEU

PRESENT EDITORS:
Betty Radice and Robert Baldick

Prosper Mérimée

CARMEN
and
COLOMBA

Translated with an Introduction by
Edward Marielle

PENGUIN BOOKS
BALTIMORE · MARYLAND

Penguin Books Ltd, Harmondsworth, Middlesex, England
Penguin Books Inc., 3300 Clipper Mill Road, Baltimore 11, Md, U.S.A.
Penguin Books Pty Ltd, Ringwood, Victoria, Australia

—

This translation first published 1965

—

Copyright © Edward Marielle, 1965

—

Made and printed in Great Britain
by Hazell Watson & Viney Ltd,
Aylesbury, Bucks
Set in Monotype Baskerville

This book is sold subject to the condition
that it shall not, by way of trade, be lent,
re-sold, hired out, or otherwise disposed
of without the publisher's consent
in any form of binding or cover
other than that in which
it is published

CONTENTS

Introduction 7
Carmen 17
Colomba 91

INTRODUCTION

It is one of the ironies of literature that the creator of Carmen and Colomba, two of the most flamboyant, colourful women in world fiction, should have been a man noted for his lacklustre personality, his conservative mode of life, and his chilly reserve.

Prosper Mérimée was born in Paris in 1803, the son of Léonor Mérimée, a mediocre painter and drawing-master who became Perpetual Secretary of the Académie des Beaux-Arts. After an undistinguished schooling at the Lycée Napoléon, which on the return of the Bourbons became the Collège Henri IV, he studied law but never practised it, preferring literature. His literary career opened with a notorious hoax, *The Theatre of Clara Gazul* (1825), a collection of plays allegedly translated from the works of a Spanish actress, and this was followed by a similar work, *La Guzla* (1827), which pretended to be a translation of Illyrian national songs. It was only in 1829, the year in which he brought out his historical novel *Chronicle of the Reign of Charles IX*, that he published the first of the short stories and novellas which have won him enduring fame. For over twenty years he went on publishing these stories in the *Revue de Paris* and the *Revue des Deux Mondes*, combining this creative work with tireless activity as Inspector General of Historic Monuments, a post in which he pioneered the classification and preservation of ancient buildings. Under the Second Empire he became a Senator and occupied a leading position at the imperial court, thanks to his friendship with the Empress Eugénie and her mother, but his literary output ceased after 1854. He died after several years of ill-health, in 1870.

His reputation for coldness was in fact largely undeserved.

INTRODUCTION

True, he was extremely reserved, and the motto which he had engraved on his ring and incorporated in his *ex-libris* was Μεμνησο ἀπιστειν (Remember to be on your guard). But all the evidence suggests that, like the character Auguste Saint-Clair in his story *The Etruscan Vase*, he was 'born with a tender, loving heart', and 'studiously concealed all the external aspects of what he considered a shameful weakness'. Certainly he had a considerable number of liaisons, some of them possibly innocent, others definitely not, with women as different as Céline Cayot, a little actress at the Théâtre des Variétés, and Valentine Delessert, the elegant, cultured wife of the Paris Prefect of Police under Louis-Philippe.

The women who provided him with the inspiration to write *Colomba*, the first of the two stories in this volume to be written and published, were not, however, Parisian actresses or hostesses, but two Corsican amazons. He met them during an archaeological mission to Corsica which he carried out from August to October 1839. In some respects this stay in Corsica was a disappointment and even an ordeal: Mérimée complained bitterly in his letters of the paucity of ancient monuments, the appalling state of the roads, and 'the excessive morality of the Corsican women which is a great trial to travellers'. But there was one great compensation. 'This country is poor in monuments,' he wrote at the end of September 1839, 'but it is nature which has pleased me most of all. I am not talking about the makis, whose only merit is that of smelling very good, and whose defect is that of tearing frock-coats to ribbons. I am not talking about the valleys, nor about the mountains, nor about the scenery, which is all the same and consequently horribly monotonous, nor about the forests, which are rather paltry, whatever people may say, but about the pure nature of MAN. This mammal is really very interesting here and I never tire of listening to tales about vendettas.'

INTRODUCTION

Probably the most remarkable of the hot-blooded natives whom the young Inspector General met in Corsica was the woman whose name and personality he lent to the central character of his great story of the island: 'a heroine, Madame Colomba, who excels in the manufacture of cartridges and is very skilled in despatching them at those individuals who have the misfortune of displeasing her.' Mérimée went on to explain that he had 'made the conquest of this illustrious lady, who is only sixty-five years old, and when we parted we kissed each other in the Corsican manner, *id est* on the lips. I had similar good fortune with her daughter, another heroine, but twenty years old, lovely as the day is long, with hair which reaches down to the ground, thirty-two pearls in her mouth, and magnificent lips, who is five feet three inches high, and who at the age of sixteen gave a tremendous drubbing to a workman on the other side. They call her La Morgana and she is a real fairy, for she has bewitched me.' The old lady mentioned in this letter was Madame Colomba Bartoli, *née* Carabelli, a great shot who had lost her only son in a gun-fight in 1833, and who maintained to all and sundry that his killers had been acquitted only because their judges had been bribed. Her daughter Catherine, who was just as good a shot as her mother, and by all accounts as beautiful as Mérimée claimed, was in fact thirty-one in 1839, not twenty. Like the fictional Colomba, she always wore mourning in memory, in her case, of her brother, and it would seem that Mérimée combined the daughter's passionate grief with the mother's murderous reputation to create his legendary character. It may be doubted, however, whether his acquaintance with the 'bewitching' Catherine ever went beyond a brief, innocent encounter, for in 1843 she married a fellow-countryman who had been her lover for a great many years, and who would probably have despatched any interfering foreigner in a typically expeditious Corsican fashion.

INTRODUCTION

It is interesting to note that the Colomba who has come down to us in Mérimée's story owes something of her character to the intervention of Madame Valentine Delessert. 'I must confess one thing to you,' the author wrote to a friend in 1840. 'At the end of the story I did not follow the plan I traced for myself at first. I intended to depict in *Colomba* that family loyalty which is so strong in your country. Once her father had been avenged, I wanted to show her busy obtaining a fortune for her brother, and I had her organizing a sort of ambush to force the English heiress to marry him. Perhaps it was truer to nature like that. A lady to whom I showed this conclusion said to me: "So far I have understood your heroine, but now I no longer understand her. The combination of such noble feelings with mercenary intentions strikes me as impossible." I have considerable respect for this lady's taste and I therefore carried out the change you have noticed, leaving Mademoiselle Colomba's plans undefined. However, this reproach of unworthiness and mercenary intentions worried me, and it is for that reason that in the final scene I exaggerated the passion of the vendetta.'

Although, by changing the ending of his story in the way suggested by Madame Delessert, Mérimée may have made his heroine less true to life in Corsica, there can be little doubt that he preserved the dignity which is one of her most admirable characteristics.

Colomba was published in the *Revue des Deux Mondes* in July 1840; *Carmen* did not appear until five years later, in October 1845, when it was published in the same periodical. It could, however, be argued that *Carmen*'s origins lay much further back than those of *Colomba*, for if the story of the gipsy girl was written only in the mid forties – Mérimée claimed to have written it 'in a week' in May 1845, but he probably began the rough draft in 1844 – the subject of the tale was furnished to the author as early as 1830. This

INTRODUCTION

is known from a letter from Mérimée to Madame de Montijo of 16 May 1845, in which he wrote:

> I have just spent a week shut up writing, not an account of the doings of the late Don Pedro, but a story which you told me fifteen years ago and which I am afraid of having spoilt. It was about a *jaque* of Malaga who had killed his mistress for devoting herself exclusively to the public. Since *Arsène Guillot* I have found nothing more moral to offer to our beautiful ladies. As I have been studying the gipsies with great care for some time, I have made my heroine a gipsy. In this connexion, do you know if there still exists in Madrid a book published by a certain Mr Borrow in *chipe calli* or the language of the Gitanos, entitled *Embeo e majaró Lucas*? It is the Gospel according to St Luke. This man Borrow has written a very amusing book entitled *The Bible in Spain*. It is a pity that he is an arrant liar and a fanatical Protestant to boot. For example, he says that there are still some Moslems in disguise in Spain, and that there was recently an Archbishop of Toledo who belonged to that religion. On the gipsies he says some very curious things, but as an Englishman and a saint he has not seen or does not want to refer to certain features which were worth mentioning. He maintains that the gipsy women are very chaste and that a *busno*, in other words a man who is not of their race, cannot obtain anything from them. Well, in Seville, Cadiz, and Granada, there were gipsy girls in my time whose virtue did not stand up to a *duro*. There was a very pretty one in the *mazmorras* near the Alhambra, who was more cruel but even so was capable of taming down. Most of those women are horribly ugly, which is one of the chief reasons for their being chaste....

This letter provides us with both the origins of *Carmen*, in an anecdote related by Madame de Montijo, and the principal source of Mérimée's information about the gipsies, in George Borrow's works. Mérimée had come to take an interest in the gipsies in 1843, when he had begun writing his *History of Don Pedro I, King of Castile*, which was not to be published until the end of 1847. He had been attracted by the Andalusian legend that Maria Padilla, the queen of

INTRODUCTION

the gipsies, had bewitched Don Pedro; and, although he had been obliged to discount it on discovering that the gipsies did not appear in Europe until a century after Don Pedro's reign, his reading of Borrow's famous books on the gipsies, *The Bible in Spain* and *The Zincali*, had revived memories of Madame de Montijo's anecdote and aroused his storytelling instincts. He may have consulted other works on the gipsies, such as Grellmann's *History of the Gipsies*, but, since all the gipsy words and proverbs which he quotes in *Carmen* are to be found in the appendix to *The Zincali*, it seems probable that he relied exclusively on Borrow.

It is still not known, and will doubtless never be known, why Mérimée thought it necessary to frame his story between a series of remarks on the location of Munda and a long essay on the gipsies. (The passage on Munda prefaced the story when it was originally published in the *Revue des Deux Mondes* in 1845, but the essay on the gipsies and the *chipe calli* was added only when *Carmen* appeared in book form in 1847.) Some commentators have suggested that Mérimée, Inspector General of Historic Monuments and member of both the Académie des Inscriptions et Belles-Lettres and the Académie Française, considered that the only fitting way in which he could offer the public a story of smugglers and gipsies was with an accompanying display of erudition: Chateaubriand, after all, had set a precedent by inserting the touching story of *Atala* in his vast work *The Genius of Christianity*. It is more likely, however, that Mérimée was anxious to maintain his reputation for restraint and reserve, and decided to show, by following the bloody ending of *Carmen* with a scholarly dissertation, that, however much the reader might be moved by Carmen's fate, he, the storyteller, retained an unimpeachable *sang-froid*.

The fact that, despite this chilling anti-climax, *Carmen* has won world-wide popular and critical success is all the

INTRODUCTION

more remarkable. This success cannot be wholly or even largely ascribed to Bizet, though that composer's opera undoubtedly did a great deal to popularize the story; nor does it owe much to what some critics have thought to be an original theme, for there were gipsy stories before *Carmen* and there have been many since, none of which has ever achieved similar fame. The decisive factor would appear rather to be Carmen's character. Unlike Colomba, who acts in complete obedience to tradition and seems almost conventional in comparison, Carmen in the last analysis obeys no law but her own nature. She admits Don José's right, as her *rom*, to kill her, but she refuses to live with a man she no longer loves. 'Carmen will always be free,' she cries. '*Calli* she was born, *calli* she will die.' It is above all else this proud affirmation of total independence and integrity which makes Carmen, thief, prostitute, and liar though she is, one of the noblest and most tragic figures in modern literature.

E.M.

CARMEN

CHAPTER ONE

I HAD always suspected the geographers of not knowing what they were talking about when they located the battlefield of Munda in the country of the Bastuli-Poeni, close to the modern Monda, about five miles north of Marbella. My own conjectures regarding the text of the anonymous author of the *Bellum Hispaniense*, and a little information culled from the Duke of Ossuna's excellent library, had led me to believe that the memorable spot where Caesar played his last game of double-or-quits with the champions of the Republic was to be found in the neighbourhood of Montilla. Happening to be in Andalusia in the early autumn of 1830, I made a fairly lengthy excursion to resolve my remaining doubts. A paper which I shall be publishing shortly will, I hope, leave no further uncertainty in the minds of archaeologists of good faith. In the meantime, until that dissertation of mine finally settles the geographical problem which has the whole of learned Europe agog, I propose to tell you a little tale, which is entirely without prejudice to the interesting question of the whereabouts of Munda.

I had hired a guide and a couple of horses at Cordova, and had set out with no luggage but Caesar's *Commentaries* and a few shirts. One day, wandering across the uplands of the Cachena plain, tired out, parched with thirst, and scorched by a burning sun, I was heartily cursing Caesar and Pompey's sons when, a fair distance from the path I was following, I caught sight of a little stretch of green sward dotted with reeds and rushes. This seemed to suggest that there was a spring nearby, and, sure enough, as I drew nearer, I saw that what I had taken for grass was a marsh, with a stream running into it which appeared to come from a narrow gorge between two lofty spurs of the Sierra de

Cabra. I concluded that if I made my way up it I should find fresh water, fewer leeches and frogs, and perhaps a little shade among the rocks.

At the entrance to the gorge, my horse whinnied, and another horse, which I could not see, whinnied in answer. I had scarcely gone a hundred yards or so before the gorge suddenly opened out, revealing a sort of natural amphitheatre completely shaded by the steep cliffs all around it. It was impossible to imagine a more promising resting-place for a traveller. At the foot of some perpendicular rocks the spring bubbled out of the ground, falling into a small pool lined with sand as white as snow. Five or six fine green oaks, perpetually sheltered from the wind and cooled by the spring, stood on the banks and shaded it with their thick foliage; and all round the pool, a stretch of soft, glossy grass offered a better bed than could have been found in any inn for thirty miles around.

The honour of having discovered this delightful spot did not belong to me. A man was already lying there, and had probably been asleep when I arrived. Awakened by the neighing of the horses, he had stood up and gone over to his own, which had been taking advantage of his master's sleep to make a hearty meal of the grass all around. The man was a strapping young fellow, of medium height, but powerfully built and with a proud, sombre expression. His complexion, which might at one time have been very fine, had been tanned by the sun until it was darker than his hair. In one of his hands he was holding his horse's halter, and in the other a brass blunderbuss.

I must admit that at first the blunderbuss and the fierce expression of the man holding it rather took me aback; but after hearing so much about robbers and meeting none, I had ceased to believe in their existence. Besides, I had seen so many honest farmers arm themselves to the teeth to go to the market that the sight of a firearm gave me no reason to doubt the stranger's respectability. 'What is more,' I said to myself, 'what would he do with my shirts and my Elzevir edition of the *Commentaries*?' I accordingly gave a friendly nod to the man with the blunderbuss, and asked him with a smile if I had disturbed his sleep. Without replying, he looked me up and down; then, as if satisfied by his scrutiny, he looked equally closely at my guide, who was then approaching. I saw the guide turn pale and stop short in obvious terror. 'An unlucky encounter!' I said to myself. But prudence immediately warned me not to show any sign of alarm. I dismounted, told the guide to unbridle the horses, and, kneeling down beside the spring, I plunged my head and hands into it; then I drank a long draught of water, lying flat on my belly, like the soldiers Gideon spurned.*

Meanwhile I watched my guide and the stranger. The former approached very reluctantly, but the other man did not seem to have any evil intentions towards us, for he had set his horse free again and his blunderbuss, which he had held horizontally at first, was now pointing at the ground.

Deciding not to take offence at the scant attention being paid to me, I stretched out on the grass and in a casual tone of voice asked the man with the blunderbuss whether he had a tinder-box on him. At the same time I took out my cigar-case. The stranger, still without saying a word, rummaged in his pocket, took out his tinder-box, and promptly gave me a light. He was obviously thawing, for he sat down opposite me, though without letting go of his gun. Once my cigar was alight, I chose the best of those that were left and asked him if he smoked.

'Yes, Señor,' he replied.

* A reference to the episode in the Book of Judges (VII, 5, 6) where Gideon chooses soldiers who scoop up water in their hands while keeping a look-out for the enemy, and rejects those who drink straight from the stream (Translator).

These were the first words he had spoken to me, and I noticed that he did not pronounce the letter *s* in the Andalusian manner,* from which I concluded that he was a traveller like myself, only less of an archaeologist.

'You will find this one quite good,' I said, offering him a real Havana *regalia*.

He bowed his head slightly, lit his cigar from mine, thanked me with another nod of the head, and then began smoking with every sign of considerable pleasure.

'Ah!' he exclaimed, slowly expelling the smoke through his mouth and nostrils. 'It's a long time since I last had a smoke!'

In Spain a cigar offered and accepted establishes a relationship of hospitality, as does the sharing of bread and salt in the East. My companion revealed himself to be more talkative than I had hoped. Moreover, although he claimed to be a native of the canton of Montilla, he did not seem to be very familiar with the district. He did not know the name of the delightful valley where we were sitting; he could not name a single village in the neighbourhood; and finally, when I asked him if he had seen any ruined walls, broad flanged tiles, or carved stones in the vicinity, he admitted that he had never paid any attention to such things. On the other hand, he showed himself to be an authority on horses. He criticized mine, which was not a difficult thing to do; then he gave me the pedigree of his, which came from the famous Cordova stud. It was indeed a splendid animal, of such endurance, so his master claimed, that he had once covered thirty leagues in a single day, at a gallop or a brisk trot. In the middle of his tirade the stranger broke off abruptly, as if surprised and annoyed at having said so much.

'You see,' he went on with a certain embarrassment, 'I

* The Andalusians aspirate the *s* like the soft *c* or the *z* which the Spanish pronounce like the English *th*. An Andalusian can be recognized by the word *señor* alone. (P.M.)

was in a great hurry to get to Cordova. I had to see the judges in connexion with a trial.' As he spoke, he looked at my guide Antonio, who lowered his eyes.

I was so delighted with the shade and the spring that I remembered that I had a few slices of excellent ham which my Montilla friends had put in my guide's saddlebag. I had them brought along and invited the stranger to share our impromptu meal. If he had not smoked for a long time, it seemed to me that he probably had not eaten for at least forty-eight hours. He ate like a ravenous wolf. I thought to myself that our meeting had been providential for the poor devil. My guide, on the other hand, ate little, drank even less, and said nothing at all, although ever since we had set out he had showed himself to be an incomparable chatterbox. He seemed to find our guest's presence embarrassing, and a certain mistrust kept them apart without my being able to guess the reason for it.

When the last crumbs of bread and ham had disappeared and we had each smoked a second cigar, I ordered the guide to bridle our horses, and I was about to take leave of my new friend when he asked me where I was planning to spend the night.

Before I could catch a sign my guide made me, I had replied that I was going to the inn at Cuervo.

'That's a poor place for somebody like you, Señor. . . . I happen to be going there, and if you will allow me to accompany you, we can travel together.'

'Gladly,' I said, mounting my horse.

My guide, who was holding the stirrup for me, made me another sign with his eyes. I replied by shrugging my shoulders, to assure him that my mind was at rest, and we set off.

Antonio's mysterious signals, his uneasiness, and a few of the things the stranger had said, particularly that thirty-league ride of his and the not very plausible explanation he had given of it, had already formed my opinion of my travelling companion. I had no doubt that I was dealing with a smuggler, and possibly a robber; but what did that matter to me? I knew the Spanish character well enough to feel sure that I had nothing to fear from a man who had shared my food and tobacco. His very presence was a reliable safeguard against any undesirable encounter. Besides, I was glad to have the chance to find out what a brigand was like. One doesn't come across them every day, and there is a certain fascination about being close to a dangerous creature, especially when that creature is obviously tame and gentle.

I hoped that I might gradually get the stranger to confide in me, and in spite of the winks my guide kept giving me I turned the conversation to highway robbers. Naturally I spoke of them in terms of respect. At that time there was a notorious bandit in Andalusia called José-Maria, whose exploits were on everybody's lips. 'What if I were riding beside José-Maria?' I asked myself. . . . I told the stories I knew about that hero, all of them incidentally to his credit, and expressed my unequivocal admiration for his courage and magnanimity.

'José-Maria is nothing but a scoundrel,' the stranger said coldly.

'Is he doing justice to himself, or is this excessive modesty on his part?' I asked myself; for, by dint of examining my companion closely, I had come to see that his appearance tallied exactly with the description of José-Maria which I had seen posted on the doors of many a town in Andalusia. 'Yes,' I thought, 'this is the man: fair hair, blue eyes, a large mouth, good teeth, small hands; a fine shirt, a velvet jacket with silver buttons, white doeskin gaiters, and a bay horse. . . . There's no doubt about it. But let's respect his incognito.'

We arrived at the inn. It was just as he had described it to me, that is to say one of the most wretched inns I had ever seen. One large room served as kitchen, dining-room, and bedroom. A fire was burning on a flat stone in the middle of the room, and the smoke went out through a hole cut in the roof, or rather, it hung in a cloud a few feet above the ground. Along the wall, five or six old mule blankets had been laid out on the floor; these were the beds for travellers. Twenty paces from this establishment, or rather, from this one room which I have just described, there was a sort of shed which served as a stable. In this delightful abode there were no other human beings, at least for the moment, except an old woman and a little girl between ten and twelve years of age, both of them as black as soot and clad in horrible rags. 'And this,' I said to myself, 'is all that remains of the population of the Munda Baetica of antiquity! O Caesar! O Sextus Pompey! How astonished you would be if you came back to earth!'

When she saw my companion, the old woman uttered an exclamation of surprise.

'Why, it's Señor Don José!' she cried.

Don José frowned and raised one hand in an authoritative gesture which silenced the old woman straight away. I turned to my guide and by an almost imperceptible sign gave him to understand that he could tell me nothing I did not know already about the man with whom I was going to spend the night.

The supper was better than I had expected. On a small table one foot high we were served an old cock fricasseed with rice and a lavish addition of peppers, then peppers in oil, and finally *gaspacho*, which is a sort of pepper salad. Three such spicy dishes obliged us to have frequent recourse to a leather bottle of Montilla wine which proved delicious. When we had finished eating, seeing a mandolin hanging on the wall – there are mandolins everywhere in Spain – I asked the little girl who had waited on us if she could play.

'No,' she replied, 'but Don José can, and very well too!'

'Do please sing something for me,' I said to him. 'I am passionately fond of your national music.'

'I can refuse nothing to such a worthy gentleman who gives me such excellent cigars,' cried Don José good-naturedly; and after asking for the mandolin he started singing, accompanying himself. His voice was harsh but pleasing, the melody sad and strange; as for the words, I did not understand a single one.

'If I am not mistaken,' I said, 'that is not a Spanish song that you have just sung. It is like the *zorzicos* I have heard in the Provinces,* and the words must be in the Basque tongue.'

'Yes,' replied Don José with a sombre air. He put down the mandolin, folded his arms, and gazed into the dying embers with a strange expression of sadness. Illuminated by a lamp on the little table, his face, at once fierce and noble, reminded me of Milton's Satan. Like him, perhaps, my companion was thinking of the paradise he had left, and of the exile he had incurred by his wrongdoing. I tried to revive the conversation, but he made no reply, absorbed as he was in his melancholy thoughts. Already the old woman had gone to bed in a corner of the room, behind a tattered blanket hung on a rope; and the little girl had followed her into that retreat reserved for the fair sex. Then my guide got up and asked me to go with him to the stable; but at this, Don José, as if waking up with a start, asked him sharply where he was going.

'To the stable,' replied the guide.

'What for? The horses have been fed. Spend the night here: the Señor won't mind.'

'I am afraid that the Señor's horse might be ill; I would

* The 'privileged provinces', which enjoy special *fueros* or rights: Alava, Biscay, Guipuzcoa, and part of Navarre. Basque is the language of this region. (P.M.)

like the Señor to see him: perhaps he will know what to do with him.'

It was obvious that Antonio wanted to speak to me in private; but I was anxious to avoid arousing Don José's suspicions, and in the circumstances it seemed to me that the best thing to do was to show complete confidence in him. I therefore told Antonio that I knew nothing about horses and that I wanted to sleep. Don José went to the stable with him, returning a little later by himself. He told me that there was nothing wrong with the horse, but that my guide considered him such a precious animal that he was rubbing him down with his jacket to make him sweat, and that he intended to spend the whole night engaged in that pleasant occupation. Meanwhile I had stretched myself out on the mule blankets, carefully wrapped in my cloak so that I should not touch them. After begging my pardon for taking the liberty of installing himself near me, Don José lay down in front of the door, but not before reloading his blunderbuss, which he took care to place under the saddle-bag which served him as a pillow. Five minutes after wishing each other a good night, we were both sound asleep.

I had thought that I was tired enough to be able to sleep even in such an inn as this, but after an hour I was awakened from my first sleep by an extremely unpleasant itching. As soon as I realized what the cause of it was, I got up, convinced that it was better to spend the rest of the night in the open than under this inhospitable roof. I tiptoed to the door, stepping over Don José, who was sleeping the sleep of the just, and managed to leave the house without awakening him. Next to the door there was a broad wooden bench; I stretched myself out on it and made myself as comfortable as I could in order to pass the rest of the night there. I was about to close my eyes for the second time when I imagined I saw the shadows of a man and a horse go by, neither of them making the slightest noise. I sat up and thought I recognized Antonio. Surprised to see him outside the stable at such an hour, I got up and went after him. He had stopped, having seen me first.

'Where is he?' Antonio whispered.

'In the inn, asleep; he isn't afraid of fleas. But why have you brought the horse out?'

I then noticed that in order not to make any noise while leaving the shed, Antonio had carefully wrapped the animal's hooves in the remnants of an old blanket.

'For God's sake,' said Antonio, 'don't speak so loudly! You don't know who that man is. He's José Navarro, the most notorious bandit in Andalusia. All day long I've been making signs to you which you refused to understand.'

'Bandit or no bandit, what does that matter to me?' I replied. 'He hasn't robbed us, and I'm willing to wager he has no desire to do so.'

'Maybe not; but there's a reward of two hundred ducats for anybody who hands him over. I know of an outpost of lancers a league and a half from here, and before daybreak I'll bring back a few stout fellows with me. I would have taken his horse, but he's such a vicious animal that nobody but Navarro can go anywhere near him.'

'Damn your eyes!' I said to him. 'What harm has that poor fellow done you that you should inform against him? Besides, are you sure that he is the brigand you mention?'

'Absolutely certain. Just now he followed me into the stable and said to me: "You seem to know me; if you tell that kind gentleman who I am, I'll blow your brains out." Stay there, Señor, stay with him; you have nothing to fear. As long as he knows you are there, he won't suspect anything.'

While talking, we had already come far enough from the inn to make it impossible for anybody to hear the horse's shoes. In the twinkling of an eye Antonio had taken off the rags which he had wrapped round the horse's hooves. He got ready to mount. I tried to detain him with both threats and entreaties.

'I am a poor man, Señor,' he said. 'Two hundred ducats aren't to be thrown away, especially when it's a question of ridding the country of vermin like that. But take care: if Navarro wakes up, he'll grab his gun, and then watch out! As for me, I've gone too far now to draw back. You must manage as best you can.'

The scoundrel was already in the saddle; he put both spurs to his horse and was soon lost from sight in the darkness.

I was very angry with my guide and not a little uneasy. After a moment's reflection I made up my mind and went back into the inn. Don José was still asleep, doubtless making up for the fatigue and vigils of several adventurous days. I had to shake him hard to awaken him. Never shall I forget the wild look in his eyes and the movement he made to seize his blunderbuss, which I had taken the precaution of placing a little way from his bed.

'Señor,' I said to him, 'I apologize for waking you, but I have a stupid question to ask you: would you be pleased to see half a dozen lancers arrive here?'

He leapt to his feet and asked me in a terrible voice:

'Who told you they will?'

'It doesn't matter where the information comes from, provided it is reliable.'

'Your guide has betrayed me, but he shall pay for it! Where is he?'

'I don't know.... In the stable, I think.... But somebody told me....'

'Who told you?... It can't be the old woman....'

'Somebody I don't know.... But without any more ado, have you or have you not any reason for not waiting to see the soldiers? If you have, then lose no time; if not, good night, and I beg your pardon for having disturbed your sleep.'

'Oh, that guide of yours! I distrusted him right from the start.... But I'll settle with him!... Good-bye, Señor. May God reward you for the service you have just rendered me. I am not quite as bad as you may think.... Yes, there is still something in me that deserves the pity of a decent man.... Good-bye, Señor.... I have only one regret, and that is that I cannot repay you.'

'To repay me for the service I have rendered you, Don José, promise me not to suspect anybody, and not to think of seeking revenge. Wait, here are some cigars for your journey. Good luck!' And I held out my hand.

Without replying, he shook it, took his blunderbuss and his saddlebag, and after saying a few words to the old woman in a jargon I could not understand, ran to the shed. A few moments later, I heard him galloping away across country.

As for me, I lay down again on my bench, but I did not go to sleep again. I asked myself whether I had done right to save a robber who was perhaps also a murderer from the gallows, merely because I had eaten some ham and some *riz à la valencienne* with him. Had I not betrayed my guide, who was upholding the law, and exposed him to the vengeance of a criminal? But what of the obligations of hospitality? A primitive prejudice, I told myself; I would be responsible for all the crimes this bandit committed in the future.... Yet is it a prejudice, that instinct of conscience which defies all argument? Perhaps I could not extricate myself from the delicate situation in which I found myself without remorse of some sort.

I was still inwardly debating the morality of my action with the greatest uncertainty when I saw half a dozen cavalrymen approaching with Antonio, who was cautiously keeping in the rear. I went to meet them, and informed them that the bandit had taken flight more than two hours before. Questioned by the sergeant, the old woman replied that she knew Navarro, but that, living alone, she would never have dared to risk her life by denouncing him. She added that when he came to her inn, he always left during the night. As for me, I had to go to a place several miles away to show my passport and sign a declaration before a magistrate, after which I was allowed to resume my archaeological researches. Antonio bore me something of a grudge, suspecting that it was I who had prevented him from earning the two hundred ducats. However, we parted amicably at Cordova, where I gave him as generous a tip as the state of my finances would allow.

CHAPTER TWO

I SPENT a few days in Cordova. I had been told about a certain manuscript in the Dominicans' library in which I should find some interesting information concerning ancient Munda. Given an excellent reception by the worthy Fathers, I spent my days in their monastery and in the evenings I strolled about the city. In Cordova, towards sunset, there are a great many idlers on the embankment which runs along the right bank of the Guadalquivir. There one breathes in the smells from a tannery which maintains the age-old fame of the region for the preparation of leather; but on the other hand one can enjoy a sight which is well worth seeing. A few minutes before the Angelus, a large number of women gather on the river bank below the embankment, which is quite high. No man would ever dare to mingle with them. As soon as the Angelus rings, it is considered to be night-time. At the last stroke of the bell, all these women undress and go into the water, making an infernal din with their shrieks and laughter. From the embankment above, the men watch the bathers, straining their eyes but not seeing very much. However, these vague white forms outlined against the dark blue of the river stir poetic minds, and with a little imagination it is not difficult to see them as Diana and her nymphs at their bathing, without having to fear the fate of Actaeon. I have been told that a few scoundrels once raised a sum of money between them to grease the palm of the cathedral bellringer so that he would ring the Angelus twenty minutes before the legal hour. Although it was still broad daylight, the nymphs of Guadalquivir did not hesitate, and, trusting the Angelus rather than the sun, they assumed with clear consciences their *toilette de bain*, which was of the very simplest nature. I was not there. In my time, the bellringer was incorruptible, the twilight dim, and only a cat could have distinguished the oldest orange pedlar from the prettiest *grisette* in Cordova.

One evening, at the hour when one can see nothing more, I was leaning on the parapet of the embankment, smoking, when a woman came up the steps leading from the river and sat down near me. In her hair she had a large bunch of jasmine, that flower whose petals give off an intoxicating scent at night. She was simply, perhaps poorly dressed, all in black, like most *grisettes* in the evening. Respectable women wear black only in the morning; in the evening they dress *à la francesca*. As she sat down near me, my bather let the mantilla covering her head slip down over her shoulders, and in the dim starlight I saw that she was small and young, with a shapely figure and large eyes. I promptly threw away my cigar. She understood this very French gesture of politeness, and hastened to tell me that she was very fond of the smell of tobacco, and that she even smoked herself when she could find some very mild *papelitos*. I was fortunate enough to have some in my case, and I lost no time in offering her one. She took one and lit it from a smouldering piece of cord which a child brought us for a sou. Mingling our smoke, we chatted so long, the beautiful bather and I, that we found ourselves almost alone on the embankment. I did not think it too indiscreet of me to suggest that we went to the *neveria** for an ice. After hesitating demurely for a moment, she accepted, but not before asking what time it was. I consulted my repeater, and its ringing seemed to astonish her greatly.

'What strange inventions you foreigners have in your

---

* A café equipped with an ice-box, or rather with a stock of snow. In Spain there is scarcely a single village without its *neveria*. (P.M.)

countries! Where do you come from Señor? You are English, I suppose.'*

'French, and your humble servant. And you, Señorita or Señora, are from Cordova, I expect.'

'No.'

'Well, at least you are an Andalusian. I think I can tell that from your soft accent.'

'If you notice people's accents so much, you must surely be able to guess who I am.'

'I think you come from the country of Jesus, two steps from Paradise.' (I had learnt this metaphor for Andalusia from my friend Francisco Sevilla, the famous picador.)

'Bah! People here say that Paradise isn't meant for us.'

'Then you must be a Moor, or . . .' I hesitated, not daring to say a Jewess.

'Come, come, you can see that I am a gipsy. Would you like me to tell your fortune? Have you ever heard of little Carmen? That's me.'

I was such a scoundrel at that time – fifteen years ago now – that I did not recoil in horror at finding myself in the company of a sorceress. 'Splendid!' I said to myself. 'Last week I supped with a highwayman: today I am going to enjoy an ice with a handmaiden of the Devil. A traveller ought to be prepared to see everything.' I had another reason for cultivating her acquaintance. After leaving school, I must confess to my shame that I had wasted a certain amount of time studying the occult sciences and had even made several attempts to conjure up the spirit of darkness. Although I had long since been cured of the passion for experiments of that sort, I none the less retained a certain curiosity about all superstitions, and I looked

* In Spain every traveller who does not carry around with him samples of calico or silk is assumed to be an Englishman. It is the same in the East. At Chalcis I have had the honour of being introduced as Μιλόρδος Φραντζέσος. (P.M.)

forward to learning how far the magic art had developed among the gipsies.

Chatting together, we entered the *neveria* and sat down at a small table lit by a candle enclosed in a glass globe. I now had the opportunity to study my *gitana* at leisure while a few respectable citizens gaped in amazement over their ices at seeing me in such company.

I very much doubt whether Mademoiselle Carmen was of pure blood, but at least she was infinitely prettier than any other woman of her race that I have ever met. For a woman to be beautiful, the Spaniards say she must satisfy thirty requirements, or, to put it another way, it must be possible to describe her by the use of ten adjectives, each applicable to three parts of her person. For example, she must have three things that are black: eyes, lashes, and eyebrows; three things that are delicate: fingers, lips, hair; and so on. Consult Brantôme for the rest. My gipsy could not lay claim to such a degree of perfection. Her skin, which incidentally was perfectly smooth, was very nearly the colour of copper. Her eyes were slanting, but beautifully shaped; her lips were rather thick but clearly defined, revealing teeth whiter than blanched almonds. Her hair, though perhaps a little coarse, was long and shiny, black with gleams of blue in it like a crow's wing. Not to weary you with too prolix a description, let me sum up by saying that every defect was matched by a quality which stood out perhaps more strongly by contrast. Hers was a strange, wild beauty, and, if her face astonished one at first, it could never be forgotten. Her eyes in particular had an expression at once voluptuous and fierce such as I have never seen since in any human gaze. 'A gipsy's eye is a wolf's eye' is a Spanish saying based on accurate observation. If you have not the time to go to the zoological gardens to study a wolf's eyes, look at your cat when it is watching a sparrow.

You will readily understand that it would have been

ridiculous for me to have my fortune told in a café. I therefore asked the pretty sorceress to allow me to see her home; she agreed readily enough, but once more she wanted to know what time it was, and asked me to make my repeater strike the hour again.

'Is it really gold?' she asked, examining it with what I considered excessive attention.

When we set off again it was pitch dark; most of the shops were closed and the streets were practically empty. We crossed the Guadalquivir bridge, and at the end of the suburb we halted in front of a house which looked like anything but a palace. A child opened the door to us. The gipsy said a few words to him in a language which was completely unknown to me, but which I later learned was Romany, or *chipe calli*, the gipsy tongue. The child promptly disappeared, leaving us in a fairly large room furnished with a small table, two stools, and a chest. I must not forget to mention that there were also a jug of water, a pile of oranges, and a string of onions.

As soon as we were alone, the gipsy took out of the chest a pack of cards which seemed to have seen considerable service, a magnet, a dessicated chameleon, and a few other objects necessary to her art. Then she told me to cross my left palm with a coin, and the magic ceremonies began. There is no point in my repeating her prophecies, but from her procedure it was obvious that she was no mean sorceress.

Unfortunately we were soon disturbed. The door was suddenly flung open, and a man wrapped up to his eyes in a brown cloak came into the room, addressing the gipsy in the most ungracious terms. I could not understand what he was saying, but the tone of his voice indicated that he was in a very bad temper. When she saw him the gipsy showed neither surprise nor anger, but ran to meet him, and with extraordinary volubility spoke several sentences to him in that mysterious tongue she had already used in my presence. The word *payllo*, which occurred repeatedly, was the only one I understood. I knew that the gipsies use it to refer to any man who is not of their race. Assuming that she was talking about me, I expected a troublesome incident; I already had my hand on the leg of one of the stools, and I was debating with myself as to the exact moment when it would be best to hurl it at the intruder's head. The man pushed the gipsy roughly aside and came towards me; then, stepping back, he cried:

'Why, Señor, it's you!'

I looked at him in my turn and recognized my friend Don José. At that moment I felt a little sorry that I had not let him hang.

'Ah, it's you, my good fellow!' I exclaimed, laughing as calmly as I could. 'You interrupted the Señorita just as she was telling me some very interesting things.'

'The same as ever! I'm going to put a stop to this,' he said between his teeth, glaring at her.

However, the gipsy went on talking to him in her own tongue. She grew more and more excited. Her eyes became bloodshot and terrifying, her features contracted, and she stamped her foot. It seemed to me that she was urging him to do something about which he was displaying a certain reluctance. What this was I thought I understood only too well when I saw her pass her little hand quickly to and fro under her chin. I was tempted to think that it was a matter of cutting somebody's throat, and I had a suspicion that that throat was my own.

To this torrent of eloquence Don José replied with only two or three words uttered in a curt voice. The gipsy shot him a look of profound contempt; then, sitting down Turkish fashion in a corner of the room, she chose an orange, peeled it, and started eating.

Don José took me by the arm, opened the door, and led

me out into the street. We walked about two hundred paces in complete silence. Then, pointing ahead, he said:

'Keep straight on, and you will come to the bridge.'

He promptly turned on his heel and walked away quickly. I went back to my inn feeling somewhat crestfallen and in a rather bad temper. The worst of it was that when I undressed I found that my watch was missing.

Various considerations prevented me from going back to ask for it the next day, or from requesting the *corregidor* to recover it for me. I finished my work on the Dominicans' manuscript and left for Seville.

After several months spent wandering about Andalusia, I decided to return to Madrid, and it was necessary for me to go by way of Cordova. I had no intention of staying there for long, for I had taken a thorough dislike to that beautiful city and the bathing girls of the Guadalquivir. However, a number of friends to see and commissions to execute were bound to keep me for at least three or four days in the ancient capital of the Moslem princes.

As soon as I reappeared at the Dominican monastery, one of the Fathers, who had always shown a keen interest in my research concerning the site of Munda, welcomed me with open arms, crying:

'Praised be the name of God! Welcome, my dear friend. We all thought that you were dead, and I myself have recited a great many *Paters* and *Aves*, which I don't regret at all, for the repose of your soul. So you weren't murdered after all – for we know for certain that you have been robbed.'

'How do you know that?' I asked, somewhat surprised.

'You remember that beautiful repeater of yours which you used to make strike the hour in the library whenever we told you that it was time to go to choir. Well, it has been found, and will be returned to you.'

'The fact is,' I broke in, rather abashed, 'that I had lost it....'

'The scoundrel is under lock and key, and as he was known to be quite capable of shooting a Christian for a sou, we were mortally afraid that he had killed you. I will go to the *corregidor* with you, and we will have your beautiful watch returned to you. After that, when you get back to France, I don't think you will be able to say that there is no justice in Spain.'

'I must admit,' I said, 'that I would rather lose my watch than give evidence which would send a poor devil to the gallows, especially since ... since. ...'

'Oh, have no fear! There are a good many charges against him, and they can't hang him more than once. When I say hang, I am wrong. This thief of yours is a nobleman, so he will be garrotted – the day after tomorrow, as it happens, with no possibility of reprieve.* You can see that one theft more or less will make no difference to his fate. Would to God that stealing were all that he had done, but he has committed several murders, each one more horrible than the last.'

'What is his name?'

'He is known in this part of the country as José Navarro, but he also has a Basque name which neither you nor I could ever pronounce. Look here, he is well worth seeing, and since you are interested in learning about all the country's peculiarities you shouldn't neglect the opportunity of finding out how scoundrels leave this world in Spain. He is in the condemned man's chapel, and Father Martinez will take you there.'

My Dominican friend insisted so strongly on my seeing the preparations for the 'pretty little hanging' that I could not refuse. I went to see the prisoner equipped with a

---

* In 1830 the nobility still enjoyed this privilege. Now, under the constitutional régime, the commoners have acquired the right to the garrotte. (P.M. – 1845)

packet of cigars which, I hoped, would persuade him to forgive my intrusion.

I was shown in to Don José while he was eating his midday meal. He nodded rather coldly to me and thanked me politely for the gift I had brought him. After counting the cigars in the packet I had handed him, he selected a certain number and gave the rest back to me, remarking that he did not need any more.

I asked him whether, with a little money or through the influence of my friends, I could obtain any alleviation of his lot. At first he shrugged his shoulders, with a sad smile; but soon afterwards, changing his mind, he asked me to have a Mass said for the repose of his soul.

'Could you,' he added hesitantly, 'could you possibly have another Mass said for a person who has done you a wrong?'

'Of course, my dear fellow,' I replied, 'but nobody, as far as I know, has done me any wrong in this country.'

He took my hand and shook it solemnly. After a moment's silence he went on:

'Dare I beg another service of you? ... When you go back to your own country, you may perhaps pass through Navarre. You will at least go through Vitoria, which is not far away.'

'Yes,' I said, 'I shall certainly go by way of Vitoria; but it is not out of the question that I should make a detour to visit Pamplona, and I would willingly make that detour on your account.'

'Well, if you do go to Pamplona, you will see more than one thing that will interest you. ... It is a beautiful city. ... I will give you this medal,' (he showed me a little silver medal which he wore hanging from his neck), 'you will wrap it in paper,' (he paused for a moment to master his feelings), 'and you will give it or arrange for it to be given to a good woman whose address I will give you. ...

You will say that I am dead, but you will not say how I died.'

I promised to do what he asked. I saw him again the next day, and I spent part of it with him. It was from his own lips that I learned the sad story which you are about to read.

CHAPTER THREE

'I was born,' he said, 'at Elizondo, in the Baztan Valley. My name is Don José Lizarrabengoa, and you know Spain well enough, Señor, to be able to tell at once from my name that I am a Basque and come from an old Christian family. If I call myself Don, that is because I am entitled to do so, and if I were at Elizondo, I would show you my family tree on parchment. It was intended that I should take Holy Orders, and I was made to study for the priesthood, but I made scarcely any progress. I was too fond of playing tennis, and that was what brought about my downfall. When we Navarrese play that game, we forget everything else. One day when I had won, a fellow from the Alava picked a quarrel with me; we set to with our *maquilas*,* and once again I won; but I was obliged to leave the country as a result. I fell in with some dragoons and enlisted in the cavalry regiment of Almanza. The men from our mountains learn the soldiering trade quickly. I soon became a sergeant, and I had been promised the rank of sergeant-major when, to my misfortune, I was put on guard duty at the tobacco factory in Seville. If you have ever been to Seville, you will have seen that big building, outside the ramparts, near the Guadalquivir. It seems to me that I can still see the main gate and the guardhouse beside it. When Spanish soldiers are on duty, they play cards or sleep, but I, as a true Navarrese, always tried to find something to do. I was making myself a chain from some brass wire, to hold my priming-needle, when all of a sudden my comrades said: "There goes the bell; the girls will be coming back to work." You see, Señor, there are a good four or five hundred women employed in that factory. It is they who roll the

* Iron-shod sticks used by the Basques. (P.M.)

cigars in a large hall which no man is allowed to enter without a permit from the local magistrate, because the women, especially the young ones, wear very little clothing when the weather is hot. When they return to work after their dinner, a lot of young men go to watch them pass, and make all sorts of remarks to them. There are very few of those young ladies who would refuse a taffeta mantilla, and men with a taste for that kind of sport have only to stoop to catch their fish. While the others were watching I stayed on my bench near the door. I was a young man at the time; I was always thinking of my home and I didn't believe that there could be any pretty girls who didn't wear blue skirts and plaits hanging down over their shoulders.* Besides, the Andalusian girls frightened me; I was not yet accustomed to their ways, always teasing with never a sensible word. So there I was, working on my chain, when I heard some townspeople say: "There's the *gitanilla*!" I looked up, and I saw her. It was a Friday, and I shall never forget it – the day I first saw that Carmen whom you met, in whose lodgings I found you a few months ago.

'She was wearing a very short red skirt which revealed a pair of white silk stockings, with more than one hole in them, and dainty red morocco shoes fastened with flame-coloured ribbons. She had thrown back her mantilla in order to show off her shoulders and a big bunch of acacia flowers in the opening of her blouse. She had another acacia flower between her teeth, and she came forward with her hips swaying like a filly from the Cordova stud. In my part of the country people would make the sign of the cross if they saw a woman dressed like that. In Seville the men all paid her some bold compliment on her appearance, and she answered every one with sidelong glances, her hands on her hips, as impudent as the true gipsy she was. At first she did

* The customary dress for the peasant-girls of Navarre and the Basque provinces. (P.M.)

not appeal to me, and I went back to my work; but, following the custom of women and cats, who don't come when you call them but come when you don't, she stopped in front of me and spoke to me.

' "Friend," she said in the Andalusian manner, "will you give me your chain to hold the keys of my cash-box?"

' "It's to hold my priming-needle," I replied.

' "Your priming-needle!" she cried, with a laugh. "So the Señor makes lace, does he, seeing that he needs a needle?"

'Everybody there burst out laughing, while I felt myself blushing and could think of nothing to say in reply.

' "Come, sweetheart," she went on, "make me seven yards of black lace for a mantilla, needle-man of my dreams!"

'And, taking the acacia flower which she had been holding in her mouth, she flicked it at me with her thumb, and it struck me straight between the eyes. Señor, I felt as if a bullet had hit me. . . . I did not know what to do with myself, and I stayed there as stiff as a plank. When she had gone into the factory, I saw the acacia flower which had fallen on the ground between my feet. I don't know what possessed me, but I picked it up without my comrades noticing, and I put it carefully away inside my jacket. That was my first act of folly!

'Two or three hours later, I was still thinking about it when a porter, panting for breath and looking quite distraught, rushed into the guardhouse. He told us that a woman had been murdered in the big hall where the cigars were rolled, and that we must send the guards in. The sergeant-major told me to take two men and go to see what had happened. I picked my men and went upstairs. Just imagine, Señor, when I went into the hall I was confronted with three hundred women, wearing their shifts or very little more, and all shrieking, howling, gesticulating, and making such a din that you couldn't have heard God's thunder. On one side there was one of them lying on her back, covered with blood, and with a cross on her face which had just been carved with two strokes of a knife. Opposite the wounded woman, who was being cared for by the best of the band, I saw Carmen being held by five or six of her cronies. The wounded woman kept shouting: "Fetch a priest! Fetch a priest! I'm dying!" Carmen said nothing; her teeth were clenched and she was rolling her eyes like a chameleon.

' "What's all this about?" I asked. I had great difficulty in finding out what had happened, because all the women spoke to me at once. It seems that the wounded woman had boasted that she had enough money in her pocket to buy a donkey at the Triana market.

' "Well, well," said Carmen, who had a sharp tongue, "so you aren't satisfied with a broomstick?"

'The other, offended by the jibe, possibly because she felt that it was not unjustified, replied that she was no judge of broomsticks, not having the honour of being a gipsy or a daughter of Satan, but that Señorita Carmencita would soon make the acquaintance of her donkey, when the *corregidor* sent her out for a ride on it with a couple of lackeys behind to whisk the flies off her.

' "Well," said Carmen, "for my part I'll make some drinking-troughs for flies on your cheeks. Yes, I'll paint a regular draughtboard on them."*

'With that, slish, slash! She started carving St Andrew's crosses on the woman's face with the knife she used to cut the ends of her cigars.

'It was a clear case. I took Carmen by the arm.

' "Sister," I said to her politely, "you'll have to come along with me."

* *Pintar un javeque:* to paint a draughtboard. Spanish draughtboards are generally painted with red and white squares. (P.M.)

'She darted a glance at me which suggested that she had recognized me, but she said with an air of resignation:

' "Let's go. Where's my mantilla?"

'She put it over her head so as to leave only one of her great eyes showing, and followed my two men as meek as a lamb. When we reached the guardhouse, the sergeant-major said that it was a serious matter, and that she had to be taken to the prison. Once again it was I who had to take her. I placed her between a couple of dragoons, and I marched along behind, as a sergeant should do in such circumstances. We set out for the town. At first the gipsy kept silent, but in the Calle Sierpes – you know the one, which deserves its name with all the bends there are in it – in the Calle Sierpes she began by letting her mantilla slip down over her shoulders, so as to show me her appealing little face, and, turning towards me as much as she could, she asked me:

' "Officer, where are you taking me?"

' "To the prison, my poor child," I replied as gently as I could, as a good soldier should speak to a prisoner, especially a woman.

' "Alas, what will become of me? Noble officer, have pity on me! You are so young, so kind!" Then, in a lower voice, she added: "Let me escape, and I will give you a piece of the *bar lachi*, which will make all women love you."

'The *bar lachi*, Señor, is the lodestone, with which the gipsies claim that you can work all sorts of magic if you know how to use it. Get a woman to drink a glass of white wine containing some filings from it, and she will no longer put up any resistance. I replied as gravely as I could:

' "We aren't here to talk nonsense. You must go to prison; those are my orders, and there's no help for it."

'We people from the Basque country have an accent by

which the Spaniards can recognize us easily; on the other hand there isn't a single one of them who can learn to say even *baï, jaona** properly. So Carmen had no difficulty in guessing that I came from the Provinces. You doubtless know, Señor, that the gipsies, having no country of their own, are always on the road and speak every language, and that most of them are quite at home in Portugal, in France, in the Provinces, in Catalonia, anywhere; they can even make themselves understood among the Moors and the English. Carmen knew the Basque tongue fairly well.

' "*Laguna, ene bihotsarena*, comrade of my heart," she said all of a sudden, "are you from our country?"

'Our language, Señor, is so beautiful that when we hear it in a foreign country, it gives us a thrill of delight. ... I should like to have a confessor from the Provinces,' the bandit added in a murmur. After a pause he went on:

' "I am from Elizondo," I replied in Basque, deeply moved at hearing her speak my native tongue.

' "And I am from Etchalar," she said. (That is a place four hours' journey from my home.) "I was carried off to Seville by some gipsies. I have been working in the factory to earn enough to go back to Navarre, to my poor mother who has only me to support her, and a little *barratcea*† with a score of cider apple trees in it. Oh, if only I were back home, looking up at the white mountain! They insulted me because I don't come from this land of swindlers and traders in rotten oranges; and those filthy women all set upon me because I told them that all their Seville *jacques*‡ with their knives wouldn't scare a single one of our lads with his blue beret and his *maquila*. Comrade and friend, won't you do something for a fellow-countrywoman?"

* Yes, sir. (P.M.)　　† Garden. (P.M.)　　‡ Braggarts. (P.M.)

'She was lying, Señor, she has always lied. I don't know whether that girl has ever spoken a true word in the whole of her life; but when she spoke, I believed her; I couldn't help it. She murdered the Basque language, yet I believed her to be Navarrese; her eyes, her mouth, her complexion – any of these should have told me that she was a gipsy. I was mad, and no longer paid attention to anything. I told myself that if some Spaniards had taken it into their heads to speak ill of my country in my presence, I would have cut open their faces, just as she had cut open her workmate's. In short, I was like a drunken man; I was beginning to think foolishly and I was on the verge of acting foolishly too.

' "If I gave you a push, and you fell down, fellow-countryman of mine," she went on in Basque, "I can promise you that these two Castillian conscripts wouldn't hold me."

'Well, I forgot my orders and everything else, and I said to her:

' "All right, my dear, my fellow-countrywoman, have a try, and may Our Lady of the Mountain help you!"

'Just then we were passing one of those narrow alleys of which there are so many in Seville. All of a sudden, Carmen turned round and struck me in the chest with her fist. I fell backwards on purpose. With one leap she jumped over me and started running, showing us a splendid pair of legs. . . . They talk about "Basque legs", but hers were just as beautiful, and they were as swift as they were shapely. As for me, I picked myself up straight away, but I held my lance* sideways so that it barred the alley, with the result that my comrades were halted in their pursuit right at the start. Then I began running myself, with them behind me; but there was no risk of catching her, encumbered as we

---

* The whole Spanish cavalry is armed with lances. (P.M. – 1845)

were with spurs, swords, and lances. In less time than it takes me to tell you about it, the prisoner had disappeared. Besides, all the women of the district helped her flight and made fun of us, giving us the wrong directions. After a great deal of marching and counter-marching, we had to go back to the guardhouse without a receipt from the prison governor.

'To avoid being punished, my men reported that Carmen had spoken to me in Basque; and to tell the truth, it didn't seem very natural that a blow from such a slip of a girl should have knocked down a strapping fellow like me so easily. It all looked rather suspicious, or rather only too obvious. When the guard was relieved, I was demoted and sentenced to a month's imprisonment. That was my first punishment since I had enlisted. It was good-bye to those sergeant-major's stripes which I had thought were mine already!

'My first days in prison went by very sadly. When I had joined the army, I had imagined that I would at least become an officer one day. After all Longa and Mina, my fellow-countrymen, have become captains-general; Chapalangarra, who is a Negro like Mina, and who like him has taken refuge in your country, was a colonel, and I have played tennis a score of times with his brother, who was a poor devil like myself. Now I told myself: "All the time you have served without any punishment is so much time wasted. Now you have a bad reputation; to get back into the good graces of your superior officers you will have to work ten times harder than when you were a new recruit. And what have you incurred this punishment for? For a hussy of a gipsy who has made a fool of you and who at this moment is busy thieving in some corner of the town."

'All the same, I could not help thinking about her. Believe it or not, Señor, I still had before my eyes those silk stockings of hers all full of holes, which she had displayed so freely to me while running away. I used to look out into the street between my prison bars, and among all the women who went by I did not see one who could compare with that diabolical girl. And then, in spite of myself, I would smell that acacia flower which she had thrown at me and which, though it had dried up, still kept its sweet scent. ... If witches really exist, then that girl was one!

'One day, the jailer came in and gave me a loaf of Alcalà bread.*

' "Here," he said, "look what your cousin has sent you."

'I took the loaf in some bewilderment, for I had no cousin in Seville. "Perhaps there is some mistake," I thought, looking at the loaf; but it looked so appetizing and smelt so good that, without asking myself where it came from or for whom it was intended, I decided to eat it. But when I tried to cut it, my knife came across something hard. I looked to see what it was, and found a tiny English file which had been slipped into the dough before the loaf was baked. There was also a two-piastre gold coin in the loaf. I could no longer have any doubt about it: this was a gift from Carmen.

'For the people of her race, freedom is everything, and they would set a whole city on fire to spare themselves one day's imprisonment. Besides, the girl was clever, and with a loaf like that I could laugh at any jailer. In an hour the thickest of bars could be sawn through with the little file; and with the two-piastre coin I could exchange my uniform tunic for a civilian coat at the first clothes shop I came to. You can imagine that a man who had many a time taken

* Alcalà de los Panaderos, a village two leagues from Seville, where delicious loaves are made. It is said that their quality is due to the water of Alcalà. Every day considerable quantities of them are brought into Seville. (P.M.)

eaglets from their nests on our crags thought nothing of getting down to the street from a window less than thirty feet up; but I didn't want to escape. I still had my sense of honour as a soldier, and desertion seemed a great crime to me. But I was touched by this token of remembrance. When you are in prison, it is pleasant to think that you have a friend outside who cares about you. The gold coin embarrassed me a little, and I would have liked to give it back; but where could I find my creditor? That did not strike me as an easy thing to do.

'After the ceremony in which I had been demoted, I thought that there was nothing more for me to suffer; but there remained another humiliation to be endured: this was when I came out of prison and was put on sentry duty as a common private. You cannot imagine what a sensitive man feels in such a situation. I believe that I would have preferred to be shot: in that case, at least a man walks by himself at the head of his squad; he is the centre of attention and feels a certain importance.

'I was put on sentry duty outside the colonel's door. He was a rich young man, a good-natured fellow who liked enjoying himself. All the young officers were at his house, and a good many citizens, as well as some women – actresses, so I was told. As far as I was concerned, it seemed to me that the whole city had agreed to meet at his door, just to stare at me. Then along came the colonel's carriage, with his valet on the seat. And whom did I see get out? The *gitanilla*! This time she was rigged out like a shrine, all bedizened and bedecked in gold and ribbons. She was wearing a spangled gown, with blue shoes also adorned with spangles, and flowers and gold lace everywhere. In her hand she held a Basque tambourine. With her there were two other gipsy women, one young and one old. There is always an old woman to take gipsy girls out, and also an old man with a guitar, another gipsy, to play for them and make them dance. You know that people often hire gipsies for their parties, to entertain them by dancing the *romalis* – their national dance – and often in other ways too.

'Carmen recognized me, and we exchanged glances. I don't know why, but at that moment I would have liked to be a hundred feet under the ground.

' "*Agur laguna*,"* she said. "What, you, an officer, on sentry duty like a conscript?"

'And before I could think of a reply, she was inside the house.

'Everybody was in the patio, and in spite of the crowd I could see almost everything that was going on through the gate.† I could hear the castanets, the tambourines, the laughter, and the applause; now and then I caught a glimpse of Carmen's head when she jumped into the air with her tambourine. Then I heard some officers saying things to her which brought a flush to my cheeks. I have no idea what she replied. It was that day, I think, that I really began to love her; for three or four times I felt tempted to rush into the patio and plunge my sword into the bellies of all those whippersnappers who were flirting with her. My torment lasted for a good hour; then the gipsies came out, and the carriage took them away. As she passed me, Carmen looked at me again with those eyes you know yourself, and said to me in a very low voice:

' "Fellow-countryman of mine, anybody who likes good fried fish goes to Lillas Pastia's at Triana."

'Then, as nimble as a kid, she leapt into the carriage, the

* 'Good day, comrade.' (P.M.)

† Most houses in Seville have an inner courtyard surrounded by porticoes. The inhabitants live there in the summertime. This courtyard is covered with an awning which is sprinkled with water during the day and removed in the evening. The street door is nearly always open, and the passage leading to the courtyard, the *zaguan*, is closed by an elegantly wrought iron gate. (P.M.)

CARMEN

coachman lashed his mules, and the whole merry band drove off I don't know where.

'You can imagine that as soon as I was relieved I went off to Triana; but first of all I had a shave and brushed myself down as if I were going on parade. Carmen was at Lillas Pastia's, an establishment belonging to an old gipsy as black as a Moor, where a great many citizens came to eat fried fish, especially, I think, since Carmen had taken up her quarters there.

' "Lillas," she said, as soon as she saw me, "I've finished for today. Tomorrow is another day.* Come, fellow-countryman, let us go for a walk."

'She drew her mantilla over her face, and there we were in the street, without my knowing where we were going.

' "Señorita," I said, "I believe that it is you I have to thank for a present you sent me when I was in prison. I ate the bread; the file will come in useful for sharpening my lance, and I shall keep it to remember you by; but here is the money."

' "Why, he's kept the money!" she exclaimed, bursting out laughing. "Well, so much the better, for I am rather low in funds; but what does that matter? A stray dog never starves.† Come, let's spend it all on food. You are going to treat me!"

'We had taken the road back to Seville. At the beginning of the Calle Sierpes she bought a dozen oranges, which she told me to put in my kerchief. A little farther on, she bought some bread, some sausage, and a bottle of manzanilla; and finally she went into a confectioner's shop. There she threw on to the counter the gold coin I had returned to her, another which she had in her pocket, and some small change in silver; and finally she asked me for all I had. I

* *Mañana será otro día:* a Spanish proverb. (P.M.)

† *Chuquel sos pirela, cocal terela* (A dog which wanders finds a bone): a gipsy proverb. (P.M.)

PROSPER MÉRIMÉE

had only a peseta and a few quartos, which I gave her, ashamed at having no more. I thought she was going to buy the entire shop. She took all that was finest and dearest, *yemas*, *turon*,* and candied fruits, until the money ran out. All this I had to carry too, in paper bags. Perhaps you know the Calle Candilejo, where there is a carved head of King Don Pedro the Justicer.†

'That ought to have given me pause. We stopped in this street, outside an old house. She went down the passage and knocked on the ground-floor door. A gipsy, a real daughter of Satan, opened it. Carmen said a few words to her in

---

* *Yemas* are sugared yolks of eggs, and *turon* is a kind of nougat. (P.M.)

† King Don Pedro, whom we call the Cruel, and whom Queen Isabella the Catholic always called the Justicer, loved to roam the streets of Seville in the evening, looking for adventures like Caliph Haroun al Raschid. One night, in a lonely street, he picked a quarrel with a man who was serenading a woman. They fought, and the King killed the amorous cavalier. Hearing the sound of the swords, an old woman put her head out of the window and lit up the scene with a small lamp, or *candilejo*, which she held in her hand. It should be added that King Don Pedro, though strong and agile, had a peculiar deformity: when he walked, his knee-caps made a loud cracking noise. From this cracking noise the old woman had no difficulty in recognizing him. The next day, the magistrate on duty came to make his report to the King.

'Sire,' he said, 'A duel was fought last night in such and such a street. One of the combatants was killed.'

'Have you discovered the identity of the murderer?'

'Yes, sire.'

'Why has he not already been punished?'

'Sire, I await your orders.'

'Carry out the law.'

Now the king had just issued a decree that anybody who fought a duel was to be beheaded, and that his head was to be exposed on the site of the duel. The magistrate extricated himself from his predicament with a nice sense of humour. He had the head of a statue of the King sawn off and exposed in a niche in the middle of the street where the killing had taken place. The King and all the Sevillians thought this an excellent device. The street took its name from the lamp of the old woman, the only witness of the affair.

CARMEN

Romany. The old woman grumbled at first. To soothe her, Carmen gave her a couple of oranges and a handful of sweets, and let her have a swig of wine. Then she put her cloak over her shoulders and led her to the door, barring it behind her. As soon as we were alone, she started dancing and laughing like a madwoman, singing: "You are my *rom* and I am your *romi*."*

'I stood there in the middle of the room, loaded with all her purchases, and not knowing where to put them. She tossed everything on the floor and threw her arms round my neck, saying:

'"I am paying my debts! I am paying my debts! That's the law of the *Calé!*"†

'Ah, Señor, what a day that was! When I think of it, I forget about tomorrow.'

The bandit was silent for a moment; then, after relighting his cigar, he went on:

'We spent the whole day together, eating, drinking – and so on. When she had eaten some of the sweets like a six-year-old, she stuffed whole handfuls into the old woman's water-jug. "To make her a water-ice," she said. She smashed *yemas* by throwing them at the wall. "So that the flies leave us in peace," she said. There wasn't a single trick or prank she didn't play. I told her that I would like to see her dance, but where were we to find any castanets? She promptly took the old woman's only plate, smashed it to

---

This is the popular tradition. Zuñiga gives a slightly different version of the story. (See *Anales de Sevilla*, vol. II, p. 136.) Be that as it may, there is still a Calle Candilejo in Seville, and in that street a stone bust which is said to be of Don Pedro. Unfortunately, this bust is modern. The old one was very weatherbeaten in the seventeenth century and the city council then had it replaced by one which can be seen today. (P.M.)

* *Rom* means husband, *romi* wife. (P.M.)

† *Calo*; feminine, *calli*; plural, *calé*; black. The word the gipsies apply to themselves in their own tongue. (P.M.)

pieces, and there she was, dancing the *romalis* and clicking the pieces of crockery together just as if she had had castanets of ebony or ivory. You couldn't be bored with the girl, I can tell you that. Evening came, and I heard the drums beating the retreat.

' "I must go back to barracks for roll-call," I told her.

' "Back to barracks?" she said scornfully. "Are you a nigger, then, to allow yourself to be ruled with a whip? You're a real canary, in coat and character.* Go on then, you chicken-hearted creature!"

'I stayed, resigned in advance to the guardroom. In the morning, it was she who spoke first of our parting.

' "Listen, Joseito," she said, "have I paid my debt? According to our law, I didn't owe you anything, since you are a *payllo*, but you are a handsome fellow and I took a fancy to you. Now we are all square. Good-bye."

'I asked her when I would see her again.

' "When you are less of a fool," she replied with a laugh. Then she went on in a more serious tone: "You know, my boy, I do believe I love you a little. But it cannot last. Dog and wolf never get on well together for long. Perhaps, if you were to accept the law of Egypt, I might choose to become your *romi*. But that's nonsense: it's out of the question. Bah! Believe me, my boy, you have got off lightly. You have met the Devil – yes, the Devil; he isn't always black, and he hasn't wrung your neck. I am dressed in wool, but I am no lamb.† Go and light a candle to your *majari*;‡ she has earned it. Come now, good-bye once more. Forget about Carmencita, or she'll marry you off to a widow with wooden legs."§

'While she was saying this, she was removing the bar

---

* Spanish dragoons are dressed in yellow. (P.M.)

† *Me dicas vriarda de jorpoy, bus ne sino braco*: a gipsy proverb. (P.M.)

‡ The Virgin Mary. (P.M.)

§ The gallows, the widow of the last man to be hanged. (P.M.)

CARMEN

across the door, and once outside she wrapped herself in her mantilla and turned on her heel.

'She was right. I would have been well advised to forget about her; but after that day in the Calle Candilejo I could think of nothing else. I roamed about all day long, hoping to meet her. I asked the old woman and the fried-fish merchant for news of her. Both of them replied that she had gone away to Laloro, the "red land", which is their name for Portugal. Probably it was on Carmen's instructions that they said this, but I soon found out that they were lying. A few weeks after that day I had spent in the Calle Candilejo, I was on sentry duty at one of the city gates. Not far from this gate a breach had been made in the city wall; work was carried out on it during the day, and at night a sentry was posted there to stop smugglers. During the day, I saw Lillas Pastia hanging around the guardhouse and chatting with some of my comrades; they all knew him, and his fish and fritters even better. He came up to me and asked me if I had any news of Carmen.

' "No," I replied.

' "Well, you soon will have, comrade."

'He was not mistaken. That night, I was put on sentry duty at the breach in the wall. As soon as the sergeant had left, I saw a woman coming towards me. My heart told me that it was Carmen. All the same, I shouted:

' "Clear off! You can't come this way!"

' "Don't be so mean," she said, revealing her identity.

' "What! Is it you, Carmen?"

' "Yes, my fellow-countryman. Let's be brief and to the point. Do you want to earn a douro? Some people are going to come along with packets; let them pass."

' "No," I replied. "I must stop them; those are my orders."

' "Your orders! Your orders! You didn't think of them in the Calle Candilejo."

' "Ah," I replied, overwhelmed by the mere memory of that day, "that was worth disobeying orders for; but I don't want any smugglers' money."

' "Well, if you don't want any money, would you like us to go and have dinner at old Dorothea's house again?"

' "No," I said, half choked by the effort I was making. "I cannot do it."

' "All right. If you are going to be difficult, I know whom to ask. I shall invite your officer to go with me to Dorothea's. He seems a good sort, and he'll have a fellow put on duty here who won't see any more than he should. Good-bye, canary. I'll have a good laugh when the orders are to string you up."

'I was weak enough to call her back, and I promised to let all the gipsies in the world pass if necessary, provided I obtained the only reward I wanted. She promptly swore that she would keep her part of the bargain the very next day, and ran off to tell her friends, who were only a little distance away. There were five of them, including Pastia, all heavily burdened with English goods. Carmen kept watch. She was to give warning with her castanets if she saw the patrol, but she had no need to do so. The smugglers had finished their work in a matter of moments.

'The next day, I went to the Calle Candilejo. Carmen kept me waiting, and was in rather a bad temper when she arrived.

' "I don't like people who have to be pressed to do a favour," she said. "You rendered me a greater service the first time, without knowing whether you would get anything in return. Yesterday you bargained with me. I don't know why I have come, for I don't love you any more. Now be off with you, and here's a douro for your trouble."

'I very nearly flung the coin in her face, and I had to make a tremendous effort to keep myself from beating her. We quarrelled for an hour, and I left in a rage. I wandered

CARMEN

about the city for some time, roaming here and there like a madman; finally I went into a church, settled down in the darkest corner, and wept bitter tears. All of a sudden I heard a voice:

' "A dragon's tears!* I should like to make a love philtre from them."

'I looked up. It was Carmen in front of me.

' "Well, my fellow-countryman, are you still angry with me?" she said. "I must love you in spite of everything, for since you left me I don't know what has been the matter with me. Come, now. This time it's my turn to ask if you will come to the Calle Candilejo."

'So we made our peace. But Carmen's moods were like the weather in our country. A storm is never so close in our mountains as when the sun is at its brightest. She had promised to see me another time at Dorothea's, but she did not come. And Dorothea assured me more emphatically than ever that she had gone to Laloro on gipsy business.

'Knowing from previous experience how much reliance I could place on this assurance, I looked for Carmen wherever I thought she might be, and I went along the Calle Candilejo a score of times a day. One evening, I was at Dorothea's – I had tamed the old woman by buying her a glass of anisette now and then – when Carmen came in, followed by a young man, a lieutenant in my regiment.

' "Get out, quick," she said to me in Basque.

'I stood there dumbfounded, with rage in my heart.

' "What are you doing here?" the lieutenant said to me. "Get out! Be off with you!"

'I couldn't move a muscle; it was as if I were paralysed. The infuriated officer, seeing that I was not leaving and

* An untranslatable play on words: in French *dragon* means both 'dragon' and 'dragoon'. (Trans.)

57

that I hadn't even taken off my cap, grabbed me by the collar and shook me roughly. I don't know what I said to him. He drew his sword and I unsheathed mine. The old woman seized my arm and the lieutenant gave me a cut on the forehead, from which I bear the scar to this day. I stepped back, and with my elbow I flung Dorothea to the floor; then, as the lieutenant came after me, I put the point of my sword to his body and he spitted himself on it.

'Carmen immediately put out the lamp and told Dorothea in her own tongue to run for it. I myself rushed out into the street and started running, without knowing where. I had the impression that somebody was following me. When I came to my senses, I found that Carmen had not left me.

' "You great ninny of a canary!" she said. "You just do one stupid thing after another. Besides, I told you I would bring you bad luck. Never mind, there's a remedy for everything when your sweetheart is a Fleming of Rome.* To begin with, put this kerchief round your head and give me that sword-belt. Wait for me in this alley. I'll be back in a couple of minutes."

'She disappeared, but soon returned, bringing me a striped cloak which she had found heaven knows where. She made me take off my uniform and put on the cloak over my shirt. Thus attired, with the kerchief which she had used to bandage the cut on my forehead, I looked passably like one of those Valencian peasants you see in Seville, who come there to sell their *chufa* syrup.† Then she

* *Flamenca de Roma*: a slang term for a gipsy woman. *Roma* here does not mean the Eternal City but the race of the *Romi* or married people, as the gipsies call themselves. The first gipsies seen in Spain probably came from the Netherlands, hence their name of Flemings. (P.M.)

† The *chufa* is a bulbous root from which a pleasant drink is made. (P.M.)

CARMEN

took me to a house rather like Dorothea's, at the end of a little alley. She and another gipsy woman washed and dressed my wound better than any army surgeon could have done, gave me something to drink, and finally laid me on a mattress, where I fell asleep.

'The women had probably put in my drink some of those soporific drugs of which they have the secret, for I did not awake until late the following day. I had a bad headache and a little fever. It was some time before I remembered the terrible scene in which I had been involved the day before. After they had dressed my wound, Carmen and her friend squatted on their heels beside my mattress and exchanged a few words in *chipe calli*, which seemed to be a medical consultation. Then they both assured me that I would soon be well again, but that I must leave Seville as soon as possible, for if I were caught there I would be shot without mercy.

' "My boy," Carmen said to me, "you must do something; now that the King isn't going to give you any more rice or dried cod,* you'll have to think about earning your living. You are too stupid to be able to steal *à pastesas*,† but you are strong and agile: if you have the courage, go off to the coast and become a smuggler. Haven't I promised to get you hanged some day? That's better than being shot. Besides, if you know how to set about it, you'll live like a prince, as long as the soldiers and the coastguards don't collar you."

'It was in this engaging fashion that that diabolical girl described to me the new career she intended for me, the only one, as a matter of fact, which was left to me, now that I had incurred the death penalty. Need I tell you, Señor, that she didn't have much trouble in convincing me? It seemed to me that I was going to be more closely attached

---

* The staple diet of the Spanish soldier. (P.M.)
† *Ustilar à pastesas*: to steal by sleight of hand. (P.M.)

to her by this life of risk and rebellion. I thought that henceforth I could be sure of her love. I had often heard of a number of smugglers who roamed Andalusia, riding good horses, blunderbuss in hand and a mistress mounted behind them. I could already see myself trotting up hill and down dale with the lovely gipsy behind me. When I spoke to her about this, she almost split her sides laughing, and told me that there was nothing more wonderful than a night spent in camp, when every *rom* went to bed with his *romi* under his little tent made of a blanket draped over three hoops.

' "If I ever have you in the mountains," I said to her, "I shall be sure of you. There'll be no lieutenant there to share you with."

' "Ah, so you're jealous!" she replied. "So much the worse for you. How can you be so stupid? Can't you see that I love you, since I've never asked you for money?"

'When she talked like that, I felt like strangling her.

'To cut a long story short, Señor, Carmen obtained a civilian coat for me, with which I left Seville without being recognized. I went to Jerez with a letter from Pastia to an anisette dealer at whose house some smugglers used to meet. I was introduced to these people, whose leader, a man called Dancaïre, accepted me in his band. We set off for Gaucin, where I found Carmen, who had arranged to meet me there. On our expeditions, she acted as a spy for our people, and there never was a better one. She had just returned from Gibraltar, and she had already come to an arrangement with a ship's captain to pick up some English merchandise which we were due to receive on the coast. We went to wait for it near Estepona, and then hid part of it in the mountains, taking the rest to Ronda. Carmen had gone there ahead of us. It was she again who told us when we could enter the town.

'That first expedition and a few others after it were

successful. I liked a smuggler's life better than a soldier's. I gave Carmen presents. I had money and a mistress. I felt scarcely any remorse, for, as the gipsies say, "Where there's pleasure, scabies don't itch".* We were well received everywhere; my companions treated me well and even showed me a certain respect. This was because I had killed a man, and there were some of them who had no such exploit on their conscience. But what pleased me more in my new life was that I saw a great deal of Carmen. She was more affectionate to me than ever; but among our comrades she would never admit to being my mistress, and she had even made me swear a solemn oath never to say anything to them about her. I was so weak in the face of that creature that I obeyed her every whim. Besides, this was the first time she had shown the modesty of a decent woman, and I was simple enough to believe that she had really given up her former ways.

'Our band, which consisted of eight or ten men, scarcely ever assembled except at decisive moments, and usually we were scattered among the towns and villages in twos and threes. Each of us pretended to have a trade; one was a coppersmith, another a horse-dealer; I myself was a haberdasher, but I scarcely ever showed my face in the bigger towns on account of my trouble in Seville. One day, or rather, one night, our rendezvous was at the foot of Vejer. Dancaïre and I arrived there before the others. He seemed to be in high spirits.

' "We are going to have another comrade with us," he told me. "Carmen has just brought off one of her finest exploits. She has just managed to get her *rom* out of the prison at Tarifa."

'I was already beginning to understand Romany, which nearly all my comrades spoke, and this word *rom* gave me a shock.

* *Sarapia sat pesquital ne punzava.* (P.M.)

' "What! Her husband? Do you mean that she is married?" I asked the captain.

' "Yes," he replied, "to One-eyed Garcia, a gipsy as cunning as she is. The poor devil was in prison, but Carmen got round the prison doctor so well that she succeeded in freeing her *rom*. Oh, that girl is worth her weight in gold, and no mistake. She has been trying to arrange his escape for the past two years. Nothing worked until they took it into their heads to change the prison doctor. It seems that she soon managed to come to an understanding with this one."

'You can imagine how pleased I was to hear this news. I soon met One-eyed Garcia, and he was undoubtedly the ugliest monster the gipsy race ever produced: with his dark skin and even darker soul, he was the most arrant scoundrel I have ever met in the whole of my life. Carmen arrived with him, and you should have seen the eyes she made at me when she called him her *rom* in my presence, and the faces she pulled when Garcia was looking the other way. I was furious, and I didn't say a word to her all night.

'In the morning, we had packed our bundles and were already on our way when we noticed that a dozen horsemen were on our heels. The boastful Andalusians, who were always breathing fire and slaughter, took fright straight away. There was a general stampede. Dancaïre, Garcia, a handsome young fellow called Remendado from Ecija, and Carmen herself did not lose their heads; but the rest abandoned the mules and took to the ravines, where the horses could not follow them. We could not save our animals, and hastily unstrapped the most valuable part of our booty and loaded it on our shoulders; then we tried to escape over the rocks down the steepest slopes. We threw our bundles in front of us and followed them as best we could, sliding on our heels. In the meantime the enemy was sniping at us; it was the first time I had heard the whistling of bullets, but it didn't make much of an impression on me. When a man is in a woman's presence, there isn't very much merit in his scorning death. We all escaped, except poor Remendado, who was hit in the back. I threw my bundle down and tried to pick him up.

' "You fool," shouted Garcia, "what do we want with a corpse? Finish him off and mind you don't lose those cotton stockings!"

' "Drop him! Drop him!" Carmen shouted at me.

'Exhaustion forced me to put him down for a moment in the shelter of a rock. Garcia came up and discharged his blunderbuss into his head.

' "He'll be a clever man who can recognize him now," said Garcia, looking at Remendado's face which had been blown to pieces by a dozen bullets.

'That, Señor, was the wonderful life I led. In the evening, we found ourselves in a thicket, utterly exhausted, with nothing to eat and handicapped by the loss of our mules. What did that devil Garcia do but take out a pack of cards and start playing with Dancaïre by the light of a fire they had lit. Meanwhile I was lying looking at the stars, thinking about Remendado, and reflecting that I would just as soon be in his place. Carmen was crouching near me, and now and then she clicked her castanets, humming to herself. Then, coming over to me as if to whisper in my ear, she kissed me two or three times, almost against my will.

' "You are a devil," I said to her.

' "I know," she replied.

'After a few hours' rest she set off for Gaucin, and the next morning a little goatherd came and brought us some bread. We stayed there all day, and at night we approached Gaucin. We waited for word from Carmen, but none came. At daybreak we saw a muleteer leading two mules, one carrying a well-dressed woman with a parasol, and the other a little girl who appeared to be her maid. Garcia said to us:

' "There are two mules and two women that St Nicholas has sent us. I'd rather have four mules, but I'll make do with what there is."

'He took his blunderbuss and went down towards the path, concealing himself in the undergrowth. Dancaïre and I followed him, a little way behind. When we were within range we showed ourselves, shouting to the muleteer to stop. The woman, instead of taking fright when she saw us – and our appearance was alarming enough – burst out laughing.

' "Ah, the *lillipendi*! They take me for an *erañi*!"*

'It was Carmen, but so well disguised that I wouldn't have recognized her if she had spoken any other language. She jumped off her mule and talked for some time in an undertone with Dancaïre and Garcia. Then she said to me:

' "Canary, we'll meet again before they hang you. I'm going to Gibraltar on gipsy business. You'll hear from me soon."

'We separated after she had told us of a place where we could find shelter for a few days. That girl was the salvation of our band. Before long we received a little money she sent us, together with some information which was worth even more to us: that on a certain day a couple of English lords would be travelling by a certain road from Gibraltar to Granada. A word to the wise is enough. They had a goodly number of guineas on them. Garcia wanted to kill them, but Dancaïre and I opposed the idea. We robbed them only of their money and their watches – and their shirts, which we needed badly.

'Señor, a man becomes a scoundrel without meaning to. A pretty girl turns your head, you fight for her, a misfortune

* 'Ah, the fools! They take me for a lady!' (P.M.)

occurs, you have to take to the mountains, and from being a smuggler you turn into a robber before you know where you are. We decided that it wouldn't be healthy for us in the vicinity of Gibraltar after the affair of the English lords, and so we went deep into the Sierra de Ronda. You once mentioned José-Maria to me; well, that was where I met him. He used to take his mistress with him on his expeditions. She was a pretty girl, sensible, demure, and well-behaved; she never spoke a coarse word, and she was utterly devoted. ... In return, he made her terribly unhappy. He was always running after other girls, he ill-treated her, and now and then he took it into his head to play the jealous lover. Once he stabbed her with his knife. Well, she only loved him all the more for it. Women are like that, especially the Andalusians. That one was proud of the scar on her arm, and used to show it off as if it were the most beautiful thing in the world. And then, apart from everything else, José-Maria was the worst of comrades. ... On one of our expeditions he so arranged matters that he reaped all the profit and we had all the trouble and fighting.

'But to return to my story, we heard no more from Carmen. Dancaïre said:

' "One of us will have to go to Gibraltar to get some news of her; she must have arranged something for us. I would go, but I am too well known in Gibraltar."

'One-eyed Garcia said:

' "So am I. They know me well there, I've played so many tricks on the lobsters.* Besides, with only one eye, it isn't easy to disguise me."

' "Does that mean that I must go?" I said in my turn, delighted at the very idea of seeing Carmen again. "Right, what do I have to do?"

'The others told me:

* The name the Spaniards give to the English on account of the colour of their uniforms. (P.M.)

' "Go there by sea or by way of San Roque, as you please, and when you arrive in Gibraltar, ask at the harbour for the house of a woman called La Rollona who sells chocolate. When you have found her, she will tell you what is happening over there."

'It was agreed that we should all set off for the Sierra de Gaucin, that I should leave my two companions there, and that I should go to Gibraltar disguised as a fruit-seller. At Ronda one of our men had obtained a passport for me, and at Gaucin I was provided with a donkey; I loaded it with oranges and melons and set out.

'When I got to Gibraltar, I found that La Rollona was well known there, but that she was dead or had gone to *finibus terrae*.* To my mind, her disappearance explained how we had lost touch with Carmen. I put my donkey in a stable, and, taking my oranges, I wandered round the town, as if in order to sell them, but really to see if I could find somebody I knew. In Gibraltar there are scoundrels from all over the world, and it's a regular Tower of Babel, for you cannot take a dozen steps in any street without hearing as many languages. I saw a good many gipsies, but I didn't dare put my trust in them; I sounded them, and they sounded me. We could tell that we were all scoundrels; the important thing was to find out whether we belonged to the same band. After spending two days vainly wandering about, I had learnt nothing about either La Rollona or Carmen, and I was thinking of rejoining my comrades after making a few purchases when, as I was walking along a street at sunset, I heard a woman call to me from a window.

' "Orange-seller!" she cried.

'I looked up and saw Carmen on a balcony, leaning on the balustrade next to a curly-headed officer in a red uniform with gold epaulets, who looked every inch a great lord.

* To prison, or to the devil. (P.M.)

As for Carmen, she was magnificently dressed, all in silk, with a shawl over her shoulders and a gold comb in her hair; and, the same as ever, the amazing girl was laughing fit to split her sides. In atrocious Spanish the Englishman called out to me to come upstairs, because the Señora wanted some oranges; while Carmen said to me in Basque:

' "Come on up, and don't be surprised at anything you see."

'By now, in fact, nothing she did could surprise me. I cannot tell whether I felt more joy or sorrow at finding her. At the door there was a tall English footman in a powdered wig who showed me into a magnificent drawing-room. Carmen immediately said to me in Basque:

' "You can't speak a word of Spanish, and you don't know me."

'Then, turning to the Englishman, she said:

' "There, didn't I tell you? I saw straight away that he was a Basque. You're going to hear what a funny language it is. Doesn't he look stupid? Just like a cat caught in a larder."

' "And you," I told her in my own tongue, "you look like a brazen hussy, and I'd like to slash your face open in front of your lover."

' "My lover?" she said. "You mean to say you guessed that all by yourself? And you are jealous of this idiot? You are even sillier than you were before our evenings together in the Calle Candilejo. Don't you see, you great ninny, that I am doing gipsy business, and doing it in great style? This house is mine, and the lobster's guineas are going to be mine too; I can lead him about by the nose, and soon I'll lead him to a place from which he'll never return."

' "As for me," I said, "if you ever do gipsy business in this way again, I'll make sure that it's the last time."

' "Will you now? Are you my *rom*, to order me about like that? One-eyed Garcia doesn't mind, so what business is it of yours? I think you ought to be satisfied to be the only man who can call himself my *minchorrò*."*

' "What is he saying?" asked the Englishman.

' "He says that he's thirsty and he wouldn't mind a drink," answered Carmen. And she threw herself on a sofa and burst out laughing at her translation.

'Señor, when that girl laughed, it was impossible to talk sense. Everybody laughed with her. That tall Englishman started laughing too, like the fool he was, and gave orders for me to be given a drink.

'While I was drinking, Carmen said:

' "Do you see that ring on his finger? If you like, I'll give it you."

' "I would give one of my fingers," I replied, "to have your lord up in the mountains, with each of us holding a *maquila*."

' "*Maquila*," said the Englishman. "What does that mean?"

' "A *maquila*," said Carmen, still laughing, "is an orange. Isn't it a funny word for an orange? He says that he would like to treat you to some *maquilas*."

' "Really?" said the Englishman. "Well, bring some more *maquilas* tomorrow."

'While we were talking the footman appeared and announced that dinner was served. Then the Englishman got up, gave me a piastre, and offered his arm to Carmen, as if she were unable to walk by herself. Still laughing, Carmen said to me:

' "I can't invite you to dinner, my lad; but tomorrow, as soon as you hear the drum beating for parade, come here with some oranges. You will find a bedroom better furnished than the one in the Calle Candilejo, and you will see whether I am still your Carmencita. And then we will talk about gipsy business."

* Sweetheart. (P.M.)

'I made no reply. I was already in the street when the Englishman shouted after me: "Bring some *maquilas* tomorrow," and I heard Carmen's peals of laughter.

'I went out without knowing what I was going to do. I slept hardly a wink, and in the morning I felt so angry with that traitress that I decided to leave Gibraltar without seeing her again. But at the first roll of the drum all my courage abandoned me: I took my basket of oranges and ran to Carmen's house. Her blind was half open, and I saw her huge dark eyes watching for me. The footman in the powdered wig showed me in straight away; Carmen sent him out on an errand, and as soon as we were alone, she gave one of her crocodile laughs and threw her arms round my neck. I had never seen her looking so beautiful. She was dressed like a madonna and perfumed .... she had silk furnishings and embroidered curtains ... and I was rigged out like the robber I was.

'"*Minchorrò*," said Carmen, "I would like to smash everything here, set fire to the house, and run away to the *sierra*."

'Then she lavished caresses on me, and laughed and sang and tore her fancy clothes: no monkey ever cut so many capers, pulled so many faces, or got up to so many tricks. When she had turned serious again, she said to me:

'"Listen – about our gipsy business: I'm going to get him to take me to Ronda, where I have a sister who is a nun. ...." (Here she burst out laughing again.) "We shall pass by way of a spot I will indicate to you. You will fall upon him, and rob him of everything. The best thing would be to kill him off, but," she added, with a diabolical smile she sometimes had – a smile which nobody ever felt like returning, "do you know what you ought to do? Make sure that One-eyed Garcia comes out first. You hang back a little. The lobster is brave and skilful; he has a good pair of pistols. .... You understand?"

'She broke off to burst into a fresh peal of laughter which made me shiver.

' "No," I said. "I hate Garcia, but he is my comrade. Some day I may get rid of him for you, but we will settle our accounts after the fashion of my homeland. I am only a gipsy by accident; and in some matters I shall always be a true Navarrese, a *Navarro fino*, as the proverb says."

' "You are a fool," she replied, "a ninny, a real *payllo*. You are like the dwarf who thought he was tall because he could spit a long way.* You don't really love me. Go away."

'When she told me to go away, I could never obey her. I promised to go back to my comrades and to lie in wait for the Englishman; for her part, she promised to feign illness until the time came to leave Gibraltar for Ronda. I spent another two days in Gibraltar. She had the audacity to come to see me at my inn, in disguise. Finally I set off; I too had my plan. I returned to our rendezvous, knowing where and when the Englishman and Carmen were due to pass. I found Dancaïre and Garcia waiting for me. We spent the night in a wood beside a fire of pine-cones which blazed magnificently. I asked Garcia to play cards with me, and he accepted. During the second game I accused him of cheating; he started laughing. I threw my cards in his face. He reached for his blunderbuss, but I put my foot on it and said to him:

' "They say you can handle a knife like the cleverest rogue in Malaga. Would you like to try your luck with me?"

'Dancaïre tried to separate us. I punched Garcia two or three times, and anger had lent him courage; he drew his knife and I drew mine. We both told Dancaïre to give us room and let us fight it out. He saw that there was no stopping us and drew back. Garcia was already bent double

* *Or esorjié de or narsichislé, sin chismar lachinguel*: a gipsy proverb. (P.M.)

like a cat ready to spring at a mouse. He was holding his hat in his left hand as a shield, and his knife thrust forward. That is the Andalusian guard. I for my part took up the Navarrese stance, right in front of him, my left arm raised, my left leg forward, and my knife down my right thigh. I felt stronger than a giant. He leapt at me like an arrow from a bow; I swung away on my left foot, so that he found nothing in front of him; but I stabbed him in the throat, and the knife went so deep that my hand was right under his chin. I twisted the blade so hard that it broke. It was all over. The blade was expelled from the wound by a jet of blood as thick as your arm. Garcia fell flat on his face, as stiff as a plank.

' "What have you done?" said Dancaïre.

' "Listen," I said, "we couldn't go on living together. I love Carmen, and I want to be the only one. Besides, Garcia was a scoundrel, and I haven't forgotten what he did to poor Remendado. There are only two of us now, but we make a good pair. Come, shall we be friends, you and I, friends for life?"

'Dancaïre gave me his hand. He was a man of fifty.

' "To hell with love affairs!" he cried. "If you had asked for Carmen, he would have sold her to you for a piastre. Now there are only two of us left; how are we going to manage tomorrow?"

' "Leave it all to me," I replied. "I could take on the whole world now."

'We buried Garcia, and pitched camp two hundred paces farther on. The next day, Carmen and her Englishman came along with two muleteers and a servant. I said to Dancaïre:

' "I'll take care of the Englishman. You scare the others away: they aren't armed."

'The Englishman was a plucky fellow. If Carmen hadn't jogged his arm, he would have killed me. In short, I won

Carmen back that day, and the first thing I told her was that she was a widow. When she found out how this had happened, she said:

' "You'll always be a *lillipendi*. Garcia ought to have killed you. That Navarrese guard of yours is ridiculous, and he has killed off better fighters than you. But his time had come. Yours will come too."

' "And yours," I replied, "if you aren't a faithful *romi* to me."

' "All right," she said. "I've seen it in the coffee grounds more than once that we two would end up together. Ah, well, what is to be, will be."

'And she clicked her castanets, as she always did when she wanted to banish some troublesome idea.

'A man forgets himself when he is talking about himself. All these details are probably boring you, but I shall soon have done.

'The life we were leading lasted quite a long time. Dancaïre and I gathered around us a few comrades who were more dependable than the original band, and we spent our time smuggling. Sometimes, I must confess, we held up travellers on the highway, but only as a last resort, when there was nothing else we could do. Besides, we did no harm to the travellers, and we confined ourselves to taking their money.

'For a few months I was quite satisfied with Carmen. She continued to help us with our operations by informing us of good hauls we could make. She stayed in Malaga, Cordova, or Granada; but at a word from me she would leave everything and join me in a lonely inn, or even in camp. Only once did she cause me a certain anxiety, and that was in Malaga. I learned that she had her eye on an extremely rich merchant, with whom she was probably planning to repeat the Gibraltar episode. In spite of all that Dancaïre could say to stop me, I set off and entered Malaga in broad

CARMEN

daylight. I sought out Carmen and took her away at once. We had a fierce quarrel.

' "You know," she said, "since you've become my *rom* for good and all, I love you less than when you were my *minchorrò*? I don't want to be pestered, let alone ordered about. What I want is to be free and do what I please. Take care not to push me too far. If you annoy me, I'll find some good fellow who'll do to you what you did to One-eyed Garcia."

'Dancaïre made peace between us; but we had said things to each other which rankled in our hearts, and things could never be the same again.

'Soon afterwards, misfortune overtook us. Some soldiers took us by surprise. Dancaïre was killed, as well as two other comrades of mine, and two more were captured. I myself was seriously wounded, and, if it had not been for my good horse, I would have been taken prisoner by the soldiers. Utterly exhausted, with a bullet in my body, I hid in a wood with the only companion left me. I fainted as I was dismounting, and I thought that I was going to die in the undergrowth like a hare full of gunshot. My comrade carried me to a cave we knew, and then went to fetch Carmen. She was in Granada, and came straight away. For a whole fortnight she did not leave me for a moment. She didn't sleep a wink, and she nursed me with a skill and devotion such as no woman had ever shown before for even the most beloved of men.

'As soon as I could stand on my two feet, she took me to Granada in the greatest secrecy. Gipsy women can always find safe refuges everywhere, and I spent over six weeks in a house only two doors away from the magistrate who was looking for me. More than once, looking out between the shutters, I saw him go by. At last I recovered, but I had done a great deal of thinking on my bed of pain, and I intended to turn over a new leaf. I spoke to Carmen about leaving Spain and trying to earn an honest living in the New World. She just laughed at me.

' "We weren't born to grow cabbages," she said: "our destiny, yours and mine, is to live at the expense of the *payllos*. Look, I've made a deal with Nathan Ben Joseph of Gibraltar. He has some cotton goods which are only waiting for you to smuggle them in. He knows that you are alive, and he is counting on you. What would our associates in Gibraltar say if you let them down?"

'I allowed myself to be persuaded, and I resumed my villainous trade.

'While I was hiding in Granada, there were some bullfights which Carmen went to watch. When she came back, she talked a great deal about an extremely skilful picador called Lucas. She knew the name of his horse and how much he had paid for his embroidered jacket. I paid no attention to this. A few days later, Juanito, my sole remaining comrade, told me that he had seen Carmen with Lucas in a shop in the Zacatin. This began to worry me. I asked Carmen how and why she had made the acquaintance of the picador.

' "He is a fellow," she said, "with whom we can do business. A river that makes a noise must have water or pebbles in it.* He has made twelve hundred reals in the bullring. We have a choice of two things: either we must have that money, or else, seeing that he's a good horseman and a man of courage, we can enrol him in our band. We've lost so-and-so and so-and-so, and you need to replace them. Take him with you."

' "I don't want either his money or his person," I replied, "and I forbid you to speak to him again."

' "Take care," she said; "if anybody forbids me to do something, it's soon done."

'Fortunately, the picador left for Malaga, and I for my

* *Len sos sonsi abela – Pani o reblendani terela:* a gipsy proverb. (P.M.)

CARMEN

part set about smuggling in the Jew's cotton goods. I had a lot to do on that expedition, and so had Carmen, and I forgot Lucas; perhaps she forgot him too, at least for the moment.

'It was about that time, Señor, that I met you, first near Montilla, then at Cordova. I shan't talk to you about our last encounter. You may know more about it than I do. Carmen stole your watch; she wanted your money too, and above all that ring I see on your finger, which she said was a magic ring which it was extremely important for her to have. We had a violent argument, and I struck her. She turned pale and burst into tears. It was the first time I had even seen her cry, and it had a terrible effect on me. I begged her forgiveness, but she sulked for a whole day, and when I left again for Montilla she wouldn't kiss me.

'I was sad at heart, but three days later she came to see me, laughing happily and as gay as a lark. All was forgotten, and we were like a couple who had just fallen in love. As we were parting, she said to me:

' "There's a *fiesta* in Cordova. I'm going to see it; then I shall find out who are the people coming away with money, and I'll tell you."

'I let her go. Once I was on my own, I thought about this *fiesta* and about Carmen's change of mood. I told myself that she must have already taken her revenge, since she had been the first to make peace. A peasant told me that there was a bullfight in Cordova. I set off like a madman, my blood boiling, and went to the bullring. Lucas was pointed out to me, and on a bench next to the barrier I saw Carmen. As I had expected, at the very first bull, Lucas paid court to her. He snatched the cockade* from the bull and took it

* *La divisa*, a knot of ribbons, the colour of which shows from which pasture the bull comes. This knot is fixed in the bull's hide by a hook, and it is the height of gallantry to tear it from the living animal and offer it to a woman. (P.M.)

to Carmen, who promptly put it in her hair. The bull then took it upon himself to avenge me. Lucas was knocked over, with his horse on his chest and the bull on top of them both. I glanced at Carmen, but she had already left her place. It was impossible for me to leave mine, and I was obliged to wait until the end of the fights. Then I went to the house you know, and lay low there all evening and part of the night. About two o'clock in the morning Carmen returned, and was somewhat surprised to see me.

' "Come along with me," I said to her.

' "All right," she said. "Let's go."

'I went to fetch my horse, I put her up behind me, and we rode along for the rest of the night without saying a single word to each other. We stopped at daybreak at a lonely inn, not far from a little hermitage. There I said to Carmen:

' "Listen, I'll forget everything, I'll never speak of this again; but swear to me one thing: that you will come with me to America and behave yourself there."

' "No," she said sulkily, "I don't want to go to America. I'm quite happy here."

' "That's because you are close to Lucas. But remember this: if he recovers, he won't make old bones. Though why should I lay the blame on him? I'm tired of killing all your lovers; it's you I shall kill next."

'She fixed me with her wild gaze and said:

' "I have always thought that you would kill me. The first time I saw you, I had just met a priest at the door of my house. And last night, leaving Cordova, didn't you notice something? A hare crossed the road between your horse's hooves. It is written."

' "Carmencita," I said, "don't you love me any more?"

'She made no reply. She was sitting cross-legged on a mat, tracing lines on the floor with one finger.

' "Let us start a new life, Carmen," I said to her beseechingly. "Let us go and live somewhere where we shall never be parted. You know that we have a hundred and twenty ounces of gold buried under an oak not far from here.... We also have some money left in the keeping of the Jew Ben Joseph."

'She started to smile, and said to me:

' "Me first, then you. I know that that is how it will be."

' "Think it over," I went on. "I am at the end of my patience and my courage; make up your mind or I shall make up mine."

'I left her and strolled in the direction of the hermitage. I found the hermit praying. I waited until he had finished; I would have liked to pray myself, but I could not. When he stood up, I went over to him.

' "Father," I said, "will you say a prayer for somebody who is in great danger?"

' "I pray for all the afflicted," he said.

' "Can you say a Mass for a soul which may be about to appear before its Creator?"

' "Yes," he replied, gazing at me hard. And, as there was something strange about my manner, he tried to draw me out.

' "I think I have seen you before," he said.

'I put a piastre on his bench.

' "When will you say the Mass?" I asked.

' "In half an hour. The innkeeper's son will come over here to serve it. Tell me, young man, isn't there something on your conscience which is troubling you? Would you care to listen to a Christian's advice?"

'I felt close to tears. I told him that I would come back, and I hurried away. I went and lay down on the grass until I heard the bell. Then I drew near, but I stayed outside the chapel. When the Mass was over, I went back to the inn. I almost hoped that Carmen had fled; she could have taken my horse and escaped ... but I found her there. She did not want it to be said that I had frightened her. During my absence she had unpicked the hem of her dress and removed the lead in it. Now she was standing at a table, gazing into a pot full of water at the lead which she had melted down and dropped inside. She was so absorbed in her magic that at first she did not notice that I had returned. First she would pick up a piece of lead and sadly turn it over and over between her fingers; then she would sing one of those magic songs in which gipsy women invoke Maria Padilla, Don Pedro's mistress, who, so they say, was the *Bari Crallisa*, or great Queen of the Gipsies.*

' "Carmen," I said, "will you come with me?"

'She got up, threw away her pot, and put her mantilla over her head as if ready to go. My horse was brought round, she mounted behind, and we set off.

' "So, Carmen," I said after we had gone a little way, "you are ready to come with me, aren't you?"

' "I will follow you to death, yes, but I shall never live with you again."

'We were in a lonely gorge; I reined in my horse.

' "Is it here?" she asked, and with one bound she had dismounted. She took off her mantilla, threw it down at her feet, and stood motionless with one hand on her hip, gazing fixedly at me.

' "You are going to kill me, I can see that clearly," she said. "It is written, but you will not make me yield."

' "I beg you," I said, "be reasonable. Listen to me. The past is all forgotten. All the same, you know, it was you who ruined me; it was on your account that I became a thief and a murderer. Carmen, Carmen my love, let me save you and save myself with you."

* Maria Padilla has been accused of having bewitched King Don Pedro. A popular legend relates that she had given Queen Blanche de Bourbon a gold girdle which to the eyes of the bewitched king looked like a live snake. Hence the repugnance which he always showed for the unfortunate queen. (P.M.)

CARMEN

' "José," she replied, "you are asking the impossible. I do not love you any more; you still love me, though, and that is why you mean to kill me. I could easily go on lying to you, but I do not want to take the trouble. Everything is over between us. As my *rom*, you have the right to kill your *romi*; but Carmen will always be free. *Calli* she was born, *calli* she will die."

' "Then you love Lucas?" I asked her.

' "Yes, I loved him for a little while, as I loved you – perhaps not as much as you. Now I love nothing any more, and I hate myself for ever having loved you."

'I threw myself at her feet, I took her hands, I moistened them with my tears. I reminded her of all the happy times we had spent together. Everything, Señor, everything; I offered her everything if only she would love me again.

' "Love you again?" she said. "That is impossible. And I do not want to live with you."

'I was filled with rage. I drew my knife. I would have liked her to be frightened and to beg for mercy, but that woman was a devil.

' "For the last time," I cried, "will you stay with me?"

' "No, no, no!" she said, stamping her foot; and she pulled the ring I had given her off her finger and threw it into the undergrowth.

'I stabbed her twice. It was One-eyed Garcia's knife that I had taken, having broken my own. She fell at the second blow, without a cry. I can still see her great black eyes staring at me; then they turned misty and closed. For a good hour I remained prostrate beside the corpse. Then I remembered that Carmen had often told me that she would like to be buried in a wood. I dug her a grave with my knife and laid her in it. For a long time I searched for her ring, and at last I found it. I put it in the grave beside her, together with a little cross. Perhaps I was wrong. Then I mounted my horse and galloped to Cordova, where I gave myself up at the first guardhouse. I said that I had killed Carmen; but I refused to say where her body was. The hermit was a holy man. He prayed for her. He said a Mass for her soul. . . . Poor child! It was the *Calé* who were to blame for having brought her up as they did.'

CHAPTER FOUR

SPAIN is one of the countries in which those nomads scattered all over Europe, and known as Bohemians, Gitanos, Gipsies, Zigeuner, and so on, are still to be found in the greatest numbers. Most of them lead a vagabond existence in the southern and eastern provinces, Andalusia, Estremadura, and the Kingdom of Murcia; and there are a great many of them in Catalonia. The latter often cross into France, and you come upon them in all the fairs in the south. The men are usually horse-dealers, veterinary surgeons, and mule-shearers; to these trades they add the mending of saucepans and copper utensils, not to mention smuggling and other illicit practices. The women tell fortunes, beg, and sell all sorts of drugs, harmless and otherwise.

The physical characteristics of the gipsies are easier to distinguish than to describe, and, when you have seen one, you could recognize a member of this race from among a thousand other men. It is in their physiognomy and expression that they differ most of all from the other inhabitants of the same country. Their complexion is very swarthy, and darker than that of the peoples among whom they live. Hence the name of the *Calé*, or 'blacks', by which they often call themselves.*

Their eyes, perceptibly oblique, deep-set, and very dark, are shaded by long, thick lashes. Their gaze can only be compared with that of a wild animal. It is at once daring and timid, and in this respect their eyes reveal quite well the character of their race, which is bold and cunning, but 'naturally afraid of violence', like Panurge. For the most part

* I have the impression that the German gipsies, although they understand the word *Calé*, do not like to be known by it. They call themselves the *Romané tchavé*. (P.M.)

the men are well-built, slim, and agile; I do not think I have ever seen one with a paunch. In Germany the gipsy women are often very pretty; but beauty is extremely rare among the *gitanas* of Spain. When very young they may appear not unattractive in their ugliness, but once they attain motherhood they become positively repulsive.

The filthiness of both sexes is unbelievable, and nobody who has never seen a gipsy matron's hair can have any idea of what it is like, even if he imagines the coarsest, greasiest, and dustiest of tresses. In some of the large towns in Andalusia, some of the girls who are slightly more attractive than the rest will take more care of their appearance. These girls perform dances for money – dances which are very like those prohibited at our public balls at carnival time.

Mr Borrow, an English missionary and the author of two very interesting books about the Spanish gipsies, whom he had set out to convert on behalf of the Bible Society, maintains that it is unheard of for any *gitana* to show the slightest partiality for a man of another race. It seems to me that there is a great deal of exaggeration in the tributes he pays to their chastity. First of all, the great majority of them are in the position of the ugly woman described by Ovid: *Casta quam nemo rogavit.** As for the pretty ones, they are like all Spanish women, fastidious in the choice of their lovers. A man must first attract them, and then merit their favours. As proof of their virtue Mr Borrow tells a story which does honour to his own, and especially to his naivety: an immoral man of his acquaintance, he says, offered a pretty *gitana* several ounces of gold, but all in vain. An Andalusian to whom I recounted this anecdote asserted that the immoral man in question would have had better luck if he had shown the girl two or three piastres, and that to offer gold to a gipsy was as poor a method of persuasion as to promise a million or two to a chambermaid in an inn.

* Chaste is she whom no man has ever courted. (Trans.)

Be that as it may, it is undeniable that the *gitanas* show the most extraordinary devotion to their husbands. There is no danger or discomfort that they will not endure to provide for their needs. One of the names by which the gipsies refer to themselves, the *Romé* or 'married people', seems to me a proof of the respect in which their race hold the married state. Generally speaking, it may be said that their principal virtue is patriotism, if one may give that name to the loyalty they show in their dealings with people of the same origin as themselves, their eagerness to help one another, and the inviolable secrecy they observe in all compromising circumstances. For that matter, something of the sort may be observed in all mysterious associations outside the law.

A few months ago, I visited a tribe of gipsies established in the Vosges. In the hut of an old woman, the oldest member of the tribe, there was a gipsy in no way related to her family, who was suffering from a mortal disease. This man had left a hospital where he was being well cared for, to come and die among his fellow gipsies. For thirteen weeks he had been confined to bed in this camp, where he received far better treatment than the sons and sons-in-law who lived in the same hut. He had a comfortable bed of straw and moss with passably clean sheets, whereas the rest of the family, which numbered eleven persons, slept on planks three feet long. So much for their hospitality. The same woman, who was so humane to her guest, said to me in the sick man's presence: '*Singo, singo, homte hi mulo*: soon, soon, he must die.' After all, these people lead such wretched lives that talk of the approach of death holds no terrors for them.

One remarkable feature of the gipsy character is their indifference to religion. This is not to say that they are free-thinkers or sceptics. They have never made any profession of atheism: far from it. The religion of the country where they live is theirs, but they change religions when they change countries. They are likewise free of the superstitions which among backward people take the place of religious beliefs. How, indeed, could superstition exist among people who live on the credulity of others? However, I have noticed that the Spanish gipsies have a peculiar horror of touching a corpse. There are few of them who would agree, even for money, to carry a dead body to the cemetery.

I have already observed that most gipsy women engage in fortune-telling. They do this extremely well. But one of their chief sources of income is the sale of charms and love philtres. Not only do they supply toads' feet to secure fickle hearts, and lodestone filings to awaken love in the unfeeling, but when required they pronounce powerful incantations which compel the Devil to lend them his aid.

Last year a Spanish lady told me the following story: One day she was walking along the Calle Alcala, very sad and pensive, when a gipsy woman squatting on the pavement called out to her: 'Pretty lady, your lover has deceived you.' (This was true.) 'Would you like me to bring him back to you?' You can imagine with what delight this proposal was accepted and what confidence was inspired by a person who could thus guess the innermost secrets of the heart at a single glance. As it would have been impossible to perform magical operations in the most crowded street in Madrid, a meeting was arranged for the following day.

'Nothing will be easier than to bring the faithless one back to your feet,' said the *gitana*. 'Do you happen to have a handkerchief, a scarf or a mantilla that he has given you?' A silk scarf was handed to her. 'Now take some crimson silk and sew a piastre into one corner of the scarf; sew a half-piastre into another corner, a peseta here, and a two-real piece there. Then you must sew a gold coin in the middle. A doubloon would be best.'

The doubloon and the other coins were duly sewn in. 'Now give me the scarf and I'll take it to the Campo Santo on the stroke of midnight. Come with me if you want to see a splendid piece of devilry. I promise you that no later than tomorrow you will be reunited with the man you love.'

The gipsy woman set off for the Campo Santo by herself, for the lady was too frightened of devils to accompany her. I leave you to guess whether the poor forsaken lady ever saw her scarf or her lover again.

In spite of their poverty and the sort of aversion they inspire, the gipsies enjoy a certain consideration among the uneducated, and they are very proud of it. They feel conscious of being a superior race with regard to intelligence, and they heartily despise the very people who show them hospitality. 'The Gentiles are so stupid,' a gipsy woman of the Vosges said to me, 'that there is no merit in fooling them. The other day, a peasant woman called to me in the street, and I went into her house. Her stove was smoking, and she asked me for a charm to make it draw. First of all, I got her to give me a good piece of bacon. Then I started muttering a few words in Romany. "You're a fool," I said, "you were born a fool, and you'll die a fool...." When I was near the door, I said to her in good German: "The surest way of stopping your stove from smoking is not to light it." And I took to my heels.'

The history of the gipsies is still very obscure. True, we know that the first bands of them, which were not very large, appeared in eastern Europe towards the beginning of the fifteenth century; but nobody can tell where they came from, or why they came to Europe, and, what is even more extraordinary, nobody knows how they multiplied so prodigiously within a short time in several countries far removed from one another. The gipsies themselves have preserved no tradition as to their origin, and, if most of them speak of Egypt as their original homeland, that is simply because they have adopted a very ancient fable about their race.

Most of the Orientalists who have studied the language of

the gipsies believe that they originated in India. It seems in fact that a great number of the roots and grammatical forms of Romany are to be found in idioms derived from Sanskrit. As may be imagined, the gipsies adopted many foreign words in the course of their long peregrinations. In every Romany dialect a good many Greek words are to be found, for instance, *cocal* (bone) from κόκκαλον, *petalli* (horseshoe) from πέταλον, *cafi* (nail) from καρφί, and so on. Today the gipsies have almost as many different dialects as there are distinct groups of their race. Everywhere they speak the language of the country they inhabit more easily than their own idioms, which they scarcely ever use except to be able to converse freely in front of strangers. If the dialect of the German gipsies is compared with that used by the Spanish gipsies, who have had no communication with the former group for centuries, a great number of words common to both dialects will be discovered; but everywhere the original language has been perceptibly affected, though in different degrees, by contact with the more developed languages which the nomads have been obliged to use. German on the one hand and Spanish on the other have so modified the basic Romany tongue that it would be impossible for a gipsy from the Black Forest to converse with one of his Andalusian brothers, although they would only have to exchange a few phrases to recognize that they were both speaking dialects derived from the same idiom. A few words in very frequent use are, I believe, common to all the dialects; thus, in every vocabulary I have been able to see, *pani* means water, *manro* bread, *mâs* meat, and *lon* salt.

The words for numbers are almost the same everywhere. The German dialect seems to me to be much purer than the Spanish dialect, for it has preserved a good many primitive grammatical forms, whereas the *gitanos* have adopted those of the Castilian language. Nevertheless, a few words are exceptions, bearing witness to a former common tongue. The preterite of the German dialect is formed by adding *-ium* to the imperative, which is invariably the root of the verb. The verbs in Spanish Romany are all conjugated on the model of the Castilian verbs of the first conjugation. The infinitive *jamar*, to eat, should normally produce the form *jamé*, I have eaten; and *lillar*, to take, should give *lillé*, I have taken. However, a few old gipsies say *jayon* and *lillon*. I know of no other verbs which have preserved this ancient form.

While I am thus showing off my slender knowledge of the Romany language, I should point out a few words of French slang which our thieves have borrowed from the gipsies. *Les Mystères de Paris* have taught honest folk that *chourin* means a knife. This is pure Romany: *tchouri* is one of those words that are common to all the gipsy dialects. Monsieur Vidocq calls a horse *grès*, and this again is a gipsy word – *gras*, *gre*, *graste*, or *gris*. Another example is the word *romanichel* which means the gipsies in Parisian slang: this is a corruption of *romané tchavé*, or gipsy lads. But one derivation of which I am proud is that of *frimousse*, a word for face or expression which all schoolboys use, or at least did in my day. Note first of all that Oudin, in his curious dictionary, wrote *firlimouse* in 1640. Now, in Romany, *firla* or *fila* means face, and *mui* has the same meaning; it is the *os* of the Latins. The combination *firlamui* was promptly understood by a gipsy purist, and I believe it to be true to the spirit of his language.

This should be quite enough to give the readers of *Carmen* a favourable impression of my Romany studies. I will conclude with this appropriate proverb: *En retudi panda nasti abela macha*: into a closed mouth no fly can enter.

COLOMBA

CHAPTER ONE

> Pè far la to vendetta,
> Sta sigur', vasta anche ella.
> VOCERO DU NIOLO

EARLY in October 181–, Colonel Sir Thomas Nevil, a distinguished Irish officer in the British army, stopped with his daughter at the Hôtel Beauveau in Marseilles on their return from a visit to Italy. The persistent admiration of enthusiastic travellers has resulted in a reaction, and, in order to set themselves apart from the common herd, many tourists nowadays adopt as their motto Horace's *nil admirari*. It was to this class of discontented travellers that Miss Lydia, the colonel's only daughter, belonged. *The Transfiguration* had struck her as mediocre, and Mount Vesuvius in eruption as barely superior to the factory chimneys of Birmingham. All in all, her great objection to Italy was that it lacked character and local colour. Let him who can, explain the meaning of these words, which I understood perfectly well a few years ago but which baffle me today. At first Miss Lydia had flattered herself that she had found things on the other side of the Alps which nobody had seen before her, and about which she could talk to 'respectable people', as Monsieur Jourdain calls them. But soon, preceded everywhere by her fellow countrymen, and despairing of finding anything unknown, she went over to the opposition. It is indeed extremely disagreeable not to be able to talk about the wonders of Italy without somebody saying to you: 'Of course you know that painting by Raphael in the Palazzo — at — ? It is the most beautiful thing in Italy.' And it is the very thing you have neglected to see. As it would take too long to see everything, the simplest course is to condemn everything out of hand.

At the Hôtel Beauveau Miss Lydia met with a bitter disappointment. She had brought back from Italy a pretty sketch of the Pelasgic or Cyclopean Gate at Segni, which she thought had been overlooked by other artists. But Lady Frances Fenwich, meeting her in Marseilles, showed her her album, in which, between a sonnet and a dried flower, there was the gate in question, liberally adorned with burnt sienna. Miss Lydia gave her Segni Gate to the chambermaid, and lost all regard for Pelasgic architecture.

This melancholy attitude was shared by Colonel Nevil, who ever since his wife's death had seen things only through Miss Lydia's eyes. To his mind, Italy suffered from the enormous disadvantage of having bored his daughter, and consequently it was the most boring country in the world. True, he had no fault to find with the pictures and the statues; but what he could say for certain was that the shooting was appalling in that country, and that you had to tramp over twenty miles in the blazing sun in the Roman *campagna* to kill a few wretched red-legged partridges.

On the day following his arrival in Marseilles, he invited to dinner Captain Ellis, his former adjutant, who had just spent six weeks in Corsica. The captain told Miss Lydia a story about bandits which had the virtue of bearing no resemblance to the stories of robbers with which she had so often been regaled on the road from Rome to Naples, and told it well. Over dessert, the two men, who had been left alone with a few bottles of claret, talked about hunting, and the colonel learnt that there is no country in which it is more excellent, varied and abundant than in Corsica. 'There are lots of wild boar,' said Captain Ellis, 'and you have to learn to tell them from the domestic pigs, to which they bear an astonishing resemblance; for if you kill any pigs you find yourself in serious trouble with the swineherds. They come out of thickets which they call *maquis*, armed to the teeth, force you to pay for their animals, and make fun of you at the same time. There's also the moufflon or wild sheep, a most peculiar animal which you won't find anywhere else, splendid game but difficult to hunt. Stags, deer, pheasants, partridges – there's no end to the kinds of game with which Corsica swarms. If you like shooting, Colonel, go to Corsica. There, as one of my hosts used to say, you can shoot at every possible kind of game, from thrushes to men.'

At tea, the captain delighted Miss Lydia again with a story of a *vendetta transversale* which was even stranger than the first tale, and he completed her enthusiasm for Corsica by describing to her the strange, wild scenery of the country, the outlandish character of its inhabitants, their hospitality and their primitive customs. Finally he offered her a pretty little dagger, less remarkable for its shape and brass handle than for its origin. A notorious bandit had given it to Captain Ellis, assuring him that it had been thrust into four human bodies. Miss Lydia put it in her belt, laid it on her bedside table, and drew it out of its scabbard twice before falling asleep. For his part, the colonel dreamt that he killed a moufflon and that the owner made him pay for it, to which he gladly agreed, for it was a most peculiar animal, like a wild boar with a stag's horns and a pheasant's tail.

'Ellis says that there's splendid shooting to be had in Corsica,' said the colonel, as he was breakfasting alone with his daughter. 'If it weren't so far, I should like to spend a fortnight there.'

'Well,' replied Miss Lydia, 'why shouldn't we go to Corsica. While you were shooting I could draw; I should love to have a sketch in my album of that grotto Captain Ellis was talking about, where Bonaparte used to go and study when he was a child.'

It was perhaps the first time that a wish expressed by the colonel had won his daughter's approval. Delighted by this unexpected approbation, he none the less had the good sense to raise a few objections in order to encourage Miss Lydia's welcome whim. It was in vain that he spoke of the wildness of the country and of the difficulties awaiting any woman who travelled there: she was afraid of nothing; she liked nothing better than travelling on horseback; she looked forward to sleeping out in the open; she threatened to go to Asia Minor. In short, she had a reply to everything, for no Englishwoman had ever been to Corsica, and consequently she felt that she must. What a joy it would be, back in St James's Place, to display her album!

'But, my dear, why are you passing over that delightful drawing?'

'Oh, that's nothing. It's just a sketch I made of a notorious Corsican bandit who acted as our guide.'

'What! You mean to say you have been to Corsica?'

Since at that time there was no steamboat service between France and Corsica, inquiries were made to find a ship about to sail for the island which Miss Lydia intended to discover. That very day, the colonel wrote to Paris to cancel the apartment which he had rented, and came to an agreement with the skipper of a Corsican schooner which was about to set sail for Ajaccio. There were two tolerable cabins available. Provisions were put on board; the skipper swore that one of his old sailors was an excellent cook and had no equal when it came to making bouillabaisse; he promised that Mademoiselle would be very comfortable and that she would have a favourable wind and a calm sea.

Finally, in deference to his daughter's wishes, the colonel stipulated that the captain should take no other passenger on board, and that he should make a point of skirting the coasts of the island, so that they could enjoy a view of the mountains.

CHAPTER TWO

ON the day fixed for their departure, everything was packed and put on board in the morning: the schooner was due to sail with the evening breeze. In the meantime, the colonel was strolling with his daughter along the Canebière when the skipper accosted him to ask his permission to take on board a relative of his, namely his eldest son's godfather's second cousin, who had to return to Corsica, his native country, on urgent business, and was unable to find a ship to take him.

'He is a delightful fellow,' added Captain Matei, 'a soldier, an officer in the Foot-guards, who would have been a colonel by now if the Other were still Emperor.'

'Seeing that he's a soldier . . . ,' said the colonel, and he was about to add: 'I shall be glad to allow him to come with us,' but Miss Lydia exclaimed in English:

'An infantry officer!' (Her father had served in the cavalry, and she looked down on any other arm of the service.) 'An uneducated fellow, perhaps, who will be seasick and spoil all the pleasure of the crossing for us!'

The skipper did not know a word of English, but he seemed to understand what Miss Lydia was saying from the pout of her lips, and he embarked on a lengthy panegyric of his relative, which he concluded by asserting that he was a highly respectable gentleman, descended from a family of *Corporals*, and that he would not inconvenience the colonel in any way, for he, the skipper, would see to it that he was installed in some corner where nobody would be aware of his presence.

The colonel and Miss Nevil thought it peculiar that there should be families in Corsica where the rank of corporal was handed down from father to son; but, as they naively imagined that the person in question was a corporal in the infantry, they concluded that he was some poor devil whom the skipper wanted to take along out of kindness. If he had been an officer, they would have been obliged to speak to him and live with him; but there was no need to bother about a corporal, who is a creature of no consequence unless his squad is with him, with fixed bayonets, ready to take you where you have no desire to go.

'Does your relative suffer from seasickness?' Miss Nevil asked in a curt tone of voice.

'Never, Mademoiselle; he's as steady as a rock, on land or sea.'

'Well then, you may bring him along,' she said.

'You may bring him along,' repeated the colonel, and they continued their stroll.

About five o'clock in the afternoon, Captain Matei came to escort them aboard the schooner. On the quayside, near the captain's yawl, they met a tall young man dressed in a blue frock-coat buttoned up to the chin, with a tanned face, dark, bright, deep-set eyes, and an open, intelligent manner. From his small curly moustache and the way he threw back his shoulders, it was easy to recognize a soldier; for at that period moustaches were far from common, and the National Guard had not yet introduced into every home the bearing and the habits of the barrackroom.

The young man doffed his cap when he saw the colonel, and thanked him politely and without any embarrassment for the good turn he was doing him.

'Delighted to be able to help you, my good fellow,' said the colonel, giving him a friendly nod. And he went on board the yawl.

'He isn't very polite, this Englishman of yours,' the young man muttered in Italian to the skipper.

The latter put his forefinger under his left eye and pulled down the corners of his mouth. To anybody familiar with sign language, this meant that the Englishman understood Italian and that he was an odd character. The young man gave a faint smile and touched his forehead in answer to Matei's sign, as if to say that all Englishmen were a little wrong in the head. Then he sat down beside the skipper and gazed attentively, but not impertinently, at his pretty fellow-traveller.

'These French soldiers cut a good figure,' the colonel said to his daughter in English; 'so it is easy to make officers of them.'

Then, addressing the young man in French, he said:

'Tell me, my good man, which regiment did you serve in?'

The young man gave a nudge with his elbow to his second cousin's godson's father, and, suppressing a sarcastic smile, replied that he had been in the Foot-guards and that he had just left the Seventh Regiment of the Light Infantry.

'Were you at Waterloo? You are very young.'

'I beg your pardon, Colonel, that was my only campaign.'

'It counts as much as two,' said the colonel.

The young Corsican bit his lip.

'Papa,' said Miss Lydia in English, 'do ask him if the Corsicans are very fond of their Bonaparte.'

Before the colonel could translate the question into French, the young man replied in fairly good English, though with a pronounced accent:

'You must know, Mademoiselle, that nobody is a prophet in his own country. We Corsicans, who are Napoleon's fellow countrymen, are probably not as devoted to him as the French. For my part, although my family used to be at daggers drawn with his, I like him and admire him.'

'You speak English!' exclaimed the colonel.

'Very badly, as you can see.'

Although somewhat shocked at his casual manner, Miss Lydia could not help laughing at the idea of a personal feud between a corporal and an emperor. This struck her as a foretaste of the peculiarities of Corsica, and she decided to make a note of it in her diary.

'Perhaps you were a prisoner in England?' asked the colonel.

'No, Colonel, I learned English in France at an early age, from an English prisoner.'

Then, addressing Miss Nevil, he went on:

'Matei tells me that you have just come back from Italy. You probably speak pure Tuscan, Mademoiselle, and I fear you will find it rather difficult to understand our dialect.'

'My daughter understands all the Italian dialects,' said the colonel. 'She has a gift for languages. Not like me.'

'Would Mademoiselle understand, for example, these lines from one of our Corsican songs? A shepherd is speaking to a shepherdess:

> '*S' entrassi 'ndru Paradisu santu, santu,*
> *E nun truvassi a tia, mi n' esciria.*'*

Miss Lydia did understand. She thought that the quotation was bold and the look which accompanied it bolder still, and she replied with a blush: '*Capisco.*'

'And are you returning to your country on leave?' asked the colonel.

'No, Colonel. They have put me on half-pay, probably because I was at Waterloo and I am a fellow-countryman of Napoleon's. I am going home, as the song says, "short of hope and short of money".' And he gave a sigh, looking up at the sky.

The colonel put his hand into his pocket and, turning a gold coin over in his fingers, hunted for a suitable phrase with which he might slip it politely into his unfortunate enemy's palm.

'I too,' he said in a good-natured voice, 'have been put on half-pay; but ... with your half-pay you can't have

* 'If I entered holy, holy Paradise, and did not find you, I would leave.' (P.M.)

enough to keep yourself in tobacco. Here, Corporal, take this.'

And he tried to thrust the gold coin into the young man's closed hand, which was resting on the gunwale of the yawl.

The young Corsican flushed, straightened up, bit his lip, and seemed to be about to make an angry retort when all of a sudden, changing his expression, he burst out laughing. The colonel, still holding his gold coin, was completely dumbfounded.

'Colonel,' said the young man, turning serious once more, 'allow me to give you two pieces of advice. The first is never to offer a Corsican money, for some of my fellow-countrymen would be rude enough to fling it back in your face; and the second is not to give people titles they don't lay claim to. You call me Corporal, and I am a lieutenant. Admittedly the difference is not very great, but. . . .'

'Lieutenant!' exclaimed Sir Thomas. 'Lieutenant! But the captain told me you were a corporal, like your father and all the other men in your family!'

At these words the young man lay back and started laughing more than ever, and so heartily that the skipper and his two sailors joined in.

'I beg your pardon, Colonel,' the young man said at last; 'but the mistake you made is really very funny, and I have only just understood it. My family does indeed pride itself on numbering several corporals among its ancestors; but our Corsican corporals have never worn stripes on their sleeves. About the year of grace 1100, a few villages rose in revolt against the tyranny of the great mountain lords and chose leaders whom they called *corporals*. On our island we account it an honour to be descended from those tribunes, as you might call them.'

'Forgive me, sir!' cried the colonel. 'A thousand pardons. Since you understand the cause of my mistake, I hope you will excuse it.' And he held out his hand.

'It is a proper punishment for my petty pride, Colonel,'

said the young man, still laughing and warmly shaking the Englishman's hand. 'I am not in the least annoyed with you. Since my friend Matei introduced me so badly, allow me to introduce myself. My name is Orso della Rebbia, a lieutenant on half-pay; and if, as I presume from those two fine dogs of yours, you are coming to Corsica to hunt, I should be extremely flattered to show you our *maquis* and our mountains ... that is, if I haven't forgotten them,' he added with a sigh.

At that moment the yawl came alongside the schooner. The lieutenant offered his hand to Miss Lydia, then helped the colonel to climb on deck. There, Sir Thomas, still very shamefaced about his mistake, and not knowing how to get a man whose family went back to 1100 to forget his impertinence, invited him to supper, repeating his apologies and handshakes, and without waiting for his daughter's approval. Miss Lydia admittedly frowned a little, but, after all, she was not sorry to know what a corporal was; she had taken rather a liking to her guest and was even beginning to find a certain aristocratic air about him; only he struck her as too frank and gay for a hero of romance.

'Lieutenant della Rebbia,' said the colonel, toasting him in the English manner, with a glass of Madeira, 'I saw a good many of your fellow-countrymen in Spain; they were splendid sharpshooters.'

'Yes, many of them stayed in Spain,' said the young lieutenant gravely.

'I shall never forget the conduct of a Corsican battalion at the Battle of Vitoria,' the colonel went on. 'I have good reason to remember it,' he added, rubbing his chest. 'All day long they had been skirmishing in the gardens, behind the hedges, and had killed heaven knows how many of our men and horses. Once the retreat had been decided on, they rallied and took to their heels as fast as they could. We had hoped to get our revenge on the plain, but those scoundrels –

I beg your pardon, Lieutenant – those brave fellows, I was saying, had formed a square and there was no way of breaking it. In the middle of the square – I can still see him now – there was an officer on a little black horse; he kept close to the eagle, smoking his cigar as if he had been in a café. Now and then their band would play a fanfare, as if to defy us. I sent my two best squadrons into action against them. Bah! Instead of charging the front of the square, my dragoons rode past them, then wheeled around and came back in utter disorder, with more than one riderless horse – and that confounded band played on. When the smoke enveloping the battalion had cleared, I again saw the officer beside the eagle, still smoking his cigar. I was furious and put myself at the head of a final charge. Their muskets, clogged by so much firing, wouldn't go off any more, but the soldiers had formed ranks six deep, with their bayonets levelled at the noses of our horses; they stood there like a wall. I kept shouting and urging on my dragoons, and I was spurring my horse forward when the officer I was telling you about, finally taking his cigar out of his mouth, pointed me out to one of his men. I heard something like: "*Al capello bianco!*" I was wearing a white plume. I heard nothing more, for a bullet went through my chest. That was a magnificent battalion, Monsieur della Rebbia: the first in the Eighteenth Regiment, and all of them Corsicans, according to what I was told later.'

'Yes,' said Orso, whose eyes had been shining as he listened to this story. 'They covered the retreat and brought back their eagle; but two thirds of those brave fellows lie sleeping today on the plain of Vitoria.'

'Do you by any chance know the name of the officer in command of them?'

'That was my father. He was then a major in the Eighteenth Regiment, and he was made a colonel for his conduct on that melancholy day.'

'Your father! Upon my soul, he was a brave man! I should be glad to see him again, and I feel sure that I would recognize him. Is he still alive?'

'No, Colonel,' said the young man, turning slightly pale.

'Was he at Waterloo?'

'Yes, Colonel, but he did not have the good fortune to die on a battlefield.... He died in Corsica ... two years ago.... Heavens, how beautiful this sea is! It is ten years since I last saw the Mediterranean. Don't you find the Mediterranean more beautiful than the Ocean, Mademoiselle?'

'I think it is too blue ... and the waves lack grandeur.'

'You like wild beauty, Mademoiselle? In that case, I think you will like Corsica.'

'My daughter,' said the colonel, 'likes anything out of the ordinary; that is why Italy did not particularly appeal to her.'

'I don't know Italy,' said Orso, 'except for Pisa, where I went to school for some time; but I cannot think without admiration of the Campo-Santo, the Duomo or the Leaning Tower – especially the Campo-Santo. Do you remember Orcagna's *Death*? I think I could draw it here and now, it made such a lasting impression on my memory.'

Miss Lydia was afraid that the lieutenant was going to launch out into an enthusiastic tirade.

'It is very pretty,' she said with a yawn. 'Excuse me, Father, I have a slight headache. I am going to go down to my cabin.'

She kissed her father on the forehead, gave a majestic nod of her head to Orso, and disappeared.

The two men then started chatting about war and hunting. They learned that at Waterloo they had been facing each other and must have exchanged a good many bullets. This knowledge strengthened their mutual liking. In turn they criticized Napoleon, Wellington, and Blücher. Then together they hunted deer, the wild boar, and the moufflon. Finally, when it was very late and the last bottle of claret was empty, the colonel shook hands once more with the lieutenant and bade him good night, expressing the hope of cultivating an acquaintance begun in such a ridiculous manner. They separated and each went off to bed.

CHAPTER THREE

IT was a beautiful night, with the moonlight playing on the waves and the ship gliding smoothly along in a gentle breeze. Miss Lydia did not feel like sleeping, and it was only the presence of an outsider which had prevented her from enjoying those emotions which every human being experiences at sea, by moonlight, if he has a grain of poetry in his heart. When she thought that the young lieutenant must be sound asleep, like the humdrum creature that he was, she got up, took a pelisse, awakened her chambermaid, and went on deck. There was nobody there but a sailor at the helm, who was singing a sort of lament in the Corsican dialect, to a wild, monotonous tune. In the calm of the night this strange music had its charm. Unfortunately Miss Lydia did not fully understand what the sailor was singing. Among a great many commonplaces, a powerful line would occasionally arouse her curiosity, but before long, at the most beautiful moment, a few words in dialect would follow whose meaning escaped her. However, she gathered that the song was about a murder. Curses directed against the murderers, threats of vengeance, and praise of the dead man were all mixed up pell-mell. She remembered a few lines, which I shall endeavour to translate here:

Neither cannons nor bayonets – could bring pallor to his brow – as serene on the battlefield as a summer sky. – He was the falcon, the eagle's friend – the honey of the sands for his friends – for his enemies an angry sea. – Prouder than the sun – gentler than the moon. – Him whom the enemies of France – never dared to fight – murderers of his own land – struck down from behind – as Vittolo killed Sampiero Corso. – Never would they have dared to look him *in* the face.

Hang on the wall, before my bed – my hard-earned Cross of the

Legion of Honour. – Red is the ribbon. – Redder is my shirt. – For my son, my son across the sea – keep my cross and my blood-stained shirt. – He will see two holes in it. – For each hole, a hole in another shirt. – But will that be vengeance enough? – I must have the hand that fired – the eye that aimed – the heart that thought. . . .

All of a sudden the sailor stopped singing.

'Why don't you go on, my good fellow?' asked Miss Nevil.

The sailor jerked his head towards a figure emerging from one of the big hatchways of the schooner: it was Orso coming to enjoy the moonlight.

'Do go on with your lament,' said Miss Lydia. 'I liked it so much.'

The sailor leant towards her and said in a very low voice:

'I don't give the *rimbecco* to anybody.'

'What? The what?'

Without replying, the sailor started whistling.

'I have caught you admiring our Mediterranean, Miss Nevil,' said Orso, walking towards her. 'You must admit that you cannot see a moon like this anywhere else.'

'I wasn't looking at it. I was completely absorbed in studying the Corsican dialect. This sailor, who was singing a most tragic lament, stopped at the most beautiful moment.'

The sailor bent down as if to read his compass better, and gave a sharp tug at Miss Nevil's pelisse. It was obvious that his lament could not be sung in Lieutenant Orso's presence.

'What were you singing, Paolo Francè?' asked Orso. 'Was it a *ballata* or a *vocero*?* Mademoiselle understands you and would like to hear the end.'

---

* When a man has died, especially if he has been murdered, his body is laid on a table, and the women of his family, or, if there are none, women friends, or even strangers reputed for their poetic talent, improvise laments in verse, in the dialect of the country, before a large

'I have forgotten, Ors' Anton',' said the sailor. And he promptly started singing a hymn to the Virgin at the top of his voice.

Miss Lydia listened absentmindedly to the hymn and did not press the singer any further, although she made a mental resolution to find out the solution to the enigma later. But her chambermaid, who, coming as she did from Florence, did not understand the Corsican dialect any better than her mistress, was just as curious to discover the truth, so, addressing Orso before Miss Lydia could give her a warning nudge, she said:

'Captain, what does giving the *rimbecco** mean?'

'The *rimbecco!*' said Orso. 'Why, that's the worst insult you can address to a Corsican: it means reproaching him for not having taken vengeance. Who has been talking to you about the *rimbecco*?'

'It was yesterday in Marseilles,' replied Miss Lydia hastily, 'that the captain of the schooner used the word.'

'And whom was he talking about?' Orso asked quickly.

'Oh, he was telling us an old story . . . about the time of . . . yes, I think it was about Vannina d'Ornano.

'I suppose, Mademoiselle, that Vannina's death didn't endear you very much to our hero, the brave Sampiero?'

---

audience. These women are called *voceratrici*, or in the Corsican pronunciation *buceratrici*, and the lament is called a *vocero*, *bucera* or *bucerata* on the east coast, and a *ballata* on the west coast. The word *vocero*, like its derivatives *vocerar*, *voceratrice*, comes from the Latin word *vociferare*. Sometimes several women take turns in improvising, and often the dead man's wife or daughter sings the funeral dirge herself. (P.M.)

* *Rimbeccare*, in Italian, means to send back, to retort, to reject. In the Corsican dialect it means to address an insulting reproach in public. One gives the *rimbecco* to the son of a murdered man if one tells him that his father's death has not been avenged. The *rimbecco* is a sort of summons to a man who has not yet washed away the stain of an offence with blood. Genoese law punished the author of a *rimbecco* very severely. (P.M.)

'But do you think that what he did was very heroic?'

'The savage ways of his time excuse his crime; and besides, Sampiero was waging a war to the death against the Genoese. How could his fellow-countrymen have trusted him if he had not punished his wife for trying to negotiate with Genoa?'

'Vannina,' said the sailor, 'had gone off without her husband's permission; Sampiero did right in wringing her neck.'

'But,' said Miss Lydia, 'it was to save her husband's life, it was out of love for him, that she went to ask the Genoese to spare him.'

'To ask for his pardon was to degrade him!' cried Orso.

'But to kill her with his own hands!' Miss Nevil went on. 'What a monster he must have been!'

'You know that she asked him as a favour to die by his hand. And what about Othello, Mademoiselle? Do you regard him as a monster too?'

'That was different! He was jealous; Sampiero was simply vain.'

'And isn't jealousy a sort of vanity – the vanity of love? But perhaps you would excuse it on account of the motive?'

Miss Nevil threw him a glance full of dignity and, speaking to the sailor, asked him when the schooner would reach port.

'The day after tomorrow,' he replied, 'if the wind holds good.'

'I wish I could already see Ajaccio, because I am finding this ship unutterably tiresome.'

She stood up, took her chambermaid's arm, and walked a little way along the deck. Orso remained motionless beside the helm, not knowing whether he ought to walk with her or abandon a conversation which seemed to have annoyed her.

'By the Madonna's blood, that's a beautiful girl!' said the

sailor. 'If all the fleas in my bed were like her, I wouldn't complain of being bitten.'

Possibly Miss Lydia overheard this naive tribute to her beauty and took offence at it, for she almost immediately went below to her cabin. Soon afterwards Orso retired too. As soon as he had left the deck, the chambermaid came up again, and, after questioning the sailor, took back the following information to her mistress: the *ballata* which had been interrupted when Orso had appeared had been composed on the occasion of the death of Colonel della Rebbia, his father, who had been murdered two years before. The sailor had no doubt that Orso was returning to Corsica to 'wreak his vengeance', as he put it, and declared that before long there would be 'fresh meat' to be seen in the village of Pietranera. This apparently meant that Signor Orso intended to murder two or three individuals suspected of having murdered his father – individuals who had in fact been brought to trial for the crime, but who had left the courtroom with characters white as snow, due to the fact that they had the judges, lawyers, prefect, and gendarmes in their pocket.

'There's no justice in Corsica,' added the sailor, 'and I put more faith in a good musket than in a judge of the Royal Court. When you have an enemy, you must choose between the three S's.'*

This interesting information produced an appreciable change in Miss Lydia's feeling and attitude towards Lieutenant della Rebbia. From that moment he became a somebody in the eyes of the romantic English girl. His nonchalant manner and his air of frank good humour, which at first had prejudiced her against him, now struck her as further points in his favour, for they were a clever disguise for an ardent nature which would not allow any

* A national expression meaning *schioppetto, stiletto, strada*: musket, dagger, flight. (P.M.)

of its inner feelings to appear on the surface. Orso appeared to her as a sort of Fiesco, hiding vast designs behind an appearance of frivolity; and, although it is less noble to kill a few scoundrels than to liberate one's country, a fine act of vengeance is still an impressive feat; and besides, women prefer their heroes not to be involved in politics. It was only now that Miss Nevil noticed that the young lieutenant had large eyes, white teeth, a good figure, education, and certain social graces. She talked with him often during the following day and found his conversation interesting. She questioned him at length about his country, and he spoke eloquently on the subject. Corsica, which he had left at an early age, to go first to school, and then to the military academy, had remained in his mind adorned with poetic colours. He grew excited as he spoke of its mountains, its forests, and the strange customs of its inhabitants. As may readily be imagined, the word 'vengeance' occurred more than once in his stories, for it is impossible to talk about the Corsicans without attacking or defending their proverbial passion. Orso somewhat surprised Miss Nevil by condemning on the whole the endless feuds of his fellow-countrymen. Among the peasants, however, he tried to excuse them, maintaining that the vendetta was the poor man's duel. 'This is so true,' he said, 'that a murder is committed only after a formal challenge has been made. "Look out for yourself, I shall do the same" – those are the time-honoured words exchanged by two enemies before they start laying ambushes for each other. There are more murders among my people,' he added, 'than anywhere else; but you will never find an ignoble motive for these crimes. We have, it is true, a great many murderers, but not a single thief.'

Whenever he uttered the words 'vengeance' and 'murder', Miss Lydia looked at him closely, but without finding the slightest trace of emotion in his face. As she had decided that he had the necessary strength of will to conceal his feelings from all eyes (except, of course, her own), she continued to hold the firm belief that the spirit of Colonel della Rebbia would not have to wait long for the satisfaction it demanded.

Already the schooner was in sight of Corsica. The skipper pointed out the principal features of the coastline, and, although they were all completely unknown to Miss Lydia, she derived a certain pleasure from learning their names. Nothing is more boring than an anonymous landscape. Now and then the colonel's telescope would make out some brown-clad islander, armed with a long gun, riding a small horse, and galloping down steep slopes. In each case, Miss Lydia believed that she was looking at a bandit, or else a son on his way to avenge his father's death; but Orso assured her that the man was a peaceable inhabitant of some nearby village travelling on business, and that he carried a gun less out of necessity than because it was the fashion, just as no dandy ever went out without an elegant cane. Although a gun is a less noble and poetic weapon than a stiletto, Miss Lydia admitted that it was more manly than a cane, and she recalled that all Lord Byron's heroes died by a bullet and not by the classical poniard.

After three days at sea, they reached the Sanguinaires, and the splendid panorama of the Gulf of Ajaccio unfolded before the eyes of our travellers. It is with good reason that it is compared with the Bay of Naples; and as the schooner was entering the harbour a burning heath, shrouding the Punta di Girato with smoke, recalled Vesuvius to mind and added to the resemblance. To make it complete, one of Attila's armies would have to descend on the suburbs of Naples and lay them waste; for everything is dead and deserted around Ajaccio. Instead of those elegant buildings which can be seen on all sides from Castellamare to Cape Miseno, there is nothing around the Gulf of Ajaccio but bleak heaths and bare mountains behind them. Not a single villa, not a single dwelling of any kind. Only, here and there, on the heights around the town, a few white edifices stand out in isolation against the green background; these are mortuary chapels, family tombs. Everything about this landscape has a grave, melancholy beauty.

The appearance of the town itself, particularly at that time, heightened the impression created by the loneliness of its surroundings. There is virtually no movement in the streets, where one comes across only a few indolent figures, always the same ones. There are no women, except for a few peasant women who come to sell their produce. There is no loud talking, laughing, or singing, as in Italian towns. Sometimes, in the shade of a tree on the promenade, a dozen armed peasants may be found playing cards or watching others playing. They never shout, never quarrel; if the game livens up, then pistol shots are heard, invariably followed by a threat. The Corsican is grave and silent by nature. In the evening, a few figures appear to enjoy the cool air, but the strollers on the *corso* are nearly all foreigners. The islanders stay in front of their doors; each seems to be on the lookout, like a falcon on its nest.

CHAPTER FOUR

AFTER visiting the house where Napoleon was born, and obtaining by more or less legitimate means a piece of its wallpaper, Miss Lydia, two days after her arrival in Corsica, began to feel intensely depressed, as is bound to happen to any foreigner who finds himself in a country whose unsociable habits seem to condemn him to complete isolation. She regretted her hasty decision; but to leave straight away would compromise her reputation as an intrepid traveller; Miss Lydia therefore resigned herself to exercising patience and whiling away the time as best she could. In order to carry out this brave resolution, she got out her pencils and paints, sketched some views of the gulf, and did a portrait of a suntanned peasant who sold melons like a market-gardener on the Continent, but who had a white beard and looked like the most ferocious scoundrel who ever lived. But as all this was not enough to keep her amused, she decided to turn the head of the descendant of the corporals, something which did not present any difficulties, for, far from making haste to return to his village, Orso seemed to be quite happy in Ajaccio, although he was not seeing any of the local citizens. Miss Lydia had also set herself a noble task, namely that of taming this mountain bear and inducing him to abandon the sinister plan which had brought him back to his island. Since she had begun taking the trouble to study him, she had told herself that it would be a pity to let this young man rush to his destruction, and that it would be a glorious achievement for her to convert a Corsican.

Our travellers spent their days in the following manner: in the morning, the colonel and Orso went hunting; Miss Lydia sketched or wrote to her friends, so as to be able to date her letters from Ajaccio; about six o'clock the men returned laden with game; they dined, Miss Lydia sang, the colonel dropped off to sleep, and the young people stayed chatting together until a late hour.

Some passport formality or other had obliged Colonel Nevil to go to see the prefect. The latter, who like most of his colleagues was extremely bored with life, had been delighted to learn of the arrival of an Englishman who was rich, a man of the world, and the father of a pretty daughter; he had accordingly given him a cordial welcome and overwhelmed him with offers of service; moreover, only a very few days later, he returned his visit. The colonel, who had just got up from table, was comfortably stretched out on the sofa, on the point of dozing off; his daughter was singing at a broken-down piano; while Orso was turning the pages of her music-book and looking at the shoulders and fair hair of the pianist. The prefect was announced; the music stopped; the colonel got up and introduced the prefect to his daughter.

'I will not introduce Monsieur della Rebbia to you,' he said, 'for you probably know him already.'

'Is Monsieur the son of Colonel della Rebbia?' asked the prefect, looking slightly embarrassed.

'Yes, Monsieur,' replied Orso.

'I had the honour of knowing your father.'

The commonplaces of conversation were soon exhausted. In spite of himself, the colonel kept yawning fairly frequently; as a liberal, Orso had no desire to speak to a henchman of the government; Miss Lydia alone kept the conversation going. For his part, the prefect did not allow it to languish, and it was obvious that he was deriving considerable pleasure from talking about Paris and the fashionable world to a woman who was acquainted with all the notabilities of European society. Now and then, while he was talking, he would look at Orso with the liveliest curiosity.

'Was it on the Continent that you met Monsieur della Rebbia?' he asked Miss Lydia.

Miss Lydia replied with some embarrassment that she had made his acquaintance on the ship which had brought them to Corsica.

'He is an excellent young man,' said the prefect in an undertone. 'And has he told you,' he went on, dropping his voice even lower, 'why he has come back to Corsica?'

Miss Lydia assumed her haughtiest expression.

'I have not asked him,' she said; 'you may question him if you wish.'

The prefect kept silent; but, a moment later, hearing Orso address a few words in English to the colonel, he said:

'It seems that you have travelled a great deal, Monsieur. You must have forgotten Corsica . . . and its customs.'

'It is true that I was very young when I left.'

'Are you still in the army?'

'I am on half-pay, Monsieur.'

'I have no doubt, Monsieur, that you have served too long in the French army not to have become a complete Frenchman.'

He laid considerable stress on these last words.

Corsicans are not particularly flattered at being reminded that they belong to the French nation. They want to be regarded as a people apart, and they justify this pretension well enough for their desire to be granted. Orso, somewhat put out, retorted:

'Do you think, Monsieur, that in order to become a man of honour a Corsican must necessarily serve in the French army?'

'No, certainly not,' said the prefect. 'That wasn't what I meant at all. I was simply referring to certain *customs* of this country, some of which are not all that a government official would wish them to be.'

He stressed the word 'customs', and assumed the most serious expression of which his features were capable. Soon afterwards, he got up and took his leave, after getting Miss Lydia to promise that she would call upon his wife at the prefecture.

When he had gone, Miss Lydia remarked:

'I had to come to Corsica to find out what a prefect is like. This one strikes me as quite pleasant.'

'For my part,' said Orso, 'I really can't say as much, and I thought him very strange with his pompous, mysterious manner.'

The colonel was fast asleep. Miss Lydia darted a glance in his direction, and, lowering her voice, said:

'I must say that I don't think he is as mysterious as you say, for I think that I understood him.'

'You are obviously very perspicacious, Miss Nevil; and if you can see any sense in what he has just been saying, then you must have put it there yourself.'

'That is one of the Marquis de Mascarille's lines, I think, Monsieur della Rebbia. But . . . would you like me to give you some proof of my perspicacity? I am something of a witch, and I can read the thoughts of people I have only just met.'

'Heavens, you frighten me. If you could read my thoughts, I don't know whether I ought to feel glad or sorry.'

'Monsieur della Rebbia,' continued Miss Lydia, blushing, 'we have known each other for only a few days. But at sea and in barbarous countries – you will pardon the expression, I hope – in barbarous countries, friendships are formed more quickly than in society. . . . So do not be surprised if I talk to you as a friend about somewhat intimate matters, in which perhaps a foreigner ought not to meddle.'

'Oh, don't say that word, Miss Nevil; I liked the other much better.'

'Well, Monsieur, I have to tell you that, without having tried to discover your secrets, I happen to have learnt some of them, and there are a few which distress me. I know,

Monsieur, the misfortune which struck your family; I have heard a lot about the vindictive character of your fellow countrymen and the way in which they avenge themselves. Wasn't it to that that the prefect was alluding?'

'Can Miss Lydia believe . . . ?' And Orso turned as pale as death.

'No, Monsieur della Rebbia,' she said, interrupting him; 'I know that you are a gentleman with a high sense of honour. You told me yourself that it was only the common people in your country who now practised the vendetta – which you are pleased to call a form of duel. . . .'

'Then do you believe me to be capable of becoming a murderer one day?'

'Since I have brought up this matter with you, Monsieur Orso, you must see that I believe in you; and if I have spoken to you,' she went on, lowering her eyes, 'it is because I have realized that back in your country, surrounded perhaps by barbarous prejudices, you would be glad to know that there is somebody who admires you for your courage in resisting them. . . . Come,' she said, getting up, 'let's not talk any more about those horrible things; they make my head ache, and besides, it is very late. You aren't angry with me, are you? Let us say good night in the English fashion.' And she held out her hand.

Orso pressed it, looking grave and deeply moved.

'Mademoiselle,' he said, 'do you know that there are moments when the instincts of my country are awakened in me? Sometimes, when I think of my poor father . . . then horrible ideas haunt me. Thanks to you, I am delivered from them forever. Thank you! Thank you!'

He was going to continue; but Miss Lydia deliberately dropped a teaspoon, and the noise awakened the colonel.

'Della Rebbia, we go hunting tomorrow at five. Don't be late.'

'No, Colonel.'

CHAPTER FIVE

THE next day, shortly before the hunters came back, Miss Nevil, returning from a walk along the seashore, was approaching the inn with her chambermaid when she noticed a young woman dressed in black, riding into the town on a small but sturdy horse. She was followed by a sort of peasant, also on horseback, wearing a brown cloth jacket which was out at the elbows; he had a flask slung across his back, a pistol hanging from his belt, and in his hand a gun whose butt was resting in a leather pocket fastened to his saddle-bow; in short, he was dressed just like a stage brigand or a Corsican on his travels. Miss Nevil's attention was drawn first of all by the remarkable beauty of the woman. She seemed to be about twenty years old, and was tall and pale, with dark blue eyes, pink lips, and teeth like enamel. In her expression one could read at once pride, anxiety, and sadness. On her head she wore that black silk veil called the *mezzaro* which the Genoese introduced into Corsica and which is so becoming to women. Long plaits of chestnut hair formed a sort of turban around her head. Her costume was neat but extremely simple.

Miss Nevil had plenty of time to study her, for the lady in the *mezzaro* had stopped in the street to question somebody about something which, judging by the look in her eyes, interested her greatly. Then, once she had been given an answer, she gave her horse a tap with her switch, and, setting off at a brisk trot, did not stop until she reached the door of the hotel where Sir Thomas Nevil and Orso were staying. There, after exchanging a few words with the innkeeper, the young woman nimbly dismounted and sat down on a stone bench beside the main door, while her groom led the horses to the stable. Miss Lydia, dressed in her Parisian clothes, passed in front of the stranger without the latter so much as looking up. A quarter of an hour later, opening her window, she saw the lady in the *mezzaro* still sitting in the same place and in the same position. Soon afterwards the colonel and Orso, back from the day's hunting, appeared. Then the innkeeper said a few words to the young lady in mourning and pointed out to her the young Della Rebbia. She flushed, got up quickly, took a few steps forward, then stood motionless, as if bewildered. Orso was quite close to her, looking at her curiously.

'Are you,' she said in a voice touched with emotion, 'Orso Antonio della Rebbia? I am Colomba.'

'Colomba!' cried Orso.

And, taking her in his arms, he kissed her tenderly, which rather surprised the colonel and his daughter, for in England people do not kiss in the street.

'Brother,' said Colomba, 'you must forgive me for coming here without your permission; but I learned from our friends that you had arrived, and it was such a great comfort for me to see you. . . .'

Orso kissed her again; then, turning to the colonel, he said:

'This is my sister, whom I would never have recognized if she had not told me her name. Colomba, Colonel Sir Thomas Nevil. Colonel, please excuse me, but I shall be unable to have the honour of dining with you today. . . . My sister. . . .'

'But my dear fellow,' exclaimed the colonel, 'where the devil will you dine? You know perfectly well that there's only one dinner served in this confounded inn, and that's for us. My daughter will be delighted if Mademoiselle will join us.'

Colomba looked at her brother, who accepted readily enough, and together they all went into the largest room in the inn, which the colonel used as his drawing-room and dining-room. Mademoiselle della Rebbia, on being introduced to Miss Nevil, made a deep curtsy to her, but did not say a word. It was obvious that she was very overawed at finding herself, perhaps for the first time in her life, in the company of strangers who were people from fashionable society. However, there was nothing provincial about her manners. Any awkwardness was concealed by her strangeness. For that very reason Miss Nevil took a liking to her; and as there was no room available in the hotel, which had been completely taken over by the colonel and his entourage, Miss Lydia pushed condescension or curiosity so far as to offer to have a bed made up for Mademoiselle della Rebbia in her own room.

Colomba stammered out a few words of thanks and hurried after Miss Nevil's chambermaid to make the small repairs to her appearance made necessary by a journey on horseback in the dust and sun.

When she returned to the drawing-room, she stopped in front of the colonel's guns, which the hunters had just placed in a corner.

'What splendid weapons!' she said. 'Are they yours, brother?'

'No, they are English guns belonging to the colonel. They are as good as they are handsome.'

'I wish,' said Colomba, 'that you had one like them.'

'There is certainly one of those three that belongs to Della Rebbia,' exclaimed the colonel. 'He uses it far too well. Today, with fourteen shots, he scored fourteen hits!'

There promptly began a contest in generosity in which Orso was defeated, to his sister's great satisfaction, as was easy to see from the expression of childlike joy which suddenly lit up her face, so serious only a moment before.

'Choose, my dear fellow,' said the colonel.

Orso refused.

'Well, then, your sister shall choose for you.'

Colomba did not wait to be asked twice. She chose the least ornate of the guns, but it was an excellent Manton of large calibre.

'This one,' she said, 'should have a long range.'

Her brother was mumbling embarrassed thanks when dinner appeared very opportunely to rescue him from his predicament. Miss Lydia was delighted to see that Colomba, who had shown a certain reluctance to sit down at table, and who had given way only at a glance from her brother, made the sign of the Cross like a good Catholic before eating.

'Good!' she said to herself. 'That's what I call really primitive.'

And she made a mental resolution to obtain a great deal of interesting information from studying this young representative of old Corsica. As for Orso, he was obviously rather ill at ease, fearing no doubt that his sister might say or do something which smacked too much of her village upbringing. But Colomba watched him unceasingly and copied all her movements from his. Sometimes she gazed at him intently with a strange expression of melancholy; and then, if Orso's eyes met hers, he would be the first to look away, as if he wanted to evade a question which his sister was asking him in thought and which he understood only too well. The conversation was in French, for the colonel expressed himself very badly in Italian. Colomba understood French, and indeed pronounced quite well the few words which she was obliged to exchange with her hosts.

After dinner, the colonel, who had noticed the sort of restraint between brother and sister, asked Orso with his habitual frankness whether he would not like to talk alone with Mademoiselle Colomba, offering, in that case, to go into the next room with his daughter. But Orso hastened to thank him and to say that they would have plenty of time to talk at Pietranera. This was the name of the village where he was due to take up residence.

The colonel accordingly assumed his usual position on the sofa, and Miss Nevil, after trying several subjects of conversation, gave up all hope of getting the fair Colomba to speak, and asked Orso to read her a canto from Dante, her favourite poet. Orso chose the canto from the *Inferno* recounting the episode of Francesca da Rimini, and started to read, accenting as best he could those sublime tercets which express so well the danger of two lovers' reading a book of love. As he read, Colomba drew nearer to the table, and raised her head, which she had kept lowered: her dilated pupils shone with an extraordinary fire; she flushed and turned pale by turns, and moved about convulsively on her chair. How admirable is the Italian nature, which, to appreciate poetry, has no need of a pedant to point out its beauties!

When the reading was finished, she exclaimed:

'How beautiful it is! Who wrote it, brother?'

Orso was a little disconcerted, and Miss Lydia replied with a smile that the author was a Florentine poet who had died several centuries before.

'I shall give you some Dante to read,' said Orso, 'when we are at Pietranera.'

'Heavens, how beautiful it is!' repeated Colomba, and she recited three or four tercets which she remembered, first in a low voice, and then, growing excited, she declaimed them aloud, with more feeling than her brother had put into reading them.

Miss Lydia said in astonishment:

'You seem to be very fond of poetry. How I envy you the joy of reading Dante for the first time!'

'You see, Miss Nevil,' said Orso, 'what power Dante's poetry must have, to move a little savage who knows only her *Pater Noster*. . . . But I am mistaken; I remember that

Colomba is something of a poet herself. Even as a child, she tried her hand at writing verse, and my father wrote to me that she was the finest *voceratrice* in Pietranera and for two leagues around.'

Colomba darted a beseeching glance at her brother. Miss Nevil had heard about the Corsican *improvisatrices* and was dying to hear one. She therefore begged Colomba to give her a sample of her talent. Orso now intervened, extremely annoyed at having recalled his sister's poetic gifts. It was no use his swearing that nothing was so insipid as a Corsican *ballata*, or protesting that to recite Corsican verse after Dante's was tantamount to betraying his country, he only exacerbated Miss Nevil's curiosity, and in the end he was obliged to say to his sister:

'Well, improvise something, but make it short.'

Colomba heaved a sigh, gazed fixedly for a minute at the table cover and then at the beams of the ceiling. Finally, putting her hand over her eyes, like those birds which take heart and think that they cannot be seen when they cannot see themselves, she sang, or rather declaimed in a faltering voice, the following *serenata*:

The Maiden and the Turtledove

In the valley, far behind the mountains – the sun shines for only an hour every day. – There is a gloomy house in the valley – and grass grows on its threshold. – The doors and windows are always shut. – No smoke rises from its chimney. – But at noon, when the sun shines – a window opens – and the orphan sits down at her spinning-wheel. – She spins and sings a sad song as she works – but no other song answers hers. – One day, one day in springtime – a turtledove alighted on a nearby tree – and heard the maiden's song. – 'Maiden,' it said, 'you do not weep alone. – A cruel sparrow-hawk has snatched away my mate.' – 'Turtledove, show me the sparrow-hawk. – Though he soar higher than the clouds – I shall soon bring him down to earth. – But who will give me back my brother, poor maiden that I am – my brother who is now in a distant land?' – 'Maiden, tell me where your brother is – and my wings will carry me to him.'

'Now there's a well-bred turtledove for you!' exclaimed Orso, embracing his sister with an emotion which contrasted with his jesting tone.

'Your song is charming,' said Miss Lydia, 'You must write it down in my album. I shall translate it into English and have it set to music.'

The good colonel, who had not understood a single word, added his compliments to his daughter's. Then he added:

'This turtledove you have been singing about, Mademoiselle – was it the bird we ate spatch-cocked for dinner today?'

Miss Nevil fetched her album and was not a little surprised to see the *improvisatrice* write down her song with extraordinary economy in the use of paper. Instead of each line being written separately, they followed straight on, one after another, as far as the width of the page would allow, so that they did not conform to the accepted rule for poetic compositions: 'Short lines of unequal length, with a margin on each side.' Something could also be said about Mademoiselle Colomba's somewhat capricious spelling, which made Miss Nevil smile more than once, while Orso's fraternal vanity was on the rack.

As it was now time for bed, the two girls retired to their room. There, while Miss Lydia was unclasping her necklace, earrings, and bracelets, she noticed her companion draw something long from her dress, like a corset-busk but very different in shape. Colomba placed it carefully and almost furtively under her *mezzaro*, which she had laid on a table; then she knelt down and devoutly said her prayers. Two minutes later, she was in her bed. As slow as any Englishwoman in undressing and extremely inquisitive by nature, Miss Lydia went up to the table, and, pretending to be looking for a pin, lifted the *mezzaro* and saw a fairly long stiletto, curiously embossed with silver and mother-of-pearl. The workmanship was remarkable, and it was an ancient weapon which would have been highly prized by a collector.

'Is it the custom here,' Miss Nevil asked with a smile, 'for young ladies to carry this little instrument in their corsets?'

'It is unfortunately essential,' answered Colomba with a sigh. 'There are so many wicked people about!'

'And would you really have the courage to stab somebody like this?'

And Miss Nevil, with the stiletto in her hand, made the gesture of stabbing with it as actors do on the stage, striking downwards.

'Yes,' said Colomba in her soft, musical voice, 'if it were necessary to defend myself or my friends. . . . But that isn't the right way to hold it; you could injure yourself if the person you intended to stab stepped backwards.' And sitting up in bed, she said: 'Look, like this, thrusting the stiletto upwards. Like this the blow is fatal, they say. Happy are those who have no need of such weapons!'

She sighed, let her head fall back on the pillow, and closed her eyes. A more beautiful, more noble, more virginal head would have been impossible to imagine. Phidias, when sculpting his Minerva, could not have wished for a finer model.

CHAPTER SIX

IT was in order to conform with the precept of Horace that I plunged straight away *in medias res*. Now that everybody is asleep – the beautiful Colomba, the colonel, and his daughter – I shall take the opportunity to inform my reader of certain details of which he must not be ignorant if he wishes to follow this true story any further. He already knows that Colonel della Rebbia, Orso's father, has been murdered. Now, a man is not murdered in Corsica, as in France, by the first escaped convict who can think of no better means of robbing you of your silver: he is murdered by his enemies; but the reason why he should have any enemies is often extremely difficult to ascertain. Many families hate one another out of a sense of tradition, and the original cause of their hatred has often been completely forgotten.

The family to which Colonel della Rebbia belonged hated several other families, but particularly that of the Barricinis; some said that in the sixteenth century a Della Rebbia had seduced a Barricini, and had then been stabbed by one of the outraged maiden's relatives. True, others told the story differently, maintaining that it was a Della Rebbia who had been seduced and a Barricini who had been stabbed. The fact remains that, to use a timehonoured expression, 'there was blood between the two houses'. None the less, contrary to custom, this murder had not led to others; this was because the Della Rebbias and the Barricinis had both been persecuted by the Genoese government, and, as all the young men had fled the country, the two families were deprived for several generations of their stronger representatives. At the end of the last century, a Della Rebbia, an officer in the service of Naples, had a quarrel in a gambling-den with some soldiers who, among other insulting names, called him a Corsican goatherd. He drew his sword, but, outnumbered three to one, he would have had a hard time of it if a stranger who was gambling in the same room had not cried out: 'I am a Corsican too!' and come to his aid. This stranger was a Barricini, who incidentally did not know his fellow-countryman. After mutual explanations the two men exchanged extravagant courtesies and promises of eternal friendship; for on the Continent, contrary to what happens on their island, the Corsicans make friends easily. This was clearly shown in this case: as long as they stayed in Italy, Della Rebbia and Barricini were close friends, but on their return to Corsica they saw each other only at rare intervals, although they both lived in the same village, and when they died it was said that they had not spoken to each other for a good five or six years. Their sons likewise lived 'on polite terms', as they say on the island. One of them, Ghilfuccio, Orso's father, was a soldier; the other, Giudice Barricini, was a lawyer. Having both become heads of families, and being separated by their professions, they had scarcely any opportunity of seeing or hearing about each other.

However, one day, about 1809, Giudice read in a newspaper at Bastia that Captain Ghilfuccio had just been decorated, and said in front of witnesses that he was not surprised, seeing that General — patronized his family. This remark was reported to Ghilfuccio in Vienna, and he said to one of his fellow-countrymen that on his return to Corsica he was sure to find Giudice a rich man, because he obtained more money from lawsuits he lost than from those he won. It was never known whether he was implying by this that the lawyer was in the habit of betraying his clients, or whether he was merely repeating that commonplace truth that a bad case is often more profitable to a lawyer than a good one. Be that as it may, the lawyer Barricini heard about the epigram and never forgot it. In 1812 he applied for the post of mayor of his commune and had every hope of obtaining it, when General — wrote to the prefect recommending a relative of Ghilfuccio's wife. The prefect hastened to comply with the general's wishes, and Barricini had no doubt that he owed his disappointment to Ghilfuccio's intrigues. After the fall of the Emperor, in 1814, the general's protégé was denounced as a Bonapartist and was replaced by Barricini. He in his turn was dismissed during the Hundred Days; but after that storm had blown over he once again took possession, with great pomp and ceremony, of the municipal seal and registers.

From that moment, his star shone more brightly than ever. Colonel della Rebbia, now living in retirement at Pietranera on half-pay, had to put up with a never-ending succession of petty attacks: once he was served with a writ for damage his horse had done to the mayor's fences; another time, the latter, under the pretext of repairing the floor of the church, had a broken flagstone removed which bore the Della Rebbia coat of arms, and which covered the tomb of some member of that family. If goats ate the colonel's seedlings, the owners of these animals found a protector in the mayor; while the grocer who kept the post office at Pietranera and the local policeman, a disabled veteran, both of whom were dependents of the Della Rebbias, were successively dismissed and replaced by henchmen of the Barricinis.

The colonel's wife died expressing a wish to be buried in the middle of a little wood where she had been fond of walking; the mayor promptly declared that she would be buried in the local cemetery, in view of the fact that he had not been given permission to allow burial elsewhere. The colonel flew into a rage and declared that pending such permission, his wife would be buried in the place she had chosen, and he had a grave dug there. The mayor for his part had one dug in the cemetery, and sent for the gendarmes, in order, so he said, that the law should be respected. On the day of the funeral, the two families came face to face, and for a moment it seemed that a fight might take place for the possession of Madame della Rebbia's mortal remains. About forty well armed peasants, brought along by the relatives of the deceased, forced the priest, on leaving the church, to go in the direction of the wood; while on the other hand, the mayor, together with two sons, his clients, and the gendarmes, came forward to bar their way. When the mayor appeared and called on the procession to turn back, he was greeted with jeers and threats; his adversaries enjoyed superiority in numbers and they looked very determined. At the sight of him, several guns were cocked, and it is even alleged that a shepherd took aim at him; but the colonel knocked the gun up and said: 'Let nobody fire without my orders!' The mayor, like Panurge, 'had a natural fear of violence', and, refusing to fight, withdrew with his escort. The funeral procession then set off, taking good care to go the longest way, in order to pass in front of the mayor's house. As it filed along, an idiot who had joined the procession took it into his head to shout: 'Long live the Emperor!' Two or three voices echoed him, and the Rebbianists, growing more and more excited, suggested killing one of the mayor's oxen, which happened to block their way. Fortunately the colonel prevented this act of violence.

As may well be imagined, a record was made of these incidents, and the mayor sent the prefect a report written in his loftiest style, in which he described how both human and divine laws had been trampled underfoot, how his dignity as mayor and that of the parish priest had been ignored and insulted, and how Colonel della Rebbia had put himself at the head of a Bonapartist plot to change the order of succession to the throne and to excite the citizens to take arms against one another – crimes provided for by articles 86 and 91 of the Penal Code.

The exaggerated tone of this complaint reduced its effect. The colonel wrote to the prefect and the public prosecutor: one of his wife's relatives was connected with one of the deputies of the island, while another was a cousin of the president of the Royal Court. Thanks to the influence of these personages, the plot came to nothing, Madame della Rebbia was left in the wood, and only the idiot was sentenced to a fortnight in prison.

The lawyer Barricini, dissatisfied with the outcome of this affair, turned his guns in a different direction. He dug up an old title-deed, on the basis of which he undertook to contest the colonel's right to the ownership of a certain stream which turned a millwheel. A lawsuit began which lasted a long time. At the end of a year the court was about to pronounce judgment, by all accounts in favour of the colonel, when Monsieur Barricini handed over to the public prosecutor a letter signed by a certain Agostini, a notorious bandit, threatening him, the mayor, with fire and death if he did not abandon his claims. It is well known that in Corsica the protection of these bandits is much sought after, and that to oblige their friends they frequently intervene in private quarrels. The mayor was turning this letter to good account when a fresh incident occurred which complicated the affair. The bandit Agostini wrote to the public prosecutor to complain that somebody had forged his handwriting and cast doubts upon his integrity by representing him as a man who made money out of his influence. 'If I ever discover the forger,' he concluded his letter, 'I shall make an example of him.'

It was obvious that Agostini had not written the threatening letter to the mayor. The Della Rebbias accused the Barricinis of having written it, and vice versa. Both families gave vent to a fresh crop of threats, and the court did not know where to look for the culprits.

In the midst of all this, Colonel Ghilfuccio was murdered.

Here are the facts as they were established by judicial inquiry: On 2 August 18—, as dusk was falling, a woman called Maddalena Pietri, who was carrying some corn to Pietranera, heard two shots in quick succession, fired, it seemed to her, in a sunken road leading to the village, about a hundred and fifty paces from where she was. Almost immediately she saw a man running along a path among the vines, bent double, in the direction of the village. This man stopped for a moment and looked back; but he was too far away for the Pietri woman to make out his features, and besides, he had a vine-leaf between his teeth which hid nearly the whole of his face. He signalled with his hand to some companion whom the witness did not see, and then disappeared among the vines.

Dropping her burden, the Pietri woman ran up the path and found Colonel della Rebbia lying in a pool of blood, suffering from two bullet wounds, but still breathing. Near him there lay his gun, loaded and cocked, as if he had just got ready to defend himself against somebody attacking him from the front when another person had shot him from behind. He was at his last gasp and was fighting against death, but he was unable to utter a single word, a circumstance which the doctors explained by the nature of his wounds, the bullets having gone through his lungs. His blood was choking him; it was flowing slowly like a red froth. It was in vain that the Pietri woman lifted him up and asked him a few questions. She could see that he wanted to speak, but he could not make himself understood. Noticing that he was trying to reach his pocket, she quickly took out of it a little notebook, which she opened and held out to him. The wounded man took the pencil from the notebook and tried to write. In fact the witness saw him laboriously trace several letters; but, being unable to read, she could not understand their meaning. Exhausted by this effort, the colonel put the notebook in the Pietri woman's hand, which he squeezed hard, as if he wanted to say – these are the witness's own words – 'This is important, it's the name of my murderer.'

The Pietri woman was running up towards the village when she met Mayor Barricini with his son Vincentello. By then it was almost dark. She related what she had seen. The mayor took the notebook and ran to his house to put on his sash and summon his secretary and the gendarmes. Left alone with the young Vincentello, Maddalena Pietri suggested that he should go to the colonel's aid, in the event of the latter still being alive; but Vincentello replied that if he went near a man who had been a bitter enemy of his family, he would be sure to be accused of having killed him. A little later the mayor arrived, found the colonel dead, had the corpse removed, and drew up an official report.

In spite of his agitation, which was natural in such circumstances, Monsieur Barricini had lost no time in putting the colonel's notebook under seal and making all the inquiries in his power; but none of these resulted in any important discovery. When the examining magistrate arrived, the notebook was opened, and on one bloodstained page a few letters were distinguished which had been written by a faltering hand but were none the less perfectly legible. They read: 'Agosti...,' and the magistrate had no doubt but that the colonel had wished to indicate Agostini as his murderer. However, Colomba della Rebbia, summoned by the magistrate, asked if she might examine the notebook. After leafing through it for a long time, she pointed at the mayor and cried: 'There's the murderer!' Then, with surprising precision and clarity, considering the agony of grief into which she had been plunged, she told how her father, a few days before, had received a letter from his son which he had burnt, but that before doing so, he had written in pencil, in his notebook, the new address of Orso, who had just changed garrison. Now, this address was no longer in the notebook, and Colomba concluded that the mayor had torn out the leaf on which it was written, which was probably the same leaf on which her father had written the murderer's name; and for that name, according to Colomba, the mayor had substituted Agostini's. The magistrate saw that one leaf was indeed missing from the section of the notebook in which the name was written; but soon he noticed that there were also leaves missing from the other sections of the same notebook, and some of the witnesses testified that the colonel had been in the habit of tearing leaves out of his notebook when he wanted to light a cigar; it was therefore extremely probable that he had accidentally burnt the address he had copied out. Moreover, it was established that after the mayor had been given the notebook by the Pietri woman, he could not have read it because of the darkness. It was proved that he had not stopped for a single moment on his way to the house, and that the sergeant of the gendarmes had accompanied him there, and had seen him light a lamp and put the notebook into an envelope, which he had sealed before his very eyes.

When the sergeant had finished his statement, Colomba, beside herself with grief, threw herself at his feet and begged him, by all that he held most sacred, to state whether he had left the mayor alone even for a moment. After a slight hesitation, the sergeant, visibly moved by the girl's distraught condition, admitted that he had gone to a nearby room to fetch a large sheet of paper, but that he had not been away for more than a minute and that the mayor had gone on talking to him all the time he had been rummaging around in a drawer for this paper. Moreover, he testified that on his return the bloodstained notebook was in the same place on the table where the mayor had thrown it when he came in.

Monsieur Barricini gave his evidence with the greatest

calm. He forgave, he said, Mademoiselle della Rebbia's wild accusation, and was willing to condescend to justify himself. He proved that he had spent the whole evening in the village; that his son Vincentello had been with him outside the house at the time the crime had been committed; and finally that his son Orlanduccio, who had been taken with a fever that very day, had never stirred from his bed. He produced all the guns in the house, not one of which had been fired recently. He added that, with regard to the notebook, he had immediately realized its importance, and that he had put it under seal and handed it over to his deputy, foreseeing that, because of the enmity between himself and the colonel, he might fall under suspicion. Finally he recalled that Agostini had threatened to kill the man who had written a letter in his name, and insinuated that that scoundrel, having probably suspected the colonel, had murdered him. In the annals of banditry, an act of vengeance of that sort for a similar motive is not without precedent.

Five days after Colonel della Rebbia's death, Agostini, surprised by a detachment of riflemen, was killed after putting up a desperate fight. They found on him a letter from Colomba begging him to declare whether or not he was guilty of the murder imputed to him. Since the bandit had made no reply, it was fairly generally assumed that he had not the courage to tell a daughter that he had killed her father. All the same, those who claimed to know Agostini's character well whispered that, if he had killed the colonel, he would have boasted about what he had done. Another bandit, known by the name of Brandolaccio, sent Colomba a statement in which he swore 'on his honour' to the innocence of his comrade; but the only proof he brought forward was the fact that Agostini had never told him that he suspected the colonel.

As a result of all this, no action was taken against the

Barricinis; the magistrate heaped praises on the mayor; and the latter put the finishing touch to his noble conduct by abandoning all his claims to the stream over which he had brought a lawsuit against Colonel della Rebbia.

In accordance with the custom of the country, Colomba improvised a *ballata* before her father's corpse, in the presence of his assembled friends. In it she gave vent to all her hatred for the Barricinis and formally accused them of the murder, at the same time threatening them with her brother's vengeance. It was this *ballata*, which had become very popular, that the sailor had sung in front of Miss Lydia. On learning of his father's death, Orso, then in the north of France, asked for leave but failed to obtain it. To begin with, on the strength of a letter from his sister, he had believed the Barricinis to be guilty, but before long he received an abstract of all the evidence given at the inquiry, and a private letter from the magistrate himself, which practically convinced him that the bandit Agostini was the sole culprit. Every three months Colomba would write to him, repeating her suspicions, which she called proofs. In spite of himself, these accusations made his Corsican blood boil, and sometimes he came close to sharing his sister's prejudices. However, every time he wrote to her, he repeated that her allegations had no solid foundation and were totally unworthy of belief. He even forbade her to mention them to him again, but always in vain.

In this way two years went by, at the end of which he was put on half-pay. He then thought of going back to his country, not to wreak vengeance on people whom he believed to be innocent, but to marry off his sister, and to sell his small property if its value was sufficient to enable him to live on the Continent.

CHAPTER SEVEN

EITHER because his sister's arrival had reminded Orso forcibly of his old home, or because Colomba's unconventional dress and manners made him feel slightly embarrassed in front of his civilized friends, he announced the very next day his intention to leave Ajaccio and to return to Pietranera. However, he made the colonel promise that when he went to Bastia he would come and stay in his humble manor, and in return he undertook to provide him with deer, pheasant, wild boar, and other game.

On the day before his departure, instead of going hunting, Orso suggested a walk along the shores of the gulf. He gave his arm to Miss Lydia, to whom he was able to talk undisturbed, for Colomba had stayed in town to do her shopping, while the colonel kept leaving them every few minutes to shoot seagulls or gannets, to the astonishment of the passers-by, who could not understand why anybody should waste his powder on such game.

They took the path leading to the Greek chapel. This vantage-point commanded the finest view of the bay, but they paid no attention to it.

'Miss Lydia,' said Orso, after a silence long enough to have become embarrassing; 'quite frankly, what do you think of my sister?'

'I like her very much,' replied Miss Nevil. 'More than I like you,' she added with a smile, 'for she is a real Corsican, while you are an over-civilized savage.'

'Over-civilized! Well, in spite of myself, I have felt myself becoming a savage again since I set foot on this island. Countless horrible thoughts disturb and torment me, and I felt I had to talk to you before plunging into my desert.'

'You must be brave, Monsieur. Look at your sister's resignation: she is setting you an example.'

'Oh, don't be taken in. You mustn't put any trust in her resignation. She hasn't said a word to me yet, but in every glance of hers I have read what she expects of me.'

'And what does she expect of you?'

'Oh, nothing. . . . Just that I should try your father's gun to see if it kills a man as well as it kills a partridge.'

'What an idea! And you can really believe that when you have just admitted that she hasn't said anything to you yet? But that's horrible of you!'

'If she weren't thinking of vengeance, she would have spoken to me straight away about our father; she did nothing of the sort. She would have mentioned the names of those whom she regards – wrongly, I know – as his murderers. But no, not a word. The point is, you see, that we Corsicans are a cunning race. My sister realizes that she doesn't hold me completely in her power, and doesn't want to frighten me while I still may escape. Once she has led me to the edge of the precipice and my head is spinning, she will push me into the abyss.'

Then Orso gave Miss Nevil a few details about his father's death, and recounted the principal proofs which had led him to regard Agostini as the murderer.

'Nothing,' he added, 'has been able to convince Colomba. I saw that by her last letter. She has sworn death to the Barricinis; and – see how I trust you, Miss Nevil – they would probably no longer be of this world if she were not convinced, thanks to one of those antiquated ideas which are excused by her savage upbringing, that the execution of vengeance falls to me in my capacity as head of the family, and that my honour is at stake.'

'Really, Monsieur della Rebbia,' said Miss Nevil, 'you slander your sister.'

'No, as you said yourself, she is a real Corsican. She

thinks as they all think. Do you know why I was so sad yesterday?'

'No, but for some time you have been subject to these fits of depression. . . . You were much more agreeable in the early days of our acquaintance.'

'Yesterday, on the contrary, I was gayer and happier than usual. You had been so kind and indulgent with my sister. We were coming back, the colonel and I in the boat. Do you know what one of the boatmen said to me in his confounded dialect? "You've killed a lot of game, Ors' Anton', but you'll find that Orlanduccio Barricini is a better shot than you are." '

'Well, what was so dreadful about those words? Are you as touchy as all that about your reputation as a hunter?'

'But don't you see that that wretch was saying that I wouldn't have the courage to kill Orlanduccio?'

'You know, Monsieur della Rebbia, you frighten me! It would seem that the air on this island of yours doesn't just give people the fever, but it makes them mad as well. Fortunately we shall soon be leaving it.'

'Not before coming to Pietranera. You promised my sister that you would.'

'And if we broke that promise, I suppose we should have to expect some terrible vengeance?'

'Do you remember what your father was telling us the other day about those Indians who threatened to starve themselves to death if the Company's agents would not grant their requests?'

'You mean that you would starve yourself to death? I doubt it. You would go without food for one day, and then Mademoiselle Colomba would bring you such an appetizing *bruccio** that you would give up your plan.'

'Your mockery is cruel, Miss Nevil; you ought to be

* A kind of baked cream cheese. It is a national dish in Corsica. (P.M.)

more gentle with me. Look, I am alone here. I had only you to prevent me from going mad, as you put it; you were my guardian angel, and now. . . .'

'Now,' said Miss Lydia in a serious tone of voice, 'to steady that reason of yours which is so easily shaken, you have your honour as a man and a soldier, and,' she went on, turning away to pick a flower, 'if it can be of any help to you, the memory of your guardian angel.'

'Oh, Miss Nevil, if only I could think that you really cared. . . .'

'Listen, Monsieur della Rebbia,' said Miss Lydia with a certain emotion, 'since you are a child, I shall treat you like a child. When I was a little girl, my mother gave me a beautiful necklace which I wanted badly; but she said to me: "Every time you put on this necklace, remember that you don't know French yet." The necklace lost some of its value in my eyes. It had become a sort of remorse for me; but I wore it, and I learned French. Do you see this ring? It's an Egyptian scarab, found, if you please, in a pyramid. This weird sign, which you may perhaps take for a bottle, means *human life*. There are people in my country who would consider this hieroglyphic very appropriate. This one, which comes after it, is a shield on an arm holding a spear: it means *fight, battle*. Thus the two signs together make up this motto, which I consider rather fine: *Life is a fight*. Don't start imagining that I can translate hieroglyphics as easily as that; a scholar explained these to me. Look, I will give you my scarab. Whenever some evil Corsican thought occurs to you, look at my talisman and tell yourself that you must win the battle which the evil passions wage against us. I'm not a bad preacher, now, am I?'

'I shall think of you, Miss Nevil, and I shall tell myself. . . .'

'Tell yourself that you have a friend who would be deeply distressed to . . . to hear that you had been hanged. Besides, that would be far too upsetting for your ancestors, the corporals.'

With these words she let go of Orso's arm, laughing, and ran towards her father.

'Papa,' she said, 'leave those poor birds alone and come along with us to write some poetry in Napoleon's grotto.'

CHAPTER EIGHT

THERE is always something solemn about a departure, even when the parting is only to be for a short time. Orso was due to set off with his sister very early in the morning, and he had taken leave of Miss Lydia the previous evening, for he could not expect her to break her habits of indolence on his account. Their farewells had been cold and grave. Since their conversation on the seashore, Miss Lydia had been afraid that she had perhaps shown too lively an interest in Orso, while Orso for his part had been hurt by her mockery and above all her frivolous tone of voice. For a moment he had thought that he could detect in the young English lady's manner a budding feeling of affection; now, disconcerted by her banter, he told himself that she regarded him simply as a mere acquaintance, who would soon be forgotten. He was therefore greatly surprised the next morning when, while he was sitting having coffee with the colonel, he saw Miss Lydia come in followed by his sister. She had got up at five o'clock, and for an English lady, particularly Miss Nevil, the effort was so great that he was bound to feel flattered by it.

'I am terribly sorry that you have put yourself out so early,' said Orso. 'No doubt it was my sister who awakened you in spite of my telling her to let you go on sleeping, and you must be inwardly cursing us. Perhaps you are already wishing that I were *hanged*?'

'No,' said Miss Lydia, in a very low voice and speaking in Italian, obviously so that her father would not understand. 'But you were sulky with me yesterday on account of my innocent teasing, and I didn't want you to go away with unpleasant memories of your humble servant. What dreadful people you Corsicans are! Good-bye, then; I hope we shall meet again soon.'

And she held out her hand.

Orso's only reply was a sigh. Colomba came up to him, took him into a window-recess, and, showing him something she was holding under her *mezzaro*, spoke to him for a moment in an undertone.

'My sister,' Orso said to Miss Nevil, 'wishes to give you a strange present, Mademoiselle; but we Corsicans have not much to give ... except our affection, which time never effaces. My sister tells me that you have looked at this stiletto with interest. It is a family heirloom. In olden times it probably hung from the belt of one of those corporals to whom I owe the honour of your acquaintance. Colomba values it so highly that she has asked my permission to give it to you, and I scarcely know whether to grant that permission, for I am afraid that you will laugh at us.'

'This stiletto is beautiful,' said Miss Lydia, 'but it is a family weapon; I cannot accept it.'

'It isn't my father's stiletto,' exclaimed Colomba eagerly. 'It was given to one of my mother's ancestors by King Theodore. If Mademoiselle accepts it, she will be giving us the greatest pleasure.'

'Come, Miss Lydia,' said Orso, 'don't scorn a king's stiletto.'

To a collector, the relics of King Theodore are more precious than those of the most powerful of monarchs. The temptation was considerable, and Miss Lydia could already imagine the effect this weapon would produce if placed on a lacquered table in her room in St James's Place.

'But,' she said, taking the stiletto with the hesitation of somebody who wants to accept a present, and giving Colomba one of her most charming smiles, 'my dear Mademoiselle Colomba, I cannot.... I would not dare let you go off unarmed like this.'

'My brother is with me,' said Colomba proudly, 'and we have the good gun your father has given us. Orso, have you loaded it?'

Miss Nevil kept the stiletto, and Colomba, in order to ward off the danger which threatens those who *give* cutting or piercing weapons to their friends, asked for a sou in payment.

At last they had to go. Orso shook hands once more with Miss Nevil; Colomba embraced her, and then offered her rosy lips to the colonel, who was delighted by this example of Corsican courtesy. From the window of the drawing-room, Miss Lydia saw the brother and sister mount their horses. Colomba's eyes were shining with a malicious joy which she had not noticed in them before. This tall, strong woman, fanatical in her ideas of barbaric honour, with pride written on her brow and her lips curled in a sardonic smile, carrying off this young man armed as if for some sinister expedition, reminded her of Orso's fears, and she fancied she was looking at his evil genius dragging him off to his destruction. Orso, already mounted, looked up and saw her. Either because he had guessed what she was thinking, or in order to bid her a final farewell, he took the Egyptian ring, which he had hung from a ribbon, and pressed it to his lips. Miss Lydia drew back from the window, blushing; then, returning to it almost immediately, she saw the two Corsicans galloping swiftly away on their little ponies, heading for the mountains. Half an hour later, the colonel showed them to her through his field-glass, skirting the far shore of the bay, and she saw that Orso kept looking back towards the town. He finally disappeared beyond the marshes, which have now been replaced by a fine nursery of young trees.

Looking at herself in the mirror, Miss Lydia thought that she seemed pale.

'What must that young man think of me?' she said. 'And

what do I think of him? And why do I think of him at all? ... A travelling acquaintance! ... What am I doing in Corsica? ... Oh, I don't love him. ... No, no; besides, that's impossible. ... And Colomba. ... Me, the sister-in-law of a *voceratrice* who wears a stiletto?' Then she noticed that she was holding King Theodore's in her hand, and threw it on her dressing-table. 'Colomba in London, dancing at Almack's! ... Heavens, what a prize to show off. ... She might well create a sensation. ... He loves me, I'm sure of that. ... He is a hero in a novel, and I have interrupted his adventurous career. ... But did he really want to avenge his father's death in the Corsican manner? ... He was a cross between Byron's Conrad and a dandy. ... I've made him a sheer dandy – a dandy with a Corsican tailor!'

She threw herself on her bed and tried to sleep, but she found it impossible. I will refrain from continuing with her soliloquy, in which she kept repeating over and over again that Monsieur della Rebbia had not been, was not, and never would be anything to her.

CHAPTER NINE

MEANWHILE Orso was riding along with his sister. At first the speed at which their horses were galloping prevented them from talking to each other; but when the path became steeper and forced them to go at a walking pace, they exchanged a few words about the friends they had just left. Colomba spoke enthusiastically of Miss Nevil's beauty, her fair hair and her gracious manners. Then she asked if the colonel was as rich as he seemed to be, and if Mademoiselle Lydia was his only child.

'She would be a good match,' she said. 'Her father appears to have taken a great liking to you.'

And, as Orso made no reply, she went on:

'Our family was rich at one time, and it is still one of the most respected on the island. All those *signori** are bastards. There is no noble blood left except in the corporals' families, and as you know, Orso, you are descended from the first corporals on the island. You know that our family came from over the mountains,† and it was the civil wars that forced us to cross over to this side. If I were in your place, Orso, I wouldn't hesitate; I would ask the colonel for Miss Nevil's hand.'

Orso shrugged his shoulders.

'With her dowry,' Colomba continued, 'I would buy the Falsetta Woods and the vineyards below our land; I would build a fine stone house, and I would add a storey to the

* The descendants of the feudal lords of Corsica are known as *signori*. There is rivalry regarding the question of noble birth between the *signori* and the *caporali*. (P.M.)

† In other words from the east coast. This widely used expression, *di là dei monti*, changes its meaning according to the location of the person using it. Corsica is divided from north to south by a chain of mountains. (P.M.)

old tower in which Sambucuccio killed so many Moors in the days of Count Henry, *il bel Missere*.'*

'Colomba, you're mad,' said Orso, galloping ahead.

'You are a man, Ors' Anton', and doubtless you know better than a woman what you ought to do. But I should like to know what objection that Englishman could raise to a marriage with our family. Are there any corporals in England?'

After a fairly long ride, spent chatting in this way, the brother and sister came to a little village, not far from Bocognano, where they stopped to dine and spend the night with a friend of their family. They were received with that Corsican hospitality which has to be experienced before it can be appreciated. The next day, their host, who had been a friend of Madame della Rebbia's, accompanied them for a league beyond his house.

'You see these woods and heaths?' he said to Orso as they were parting. 'A man who had *done something* could live here in peace for ten years without any gendarmes or riflemen coming to look for him. These woods border on the Vizzavona Forest; and, if a man has friends at Bocognano or in the vicinity, he needs want for nothing. That's a fine gun you have there. It must have a long range. By the Madonna's Blood, what a calibre! You can kill better game than wild boar with that.'

Orso replied coldly that it was an English gun and that it did indeed have a long range. They embraced and went their different ways.

Our travellers were only a short distance from Pietranera

---

* Cf. *Filippini*, Book II. Count Arrigo bel Missere died about the year 1000; it is said that at his death a voice was heard in the air singing these prophetic words:

> *E morto il conte Arrigo bel Missere*
> *E Cursica sara di male in peggio.*

(P.M.)

when, at the entrance to a gorge which they had to cross, they saw seven or eight men, armed with guns, some sitting on rocks, others lying in the grass, and a few standing around, apparently keeping watch. Their horses were grazing a little way off. Colomba inspected them for a moment through a field-glass, which she took out of one of those big leather bags which all Corsicans carry on their travels.

'They're our men!' she exclaimed joyfully. 'Pieruccio has done his work well.'

'What men?' asked Orso.

'Our herdsmen,' she replied. 'The night before last, I sent Pieruccio off to gather these good fellows together to accompany you home. It would never do for you to enter Pietranera without an escort, and besides, you know very well that the Barricinis are capable of anything.'

'Colomba,' said Orso in a stern voice, 'I have asked you time and again not to mention the Barricinis or your groundless suspicions to me any more. I'm certainly not going to make a fool of myself by returning home with that gang of good-for-nothings, and I'm very angry that you brought them together without informing me beforehand.'

'Brother, you have forgotten what your country is like. It is my duty to protect you when your imprudence exposes you to danger. I had to do what I did.'

At that moment the herdsmen, who had caught sight of them, ran to their horses and came galloping downhill to meet them.

'*Evviva* Ors' Anton'!' cried a sturdy old man with a white beard, dressed, in spite of the heat, in a hooded cloak of Corsican cloth thicker than the fleece of his goats. 'Why, he's the spitting image of his father, only taller and stronger. What a beautiful gun! We're going to hear a lot about that gun, Ors' Anton'.'

'*Evviva* Ors' Anton'!' chorussed the rest of the herdsmen. 'We knew that he'd come back in the end!'

'Ah, Ors' Anton',' said a tall, strapping fellow with a brick-coloured complexion, 'how happy your father would be if he were here to greet you! You'd see the dear man here now if only he had listened to me, if only he had let me take care of Giudice.... The poor fellow! He wouldn't believe me. Now he knows that I was right.'

'Never mind,' said the old man. 'Giudice won't lose anything by waiting.'

'*Evviva* Ors' Anton'!'

And a dozen shots accompanied this greeting.

Orso, who was in a very surly mood in the midst of this band of mounted men, all talking at once and crowding round to shake hands with him, could not make himself heard for some time. At last, assuming the expression he wore in front of his company when issuing reprimands or sending men to the guardroom, he said:

'Thank you, my friends, for the affection you have shown me today, and for the affection you had for my father. But I do not want anybody to give me any advice. I know what I have to do.'

'He's right! He's right!' cried the herdsmen. 'You know that you can count on us.'

'Yes, I am counting on you. But I don't need anybody now, and my house is in no danger. So begin by turning round and go back to your goats. I know the way to Pietranera, and I don't need any guides.'

'Have no fear, Ors' Anton',' said the old man. '*They* wouldn't dare to show themselves today. The mouse runs back into its hole when the tomcat returns.'

'Tomcat yourself, you old greybeard!' said Orso. 'What's your name?'

'What! Don't you recognize me, Ors' Anton', me that's taken you up behind me so often on that biting mule of mine? You don't recognize Polo Griffo? He's a good sort, you know, and devoted to the Della Rebbias. Just say the word, and, when your big gun speaks, this old musket of mine, as old as its master, won't keep silent. You can count on that, Ors' Anton'!'

'All right, all right. But now, in the devil's name, be off with you, and let us go on our way.'

The herdsmen finally rode off, heading towards the village at a brisk trot; but every now and then they would stop at all the high points of the road, as if to make sure that there was no hidden ambush, and all the time they remained close enough to Orso and his sister to be able to come to their aid if necessary. And old Polo Griffo said to his companions:

'I understand him! I understand him! He won't say what he's going to do, but he'll do it. He's the spitting image of his father. He can say he doesn't bear a grudge against anybody: he's made a vow to St Nega.* All right! But I wouldn't give a fig for the mayor's hide. Before the month is out, it'll be as full of holes as a sieve.'

Preceded in this way by this band of scouts, the scion of the Della Rebbias entered his village and rode to the old manor of his ancestors, the corporals. The Rebbianists, who had been deprived of a leader for a long time, had turned out en masse to greet him, and those inhabitants of the village who were neutral were all on their doorsteps to see him pass by. The Barricinists stayed inside their houses and peered through the slits in their shutters.

The village of Pietranera is laid out in a very haphazard fashion, like all the villages in Corsica; for to see a real street one has to go to Cargese, which was built by Monsieur de Marboeuf. The houses in Pietranera, scattered about at random without the slightest attempt at alignment, occupy the top of a small plateau, or rather a mountain ledge. Towards the middle of the village there stands a tall green oak,

* This saint is not to be found in the calendar. To make a vow to St Nega means to deny everything as a matter of course. (P.M.)

and near it there is a granite trough into which water is brought from a nearby spring through a wooden pipe. This monument of public utility was paid for jointly by the Della Rebbias and the Barricinis; but anybody who took this as an indication of a former period of friendship between the two families would be sorely mistaken. On the contrary, it is a product of their jealousy. At some time in the past, Colonel della Rebbia sent the municipal council of his commune a small sum of money towards the erection of a fountain, and the lawyer Barricini hastened to make a similar donation: it is to this rivalry in generosity that Pietranera owes its water. Around the green oak and the fountain there is an open space known as the square, where idlers forgather in the evening. Sometimes they play cards there, and once a year, at carnival time, there is dancing. At opposite sides of the square there stand two buildings, higher than they are wide, made of granite and shale. These are the rival 'towers' of the Della Rebbias and the Barricinis. Their architecture is uniform, their height identical, and it can be seen that rivalry between the two families has always continued without fortune deciding between them.

Perhaps it would be as well to explain the meaning of this word 'tower'. It is a square building about forty feet high, which in any other country would be called simply a dovecot. The entrance consists of a narrow door, eight feet above the ground, which is reached by a steep flight of steps. Above the door there is a window with a sort of balcony which has holes in it underneath like a machicolation, so that unwelcome visitors may be overwhelmed without any danger to the occupants of the tower. Between the window and the door can be seen two crudely carved escutcheons. One of these used to bear the Genoese cross, but today it is so worn away that only antiquarians could decipher it. On the other escutcheon is carved the coat of arms of the family to which the tower belongs. Add to this, to complete the decoration, a few bullet scars on the escutcheons and the window casing, and you will have a fair idea of a medieval manor in Corsica. I forgot to say that the living quarters are adjacent to the tower, and are often connected with it by an inner passage.

The Della Rebbia tower and house occupy the north side of the square at Pietranera, and the tower of the Barricinis' house the south side. The space between the north tower and the fountain is the Della Rebbias' walk, while the Barricinis' walk is on the opposite side. Since the funeral of the colonel's wife, nobody had ever seen a member of either of these two families appear on any side of the square other than that assigned to his family by a sort of tacit agreement. To avoid making a detour, Orso was about to pass in front of the mayor's house when his sister stopped him and urged him to take a lane which would bring them to their house without having to cross the square.

'Why should we go out of our way?' asked Orso. 'Doesn't the square belong to everybody?' And he spurred his horse on.

'Brave heart!' murmured Colomba. 'Father, you will be avenged!'

When they reached the square, Colomba placed herself between the Barricinis' house and her brother, and kept her eyes fixed on her enemies' windows. She noticed that they had recently been barricaded and provided with *archere*. These *archere* are narrow openings shaped like loopholes which are left between the thick logs used to block the lower part of a window. When an attack is expected, Corsicans barricade themselves in like this, so that, protected by the logs, they can safely fire at their assailants.

'The cowards!' said Colomba. 'Look brother, they are already beginning to take cover; they are barricading themselves in! But they'll have to come out one day!'

Orso's presence on the south side of the square created a tremendous sensation at Pietranera, and was regarded as a proof of boldness verging on temerity. For the neutrals who gathered that evening around the green oak, it was the subject of endless comment.

'It's a good thing,' they said, 'that the Barricini sons aren't back yet, because they aren't as long-suffering as the lawyer, and they might not have let their enemy go past on their ground without making him pay for his bravado.'

'Remember what I'm going to tell you, neighbour,' added an old man who was the village oracle. 'I had a good look at Colomba's face today: she has something in mind. I can smell gunpowder in the air. Before long there'll be butcher's meat going cheap at Pietranera.'

CHAPTER TEN

SEPARATED from his father at an early age, Orso had scarcely had time to know him. He had left Pietranera when he was fifteen to study in Pisa, and from there he had gone to the military academy while Ghilfuccio was bearing the imperial eagles across the length and breadth of Europe. On the Continent, Orso had seen him at rare intervals, but it was only in 1815 that he had found himself in the regiment which his father commanded. But the colonel, inflexible in matters of discipline, treated his son like all the other young lieutenants, in other words very strictly. The memories which Orso had retained of him were of two sorts. He remembered him at Pietranera entrusting his sword to him, allowing him to fire his gun when he came home from a hunting expedition, or letting him sit down for the first time, when he was a child, at the family table. Then he recalled Colonel della Rebbia putting him under arrest for some blunder, and never calling him anything but Lieutenant della Rebbia:

'Lieutenant della Rebbia, you are not in your battle order. Three days under arrest.'

'Your riflemen are five yards too far from the reserves. Five days under arrest.'

'You are still wearing a forage cap five minutes past noon. A week under arrest.'

Only once, at Quatre-Bras, he had said to him:

'Well done, Orso. But be careful.'

In any case, these last memories were not the ones conjured up by Pietranera. The sight of the places he had known in childhood, and of the furniture used by his mother, to whom he had been deeply attached, aroused in his soul a host of sweet and sad emotions. Then the grim future which lay before him, the vague uneasiness his sister caused him, and, above all else, the idea that Miss Nevil was going to come to his house, which now struck him as so small, so poor, so unsuitable for somebody accustomed to luxury, and the disdain she might feel for it – all these thoughts raced chaotically through his head and plunged him into profound discouragement.

At suppertime he sat down in a big armchair of blackened oak in which his father had always presided over the family meals, and he smiled as he saw Colomba hesitate to sit down at table with him. He was grateful to her though for the silence she maintained during supper and the speedy retreat she beat afterwards, for he felt too deeply moved to be able to resist the attacks she was doubtless preparing to launch upon him; but Colomba was dealing gently with him, wanting to give him time to get his bearings. He sat motionless for a long time, his head resting on one hand, turning over in his mind the scenes of the last fortnight. He realized with a certain alarm everybody's apparent expectation as to how he was going to behave towards the Barricinis. Already he was conscious that the opinion of Pietranera was beginning to appear to him as that of the world in general. He had to avenge his father's death or be taken for a coward. But on whom was he to wreak his vengeance? He could not believe that the Barricinis were guilty of murder. True, they were his family's enemies, but only somebody infected with the crude prejudices of his fellow-countrymen could suspect them of being murderers. Now and then he would look at Miss Nevil's talisman and murmur the motto: 'Life is a fight!' At last he said to himself in a firm voice: 'I shall win it!' With this cheering thought he got up, and, picking up the lamp, he was about to go upstairs to his room when somebody knocked at the outside door. It was an odd hour for anybody to pay a call.

Colomba promptly appeared, followed by the woman who worked for them.

'It's nothing,' she said, running to the door.

However, before opening it, she asked who was knocking. A soft voice replied:

'It's me.'

The wooden bar placed across the door was promptly removed, and Colomba came back into the dining-room, followed by a little girl about ten years old, barefoot and in rags, her head covered with a shabby kerchief from which there escaped long locks of hair as black as a raven's wing. The child was thin and pale, and her skin was sunburnt; but the fire of intelligence glowed in her eyes. When she saw Orso, she stopped shyly and curtsied to him in the peasant style; then she said something in an undertone to Colomba and gave her a freshly killed pheasant.

'Thank you, Chili,' said Colomba. 'And thank your uncle. Is he keeping well?'

'Very well, Mademoiselle, at your service. I couldn't come earlier because he was very late. I waited three hours for him in the *maquis*.'

'And you haven't had any supper?'

'Heavens, no, Mademoiselle, I haven't had time.'

'Then you'll have some supper here. Has your uncle enough bread left?'

'Not much, Mademoiselle, but it's powder that he lacks most of all. Now that the chestnuts have come, all he needs is powder.'

'I'll give you a loaf for him and some powder. Tell him to use it sparingly – it is dear.'

'Colomba,' Orso said in French, 'to whom are you giving alms like that?'

'To a poor bandit from this village,' Colomba replied in the same language. 'This little girl is his niece.'

'It seems to me that you could place your gifts better.

Why send powder to a scoundrel who will only use it to commit crimes? If it weren't for the deplorable weakness everybody seems to have here for bandits, they would have disappeared from Corsica long ago.'

'The worst men on our island are not those who are in the country.'*

'Give them bread if you like: one should never refuse that to anybody. But I won't have you providing them with ammunition.'

'Brother,' Colomba said in grave tones, 'you are the master here, and everything in this house belongs to you. But I warn you that I shall give my *mezzaro* to this little girl for her to sell it rather than refuse powder to a bandit. Refuse to give him powder! Why, we might as well hand him over to the gendarmes. What protection has he against them, apart from his cartridges?'

Meanwhile the little girl was greedily eating a piece of bread and gazing intently at Colomba and her brother in turn, trying to understand from their eyes the meaning of what they were saying.

'And what has he done, this bandit of yours? What crime has made him take to the *maquis*?'

'Brandolaccio has not committed any crime,' exclaimed Colomba. 'He killed Giovan' Opizzo, who had murdered his father while Brandolaccio was in the army.'

Orso turned his head away, picked up the lamp, and, without making any reply, went upstairs to his room. Then Colomba gave the child some powder and food, and showed her to the door, repeating several times:

'Above all, see to it that your uncle watches carefully over Orso!'

* To be in the country, or *alla campagna*, means to be a bandit. The word 'bandit' is not a term of opprobrium; it is to be taken in the sense of 'banished'. A 'bandit' is the 'outlaw' of the English ballads. (P.M.)

CHAPTER ELEVEN

ORSO was a long time getting to sleep, and consequently he awoke late, at least for a Corsican. He had scarcely got up when the first object which caught his eye was his enemies' house and the *archere* which they had just installed there. He went downstairs and asked for his sister.

'She's in the kitchen casting bullets,' replied the servant Saveria.

He clearly could not take a single step without being pursued by tokens of war.

He found Colomba sitting on a stool, surrounded by freshly cast bullets, trimming off the lead ridges.

'What the devil are you doing?' asked her brother.

'You had no bullets for the colonel's gun,' she replied in her sweet voice. 'I found a mould of the right calibre, and you shall have twenty-four cartridges today, brother.'

'I don't need them, thank heavens!'

'You mustn't be taken unawares, Ors' Anton'. You have forgotten what your country and the people who live here are like.'

'If I had really forgotten, you would have reminded me soon enough. Tell me, didn't a big trunk arrive a few days ago?'

'Yes, brother. Do you want me to take it up to your room?'

'You take it up! But you wouldn't have the strength to lift it off the ground.... Isn't there some man here who could do it?'

'I'm not as weak as you think,' said Colomba, rolling up her sleeves and revealing a pair of round white arms, perfectly shaped but suggesting unusual strength. 'Come on, Saveria,' she said to the servant, 'give me a hand.'

She was already lifting the trunk by herself when Orso rushed forward to help her.

'There is something in this trunk for you, my dear Colomba,' he said. 'You must forgive me for giving you such poor presents, but the purse of a lieutenant on half-pay is not very well lined.'

As he spoke, he opened the trunk and took out of it a few dresses, a shawl, and some other things suitable for a young woman.

'What a lot of beautiful things!' exclaimed Colomba. 'I'll put them away at once so that they don't come to any harm. I'll keep them for my wedding,' she added with a sad smile, 'for now I am in mourning.'

And she kissed her brother's hand.

'There's a certain affectation, sister, about staying in mourning so long.'

'I have sworn to,' said Colomba firmly. 'I shan't come out of mourning....'

And she looked out of the window at the Barricinis' house.

'Until your wedding day?' said Orso, trying to avoid the end of her sentence.

'I shall only marry a man who has done three things,' said Colomba.

And she went on gazing in a sinister fashion at the enemy's house.

'You are so pretty, Colomba, I am surprised that you aren't married already. Come, you must tell me who is courting you. In any case I'll hear the serenades. They must be very beautiful to please a great *voceratrice* like you.'

'Who would want to marry a poor orphan girl? Besides, the man who makes me come out of mourning will have to make the women over there go into mourning!'

'This is becoming a positive mania,' Orso thought to himself.

PROSPER MÉRIMÉE

But he said nothing in order to avoid any discussion.

'Brother,' said Colomba in a wheedling tone, 'I have something to give you too. The clothes you are wearing are too good for this country. Your pretty frock-coat would be in rags in two days if you wore it in the *maquis*. You must keep it for the time when Miss Nevil comes.'

Then, opening a wardrobe, she took out a complete hunting outfit.

'I have made you a velvet jacket, and here's a cap such as our well-dressed men wear; I embroidered it for you a long time ago. Will you try them on?'

And she helped him into a loose green velvet jacket with a huge pocket at the back. On his head she put a pointed black velvet cap, embroidered with jet and silk of the same colour and finished with a sort of tassel.

'Here is our father's cartridge-belt,' she said. 'His stiletto is in the pocket of your jacket. I'll go and fetch his pistol.'

'I look just like a brigand at the Ambigu-Comique,' said Orso, looking at himself in a small mirror which Saveria was holding out for him.

'You look real good like that, Ors' Anton',' said the old servant, 'and the most handsome *pinsulo** in Bocognano or Bastelica isn't any smarter.'

Orso breakfasted in his new costume, and during the meal he told his sister that his trunk contained a number of books, and that he intended to send for more from France and Italy, as he planned to make her study a great deal.

'For it is disgraceful, Colomba,' he added, 'that a grown woman like you should still be ignorant of things which children on the Continent know by the time they leave their wet-nurses.'

'You are right, brother,' said Colomba; 'I know what I

* A *pinsulo* is somebody who wears the huntsman's pointed cap. (P.M.)

lack, and I ask for nothing better than to study, especially if you will give me lessons.'

A few days went by without Colomba's mentioning the Barricinis. She lavished little attentions on her brother and often talked to him about Miss Nevil. Orso gave her some French and Italian books to read, and was surprised on the one hand by the soundness and good sense of her comments and on the other by her complete ignorance of the most elementary things.

One morning, after breakfast, Colomba left the room for a moment, and, instead of returning with a book and some paper, reappeared with her *mezzaro* on her head. The expression she wore was even more serious than usual.

'Brother,' she said, 'I should like you to come out with me.'

'Where do you want me to take you?' asked Orso, offering her his arm.

'I don't need your arm, brother, but take your gun and your cartridge-box. A man should never go out without his weapons.'

'All right. I suppose I must follow the fashion. Where are we going?'

Without replying, Colomba drew the *mezzaro* tightly round her head, called the watchdog, and went out, followed by her brother. Striding out of the village, she took a sunken road which twisted among the vines. She had sent the dog on ahead, after giving him a command with which he seemed to be familiar, for he promptly started running along in zigzags, plunging into the vines first on one side and then on the other, always within fifty paces of his mistress, and sometimes stopping in the middle of the road to look at her and wag his tail. He seemed to be performing his duties as a scout to perfection.

'If Muschetto barks,' said Colomba, 'cock your gun, brother, and keep perfectly still.'

Half a mile from the village, after a good many detours, Colomba stopped all of a sudden at a bend in the road. Here there stood a little pyramid of branches, some green and the others dried, piled up about three feet high. The tip of a wooden cross painted black could be seen poking out at the top. In several Corsican cantons, particularly in the mountains, a very ancient custom, which may be connected with some pagan superstition, obliges passers-by to throw a stone or a branch on the spot where a man has died a violent death. For years and years, as long as the recollection of his tragic end lasts in the memory of men, this strange offering accumulates like this, day by day. It is called the heap, or *mucchio*, of the man in question.

Colomba stopped in front of this heap of foliage, and, breaking off an arbutus twig, added it to the pyramid.

'Orso,' she said, 'this is where your father died. Let us pray for his soul, brother!'

And she knelt down. Orso promptly followed her example. At that moment the bell of the village church started tolling, for a man had died during the night. Orso burst into tears.

After a few minutes Colomba stood up, her eyes dry but her face flushed. With her thumb she hurriedly crossed herself after the fashion of her compatriots, who usually make the sign of the Cross when making solemn oaths. Then, leading her brother, she set off on the way back to the village. They entered their house in silence. Orso went upstairs to his room. A moment later Colomba joined him there, carrying a small casket which she placed on the table. She opened it and took out a shirt covered with large bloodstains.

'This is your father's shirt, Orso.'

And she threw it on to his lap.

'This is the lead that killed him.'

And she placed two blackened bullets on the shirt.

'Orso, my brother!' she cried, throwing herself into his arms and clasping him tightly. 'Orso, you will avenge his death!'

She embraced him in a sort of frenzy, kissed the bullets and the shirt, and went out of the room, leaving her brother sitting in his chair as if he were petrified.

For some time Orso remained motionless, not daring to push away those horrifying relics. Finally, making a tremendous effort, he put them back in the casket and ran to the other end of the room, where he threw himself on his bed, his head turned towards the wall and buried in the pillow, as if he were trying to hide from the sight of some ghost. His sister's last words went on ringing in his ears, and it seemed to him that he could hear a fateful unescapable oracle asking him for blood, and innocent blood at that. I shall not try to convey to you the thoughts and feelings of the unhappy young man, which were as confused as those which haunt a madman's head. For a long time he remained in the same position, without daring to turn his head. At last he got up, closed the casket, and rushed headlong out of the house, taking to the open country, where he ran and walked without knowing where he was going.

Gradually the fresh air soothed him; he grew calmer and began to consider with a certain composure his position and the means of extricating himself from it. He did not for a moment suspect the Barricinis of murder, as you already know, but he did think them guilty of having forged the letter from the bandit Agostini; and that letter, or so at least he believed, had caused his father's death. To have them prosecuted for forgery was, he knew, impossible. Now and then, when the prejudices or instincts of his country returned to assail him and to suggest an easy vengeance at the bend in some path, he banished them with horror by thinking of his comrades in the regiment, of the drawing-rooms of Paris, and above all of Miss Nevil. Then he would think of his sister's reproaches, and that part of his character which was still Corsican justified those reproaches and rendered them more poignant. Only one hope was left to him in this conflict between his conscience and his prejudices, and that was to pick a quarrel, under some pretext or other, with one of the lawyer's sons and fight a duel with him. To kill a man with a bullet or a sword-thrust would reconcile his Corsican ideas with those he had acquired in France. Once he had accepted this plan and had begun to consider the means of carrying it out, he already felt that a great burden had been taken off his mind; and then other, gentler thoughts occurred to him which contributed still further to calm his feverish agitation. Cicero, plunged into despair by the death of his daughter Tullia, forgot his grief by turning over in his mind all the beautiful things he could say about it. By discoursing in similar fashion, Tristram Shandy consoled himself for the death of his son. Orso cooled his blood by thinking that he might describe his state of mind to Miss Nevil, and that such a description could not fail to interest that beautiful person.

He was drawing near to the village, from which he had walked a long way without noticing it, when he heard the voice of a little girl, who probably imagined that she was alone, singing on a path along the edge of the *maquis*. The melody was that slow, monotonous air used in funeral laments, and the words were: 'For my son, my son across the sea – keep my cross and my bloodstained shirt.'

'What are you singing, child?' Orso asked angrily, suddenly appearing before her.

'Oh, it's you, Ors' Anton'!' exclaimed the child, a little frightened. 'It's a song by Mademoiselle Colomba. . . .'

'I forbid you to sing it,' said Orso in a terrible voice.

The child kept turning her head this way and that, as if

she were wondering which way she could escape, and she would doubtless have taken to her heels if she had not been held back by the need to take care of a large bundle which lay in the grass at her feet.

Orso felt ashamed of his angry outburst.

'What have you there, child?' he asked her as gently as he could.

And as Chilina hesitated to answer, he lifted the cloth which was wrapped round the bundle and saw that it contained a loaf of bread and some other food.

'To whom are you taking this bread, my dear?' he asked.

'You know very well, Monsieur; to my uncle.'

'And isn't your uncle a bandit?'

'At your service, Monsieur Ors' Anton'.'

'If you met the gendarmes, they would ask you where you were going....'

'I would tell them,' the child replied without any hesitation, 'that I was taking food to the men from Lucca who are cutting the *maquis*.'

'And what if you ran into some hungry huntsman who wanted to dine at your expense and took all your food?'

'He wouldn't dare. I would say it was for my uncle.'

'Yes, it's true that he isn't the sort of man to let somebody else take his dinner.... Is your uncle fond of you?'

'Oh, yes, Ors' Anton'. Ever since my father died, he has taken care of the whole family – my mother, myself, and my little sister. Before mother fell ill, he recommended her to rich people who gave her sewing to do. The mayor has given me a dress every year and the curé has been teaching me the catechism and how to read ever since my uncle spoke to them. But it's your sister who is kindest of all to us.'

At that moment a dog appeared in the pathway. The little girl put two fingers in her mouth and gave a shrill whistle: her dog promptly came running up to her, licked her hand, and then plunged into the *maquis*. Soon two men, shabbily dressed but well armed, rose behind a clump of shoots a few paces away from Orso. It was as if they had slithered like snakes through the rock-rose and myrtle which covered the ground.

'Oh, Ors' Anton', welcome!' said the older of the two men. 'Why, don't you recognize me?'

'No,' said Orso, gazing hard at him.

'It's odd how a beard and a pointed cap can change a man! Come now, Lieutenant, have a good look. Have you forgotten the veterans of Waterloo? Don't you remember Brando Savelli, who bit open many a cartridge beside you on that unhappy day?'

'What! It's you?' said Orso. 'But you deserted in 1816!'

'As you say, Lieutenant. Dammit all, army life is boring, and besides, I had an account to settle in this country. Ah, Chili, you're a good girl. Give us something to eat quickly, for we're hungry. You can't imagine, Lieutenant, what an appetite living in the *maquis* gives you. Who sent us this? Mademoiselle Colomba or the mayor?'

'No, Uncle; it was the miller's wife who gave me this for you and a blanket for Mother.'

'What does she want from me?'

'She says that the men from Lucca she hired to clear her land are now asking her for thirty-five sous and the chestnuts, because of the fever in the lower part of Pietranera.'

'The lazy good-for-nothings! . . . I'll take care of them. . . . Without standing on ceremony, Lieutenant, will you share our dinner? We've eaten worse meals together in the days of that poor fellow-countryman of ours who has been put on the retired list.'

'No, thank you. . . . I've been put on the retired list too.'

'Yes, so I've heard. But I bet you weren't too annoyed. After all, now you can settle your own account. . . . Come on, Curé,' the bandit said to his comrade, 'let's eat! Monsieur Orso, allow me to introduce the curé. As a matter of fact, I'm not too sure that he is a curé, but he certainly knows as much as any priest.'

'A poor theology student, Monsieur,' said the second bandit, 'who was prevented from following his vocation. Who knows? I might have become Pope, Brandolaccio.'

'And what was it that deprived Holy Mother Church of your learning?' asked Orso.

'A mere trifle, an account that had to be settled, as my friend Brandolaccio puts it. A sister of mine had made a fool of herself while I was working at my books at the University of Pisa. I had to come back to Corsica to marry her off. But her intended, who had been in too much of a hurry, died of the fever three days before I arrived. So I turned, as you would have done in my place, to the dead man's brother. I was told he was married. What was I to do?'

'It was certainly a difficult situation. What did you do?'

'It was one of those cases where you have to resort to a gun-flint.'

'You mean that. . . .'

'I put a bullet through his head,' said the bandit calmly.

Orso gave a start of horror. However, curiosity, and also perhaps the desire to postpone the moment when he would have to return home, induced him to stay where he was and continue his conversation with these two men, each of whom had at least one murder on his conscience.

While his comrade was talking, Brandolaccio was putting bread and meat in front of him. He helped himself and then gave some food to his dog, which he introduced to Orso as Brusco, an animal endowed with the wonderful ability to recognize a rifleman, whatever the disguise he might be wearing. Finally he cut a piece of bread and a slice of raw ham which he gave to his niece.

'Oh, it's a wonderful life being a bandit!' exclaimed the

theology student after he had eaten a few mouthfuls. 'Perhaps you'll try it one day, Monsieur della Rebbia, and then you'll see how delightful it is to have no other master than your own fancy.'

So far the bandit had spoken in Italian; he went on in French:

'Corsica isn't a very amusing country for a young man to live in; but for a bandit, it's a very different matter. The women are crazy about us. Why, I myself have three mistresses in three different cantons. I'm at home wherever I go. And one of them is the wife of a gendarme.'

'You speak a great many languages, Monsieur,' said Orso gravely.

'If I talk in French, it's because, you see, *maxima debetur pueris reverentia*. Brandolaccio and I want the little girl to turn out well and go straight.'

'When she's fifteen,' said Chilina's uncle, 'I'll find her a good husband. I already have somebody in mind.'

'Will it be you that makes the proposal?' asked Orso.

'Naturally. Do you think that if I say to a rich man from these parts: "I, Brando Savelli, would like your son to marry Michelina Savelli," he'll wait to be asked twice?'

'I wouldn't advise him to,' said the other bandit. 'My comrade has a rather heavy hand.'

'If I were a scoundrel,' Brandolaccio went on, 'a rogue or an impostor, I'd only have to open my purse and five-franc pieces would rain into it.'

'Then is there something in your purse that attracts them?' asked Orso.

'Nothing. But if I wrote to a rich man, as some people have done: "I need a hundred francs," he'd send them to me double quick. But I'm a man of honour, Lieutenant.'

'Do you know, Monsieur della Rebbia,' said the bandit whom his comrade called the curé, 'that in this country, with its simple ways, there are none the less a few wretches who take advantage of the respect inspired by our passports' (here he pointed to his gun) 'to draw bills of exchange by forging our handwriting?'

'I know,' Orso said brusquely. 'But what bills of exchange?'

'Six months ago,' the bandit continued, 'I was walking along near Orezza when a villager came up to me, taking his cap off when he was still some way off, and said: "Oh, Monsieur le Curé," (they always call me that), "forgive me, give me time. I've only been able to find fifty-five francs. Honestly, that's all I've been able to scrape together." I was astonished. "What do you mean, you scoundrel," I said, "fifty-five francs?" "I mean sixty-five," he replied, "but as for the hundred you're asking me for, that's impossible." "What, you rascal, I'm asking you for a hundred francs? I don't even know you." Then he showed me a letter, or rather a dirty scrap of paper, which called upon him to deposit a hundred francs at a spot which was indicated, on pain of seeing his house burnt down and his cows killed by Giocanto Castriconi, which is my name. And somebody had had the gall to forge my signature! What annoyed me most of all was that the letter was written in dialect and full of spelling mistakes.... The idea that I should make spelling mistakes – I who won all the prizes at the University! I began by giving the rascal a slap that sent him spinning. "Oh, so you take me for a thief, do you, you blackguard?" I said to him, and I gave him a good kick you know where. Feeling a little better, I asked him: "When are you due to take this money to the place mentioned?" "Today." "Good! Then go and take it there." It was at the foot of a pine-tree, and the place was clearly indicated. He took the money, buried it at the foot of the tree, and came and joined me. I had hidden myself nearby. I stayed there with my man for six mortal hours. Monsieur della Rebbia, I would have stayed three days if it had been necessary. After six hours a *Bastiaccio*,* a vile moneylender, appeared. As he bent down to dig up the money, I fired, and I had aimed so well that he fell with his head on the coins he was unearthing. "Now, you scoundrel," I said to the peasant, "take your money and don't ever suspect Giocanto Castriconi again of a mean action like that." The poor devil, trembling all over, picked up his sixty-five francs without even bothering to wipe them. He thanked me, I gave him a good parting kick, and he's probably still running.'

'Ah, Curé,' said Brandolaccio, 'I envy you that shot. What a good laugh you must have had!'

'I had shot the *Bastiaccio* in the temple,' the bandit went on, 'and that reminded me of these lines from Virgil:

> ... *Liquefacto tempora plumbo*
> *Diffidit, ac multa porrectum extendit arena.*

Liquefacto! Do you think, Monsieur Orso, that a lead bullet travels so fast through the air that it melts? You, who have studied ballistics, ought to be able to tell me whether that is true or false.'

Orso preferred discussing this problem of physics to arguing with the theology student about the morality of his action. Brandolaccio, who was rather bored by this scientific discussion, interrupted it to observe that the sun was about to set.

'Since you wouldn't have dinner with us, Ors' Anton',' he said, 'I advise you not to keep Mademoiselle Colomba waiting any longer. Besides, it isn't always safe to be on the roads after sunset. Why did you come out without a gun? There are some bad characters in these parts: take care.

---

* The Corsicans who live in the mountains loathe the inhabitants of Bastia, whom they do not regard as their fellow-countrymen. They never call a citizen of Bastia a *Bastiese*, but a *Bastiaccio*: as is well known, the ending – *accio* has a pejorative sense. (P.M.)

Today you've nothing to fear; the Barricinis are bringing the prefect home with them; they have gone to meet him on the road, and he's staying for a day at Pietranera before going to Corte to lay what they call a foundation-stone ... a lot of nonsense! He is spending the night at the Barricinis', but tomorrow they'll be free. There is Vincentello, who is a bad lot, and Orlanduccio, who is not much better.... Try to meet them separately, one today, the other tomorrow. But watch out, that's all I can say.'

'Thank you for the advice,' said Orso; 'but I have no quarrel with them. Until they come looking for me, I have nothing to say to them.'

The bandit put his tongue in his cheek and clicked it ironically, but made no reply. Orso got up to go.

'By the way,' said Brandolaccio, 'I haven't thanked you for your powder; it reached me just when I needed it. Now I've everything I want ... except for shoes ... but I'll make myself a pair from the skin of a moufflon one of these days.'

Orso slipped a couple of five-franc pieces into the bandit's hand.

'It was Colomba who sent you the powder; this is to buy you some shoes.'

'No, I can't have that, Lieutenant,' exclaimed Brandolaccio, giving him back the two coins. 'Do you take me for a beggar? I accept bread and powder, but I'll have nothing else.'

'I thought one old soldier could help another. Well, goodbye!'

But, before leaving, he had put the money in the bandit's bag without his noticing.

'Good-bye, Ors' Anton',' said the theologian. 'Perhaps we'll meet again in the *maquis* one of these days, and then we'll continue our study of Virgil.'

Orso had left his good companions a quarter of an hour

when he heard a man running after him as fast as his legs could carry him. It was Brandolaccio.

'This is going too far, Lieutenant,' he exclaimed breathlessly, 'a bit too far! Here are your ten francs. I wouldn't let it pass if any other man had played that trick on me. Give my regards to Mademoiselle Colomba. You've put me right out of breath. Good night.'

CHAPTER TWELVE

ORSO found Colomba somewhat alarmed at his prolonged absence; but, as soon as she saw him, she resumed that air of melancholy serenity which was her habitual expression. During the evening meal, they talked only of trivial matters, and Orso, emboldened by his sister's composure, told her about his encounter with the bandits and even hazarded a few pleasantries concerning the moral and religious education which little Chilina was receiving from her uncle and his esteemed colleague, Monsieur Castriconi.

'Brandolaccio is a good fellow,' said Colomba; 'but as for Castriconi, I have heard that he's an unprincipled scoundrel.'

'I think,' said Orso, 'that he is just as good as Brandolaccio, and Brandolaccio as good as he. Both of them are at open war with society. Their first crime leads them to commit other crimes every day, and yet perhaps they are not as guilty as a good many people who don't live in the *maquis*.'

A flash of joy lit up his sister's face.

'Yes,' Orso went on, 'those wretches have their own code of honour. It was a cruel tradition and not base greed which thrust them into the life they are leading.'

There was a moment's silence.

'Brother,' said Colomba, as she poured out his coffee, 'perhaps you know that Carlo-Battista Pietri died last night? Yes, he died of the swamp-fever.'

'Who was this Pietri?'

'He was a man from this village, the husband of Maddelena, to whom our dying father gave his notebook. His widow came to ask me to attend his wake and to sing something there. It would be fitting for you to come too. They are our neighbours, and this is a courtesy which we cannot fail to perform in a small place such as this.'

'Oh, confound your wake, Colomba! I don't like seeing my sister making an exhibition of herself like that.'

'Orso,' replied Colomba, 'everybody honours his dead in his own way. The *ballata* has come down to us from our ancestors, and we must respect it as an ancient custom. Maddalena hasn't the "gift", and old Fiordispina, who is the best *voceratrice* in these parts, is ill. There has to be somebody for the *ballata*.'

'Do you think that Carlo-Battista won't find his way into the next world unless somebody sings some bad verse over his bier? Go to the wake if you like, Colomba, and I'll go with you if you think I should. But don't improvise the *ballata*: it's not fitting at your age, and ... please, sister.'

'Brother, I have promised. It is the custom here, as you know, and, as I have already said, I am the only one who can improvise.'

'It's a stupid custom!'

'It distresses me terribly to sing like that. It reminds me of all our own misfortunes. Tomorrow I shall be ill because of it; but I must do it. Allow me to, brother. Remember that in Ajaccio you told me to improvise to amuse that young English lady who laughs at our old customs. So may I not improvise today for some poor people who will be grateful for my singing, and whose grief it will help them to bear?'

'Very well, do as you please. I'm willing to wager that you have already composed your *ballata* and don't want to waste it.'

'No, brother, I couldn't possibly compose it in advance. I stand before the dead man and I think of those whom he has left behind. Tears spring to my eyes, and then I sing whatever comes into my mind.'

All this was said with such simplicity that it was impossible to suspect Mademoiselle Colomba of the slightest poetic vanity.

Orso allowed himself to be persuaded and accompanied his sister to Pietri's house. The dead man had been laid out on a table, with his face uncovered, in the largest room in the house. The doors and windows were open, and several tapers were burning round the table. At the head of the table there stood the widow, and behind her a considerable number of women occupied the whole of one side of the room; on the other side stood the men, bareheaded, their eyes fixed on the corpse, and all absolutely silent. Each new arrival went up to the table, kissed the dead man,* bowed his head towards the widow and her son, and then took his place in the circle, without uttering a single word. Now and then, however, one of those present would break the solemn silence to address a few words to the dead man.

'Why did you leave your good wife?' said one old woman. 'Didn't she look after you well? What did you lack? Why didn't you wait another month? Your daughter-in-law would have borne you a grandson.'

A tall young man, Pietri's son, pressing his father's cold hand, cried:

'Oh, why didn't you die of the *mala morte*?† Then we could have avenged you.'

These were the first words Orso heard as he came in. At the sight of him the circle opened up, and a faint murmur of curiosity revealed the expectations aroused by the presence of the *voceratrice*. Colomba embraced the widow, took one of her hands, and stood meditating for a few minutes with her eyes lowered. Then she threw back her *mezzaro*, and, bending over the dead man, her face almost as pale as his, she began thus:

'Carlo-Battista! May Christ receive your soul! – To live

* This custom still exists at Bocagnano in 1840. (P.M.)
† The *mala morte* means a violent death. (P.M.)

is to suffer. You are going to a place – where there is neither sunshine nor cold. – You no longer need your bill-hook – nor your heavy pick. – No more work for you. – Henceforth all your days are Sundays. – Carlo-Battista, may Christ take your soul. – Your son rules over your house. – I saw the oak-tree fall – dried up by the Libeccio. – I thought that it was dead. – I passed by again, and its roots had put forth a sapling. – The sapling has become an oak – giving vast shade. – Under its strong branches, Maddalè, take your rest – and think of the oak that is no more.'

At this point Maddalena began sobbing loudly, and two or three men who, if the opportunity arose, would have shot at Christians as calmly as at partridges, started wiping big tears from their suntanned cheeks.

Colomba went on in this way for some time, addressing herself sometimes to the corpse, sometimes to the family, and sometimes – by means of a personification often employed in a *ballata* – making the dead man himself speak to console his friends or give them advice. As she improvised, her face took on a sublime expression, her complexion turning a transparent pink which set off even more the whiteness of her teeth and the fire in her dilated pupils. She was like a soothsayer on her tripod. Apart from a few sighs and muffled sobs, not the slightest murmur could be heard from the crowd pressing around her. Although he was less liable than other people to be swayed by this wild poetry, Orso soon felt affected by the general emotion. Unnoticed in a dark corner of the room, he wept as Pietri's own son was weeping.

All of a sudden a slight movement occurred in the gathering: the circle opened, and several strangers came in. From the respect shown to them and the eagerness with which room was made for them, it was obvious that they were people of importance whose visit was a great honour for the house. However, out of respect for the *ballata*, nobody spoke to them. The man who had come in first appeared to be about forty years old. His dress coat, his rosette, and his expression of confident authority identified him immediately as the prefect. Behind him came a bent old man with a bilious complexion, trying in vain to conceal behind green spectacles a timid, anxious gaze. He was wearing a dress coat which was too big for him, and which, although only a little worn, had obviously been made several years before. He kept close to the prefect all the time, as if he wanted to hide himself in his shadow. Lastly, behind him, two tall young men came in, their faces tanned by the sun, their cheeks hidden by bushy sidewhiskers, their eyes proud, arrogant, and full of an impertinent curiosity. Orso had been away long enough to forget the faces of the people of his village; but the sight of the old man in the green spectacles promptly awakened old memories in his mind. His presence in the prefect's company was enough to identify him. It was the lawyer Barricini, the mayor of Pietranera, who had come with his two sons to show the prefect what a *ballata* was like. It would be difficult to say exactly what happened at that moment in Orso's mind, but the presence of his father's enemy filled him with a kind of horror, and, more than ever before, he felt swayed by the suspicions which he had resisted for so long.

As for Colomba, at the sight of the man for whom she had vowed deadly hatred, her mobile features immediately took on a sinister expression. She turned pale, her voice became hoarse, and the line she had begun died on her lips. . . . But soon, taking up the *ballata* again, she continued with fresh vehemence:

'When the sparrow-hawk mourns – before his empty nest – the starlings flutter around – insulting his grief.'

At this point there was a muffled laugh; it came from the two young men who had just arrived, and who doubtless considered the comparison too bold.

'The sparrow-hawk will awaken and spread his wings. – He will wash his beak in blood! – As for you, Carlo-Battista, let your friends – bid you their last farewell. – Their tears have flowed long enough. – Only the poor orphan maid will not weep for you. – Why should she weep for you? You have fallen asleep full of years – in the midst of your family – ready to appear – before the Almighty. – The orphan maid weeps for her father – taken by surprise by cowardly murderers – struck down from behind – her father whose blood is red – beneath the heap of green leaves. – But she has gathered up his blood – that noble, innocent blood. – She has poured it over Pietranera – so that it may become a deadly poison. – And Pietranera shall remain stained and sullied – until guilty blood – has effaced all trace of innocent blood.'

With these last words Colomba dropped on to a chair; she pulled her *mezzaro* over her face, and they heard her sobbing. The weeping women gathered around the *improvisatrice* to comfort her; several men threw fierce glances at the mayor and his sons; a few old men murmured protests at the scandal they had caused by their presence. The dead man's son pushed his way through the crowd and was about to ask the mayor to leave the house at once; but Barricini had not waited for this request. He was making for the door, and his two sons were already in the street. The prefect expressed his condolences to young Pietri and followed them almost immediately. As for Orso, he went over to his sister, took her arm, and led her out of the room.

'Go with them,' young Pietri said to some of his friends. 'Make sure that nothing happens to them!'

Two or three young men hastily slid their stilettos up the left sleeve of their jackets and escorted Orso and his sister to the door of their house.

CHAPTER THIRTEEN

COLOMBA, panting and exhausted, was incapable of uttering a single word. Her head rested on her brother's shoulder, and she was holding one of his hands tightly in hers. Although he was inwardly rather angry with her about her peroration, Orso was too alarmed to address even the mildest reproach to her. He was waiting in silence for the end of what appeared to be a fit of hysterics when there was a knock at the door, and a flustered Saveria came in to announce the prefect. At this, Colomba got up, as if she were ashamed of her weakness, and stood there leaning on a chair which trembled visibly under her hand.

The prefect began with a few conventional apologies for the unseemly hour of his visit, offered Mademoiselle Colomba his sympathy, and spoke of the dangers of strong emotions. He criticized the custom of composing funeral laments, which the very talent of the *voceratrice* rendered still more harrowing for the mourners; and he skilfully insinuated a mild reproof regarding the character of this latest improvisation. Then, changing his tone of voice, he said:

'Monsieur della Rebbia, your English friends have asked me to give you their kindest regards, and Miss Nevil wishes to be remembered to your sister. I have a letter for you from her.'

'A letter from Miss Nevil?' exclaimed Orso.

'Unfortunately I haven't the letter on me, but you shall have it in five minutes. Her father has been ill. For a while we were afraid he had caught one of our terrible fevers. Fortunately he is now fully recovered, as you can judge for yourself, for I imagine you will be seeing him soon.'

'Miss Nevil must have been very worried.'

'Luckily she did not realize the danger until it was already past. Monsieur della Rebbia, Miss Nevil has spoken to me a great deal about you and your sister.'

Orso bowed.

'She is extremely fond of you both. Beneath an exterior of great charm, and behind an air of apparent frivolity, she conceals a wealth of good sense.'

'She is a delightful person.'

'It is almost at her request that I have come here, Monsieur. Nobody is better acquainted than I with the tragic story which I would much prefer not to have to recall to you. Since Monsieur Barricini is still the mayor of Pietranera, and I am the prefect of this department, I have no need to tell you how little importance I attach to certain suspicions which, if I have been correctly informed, certain imprudent persons have expressed to you, and which I know you have rejected with the indignation one would expect from your position and your character.'

'Colomba,' said Orso, shifting about in his chair, 'you are very tired. You ought to go to bed.'

Colomba shook her head. She had recovered her usual calm and was gazing at the prefect with burning eyes.

'Monsieur Barricini,' the prefect continued, 'would very much like to see an end to this sort of enmity. . . . I mean this state of uncertainty which exists between you. . . . For my part, I would be delighted to see you establish the kind of relations with him which should exist between people who ought to feel esteem for one another. . . .'

'Monsieur,' interrupted Orso in a trembling voice, 'I have never accused Barricini of having murdered my father, but he is guilty of an action which will always prevent me from having friendly relations with him. He forged a threatening letter in the name of a certain bandit . . . or at least, he insinuated that my father had forged it. And that letter, Monsieur, was probably the indirect cause of my father's death.'

The prefect thought for a moment.

'That your father should have believed Monsieur Barricini to be guilty of forgery at a time when, carried away by his impetuous nature, he was engaged in a lawsuit with him is pardonable; but there can be no excuse for similar blindness on your part. Remember that Barricini could have gained no advantage from forging that letter. . . . I will not say anything of his character – you don't know him and you are prejudiced against him – but you cannot imagine that a man familiar with the law. . . .'

'But, Monsieur,' said Orso, getting to his feet, 'kindly remember that to tell me that that letter was not forged by Barricini is tantamount to attributing it to my father. His honour, Monsieur, is mine.'

'Nobody, Monsieur,' continued the prefect, 'is more convinced of Colonel della Rebbia's honour than I am . . . but . . . the author of that letter is now known.'

'Who is it?' exclaimed Colomba, walking towards the prefect.

'A rascally fellow who has committed several crimes – the sort of crimes you Corsicans never forgive – a thief called Tomaso Bianchi, at present held in the prison at Bastia, has revealed that he wrote that fateful letter.'

'I don't know the man,' said Orso. 'What could his motive have been?'

'He comes from these parts,' said Colomba. 'He is the brother of a former miller of ours. He is a scoundrel and a liar, unworthy of belief.'

'You will see in a moment,' the prefect went on, 'what his interest in the matter was. The miller your sister referred to – he was called Teodoro, I think – rented a mill from the colonel, on the stream which was the subject of dispute between Monsieur Barricini and your father. The colonel, with his usual generosity, derived scarcely any profit from his mill. Now, Tomaso thought that if Monsieur Barricini obtained possession of the stream, he would have to pay him a very high rent, for it is well known that Monsieur Barricini is rather fond of money. In short, to oblige his brother, Tomaso forged the bandit's letter – and that's the whole story. You know that family ties are so strong in Corsica that they sometimes lead to crime.... Please read this letter which I have received from the attorney general: it will confirm what I have just told you.'

Orso glanced through the letter, which recounted Tomaso's confession in detail, and at the same time Colomba read it over her brother's shoulder.

When she had finished, she exclaimed:

'Orlanduccio Barricini went to Bastia a month ago, when he heard that my brother was coming home. He must have seen Tomaso and paid him to tell this lie.'

'Mademoiselle,' said the prefect impatiently, 'you explain everything with odious suppositions; is that the way to discover the truth? You, Monsieur, are quite calm; tell me, what do you think now? Do you believe, like Mademoiselle, that a man with only a light sentence to fear would deliberately lay himself open to a conviction for forgery to oblige somebody he doesn't even know?'

Orso read the attorney general's letter again, weighing every word with extraordinary care, for now that he had seen Barricini he felt less open to persuasion than he would have been a few days earlier. At last he found himself obliged to admit that the explanation struck him as satisfactory. Colomba, however, exclaimed vehemently:

'Tomaso Bianchi is a crafty scoundrel. He won't be convicted, or he'll escape from prison, I'm sure of that.'

The prefect shrugged his shoulder.

'I have passed on to you, Monsieur,' he said, 'the information I have received. I will go now, and leave you to your thoughts. I shall wait for your reason to enlighten you, and I hope that it will prove stronger than your sister's ... suppositions.'

Orso, after a few words of apology for Colomba, repeated that he now believed Tomaso to be the sole culprit.

The prefect had got up to go.

'If it were not so late,' he said, 'I would suggest that you come along with me to collect Miss Nevil's letter. At the same time you could tell Monsieur Barricini what you have just told me, and the whole affair would be finished.'

'Orso della Rebbia will never set foot in the house of a Barricini!' Colomba cried impetuously.

'Mademoiselle would seem to be the *tintinajo** of the family,' remarked the prefect sarcastically.

'Monsieur,' said Colomba in a firm voice, 'you have been taken in. You don't know the lawyer. He is the most cunning and unscrupulous of men. I beg you not to make Orso do something which would cover him with shame.'

'Colomba,' exclaimed Orso, 'your hatred is making you talk nonsense.'

'Orso, Orso, by the casket I gave you, I beg you to listen to me. There is blood between you and the Barricinis; you shall not go to their house!'

'Sister!'

'No, brother, you shall not go, or I shall leave this house and you will never see me again. . . . Orso, have pity on me.'

And she fell to her knees.

'I am sorry,' said the prefect, 'to see Mademoiselle della Rebbia being so unreasonable. You will convince her, I feel sure.'

He half-opened the door and paused, apparently waiting for Orso to follow him.

'I cannot leave her now,' said Orso. 'Tomorrow, if. . . .'

'I shall be leaving early,' said the prefect.

'At least, brother,' cried Colomba, clasping her hands

---

* This is the name given to the ram with the bell round its neck which leads the flock, and, by metaphor, to the member of a family who directs it in all important matters. (P.M.)

together, 'wait until tomorrow morning. Let me look through my father's papers again.... You cannot refuse me that.'

'Very well, you shall see them tonight, but after that you must stop tormenting me with that violent hatred of yours.... A thousand pardons, Monsieur.... I myself feel extremely upset.... It would be better to wait until tomorrow.'

'Sleep on it,' said the prefect as he went out. 'I hope that by tomorrow all your irresolution will have disappeared.'

'Saveria,' cried Colomba, 'take the lantern and go with the prefect. He will give you a letter for my brother.'

She added a few words which only Saveria could hear.

'Colomba,' said Orso when the prefect had gone, 'you caused me considerable embarrassment. Will you always refuse to accept the facts?'

'You have given me till tomorrow,' she replied. 'I have very little time, but I still have hope.'

Then she took a bunch of keys and ran up to a room on the next floor. There he could hear her hurriedly opening drawers and rummaging about in a desk in which Colonel della Rebbia used to keep his important papers.

CHAPTER FOURTEEN

SAVERIA was away a long time, and Orso's patience was almost exhausted by the time she finally reappeared, holding a letter, and followed by little Chilina, who was rubbing her eyes, for she had been awakened from her first sleep.

'Child,' said Orso, 'what are you doing here at this hour?'
'Mademoiselle sent for me,' replied Chilina.
'What the devil does she want with her?' wondered Orso; but he hastened to open Miss Lydia's letter, and, while he was reading it, Chilina went upstairs to join his sister.

My father, Monsieur, has been rather unwell [wrote Miss Nevil], and besides, he is so lazy about writing that I have to act as his secretary. You will remember that the other day he got his feet wet on the seashore instead of admiring the scenery with us, and that is quite enough to give somebody the fever on your delightful island. I can imagine the scowl you are making now; you are probably reaching for your stiletto, but I hope that you no longer have one. As I was saying, my father had a little fever and I had a great fright; the prefect, whom I still consider a very pleasant man, sent us a doctor who was also very pleasant and who pulled us through in a couple of days. The fever has not returned, and my father wants to go hunting again, but I have forbidden him to do so yet.

How did you find your château in the mountains? Is your north tower still in the same place? Is it haunted? I am asking you all this because my father remembers that you promised him deer, boar, and moufflon ... is that the right name for those weird animals? On our way to take the boat at Bastia we are planning to impose upon your hospitality, and I hope that the Della Rebbia Castle, which you say is so old and dilapidated, will not collapse on our heads.

The prefect is so charming that with him there is never any lack of a subject of conversation – by the way, I flatter myself that I have turned his head. We have talked about your lordship. The authorities at Bastia have sent him certain revelations made by a scoundrel they are holding in custody, and which are such as to destroy your last suspicions; your feud, which sometimes made me uneasy, must come to an end now. You have no idea how delighted I was to learn all this. When you left with the beautiful *voceratrice*, with your gun in your hand and thunder on your brow, you struck me as more of a Corsican than usual . . . too much of a Corsican, indeed. *Basta!* I am writing you such a long letter because I am bored.

The prefect, alas, is leaving. We shall send word to you when we are about to set off for your mountains, and I shall take the liberty of writing to Mademoiselle Colomba to ask her for a *bruccio, ma solenne*. In the meantime, give her my love. I am using her stiletto a great deal, to cut the pages of a novel I brought with me; but this terrible weapon is indignant at being employed for such a purpose and tears my book in the most dreadful fashion.

Farewell, Monsieur. My father sends you 'his best love'. Listen to the prefect. He is a sensible man, and is going out of his way, I believe, on your account. He is going to lay a foundation-stone at Corte; I imagine that it will be an impressive ceremony, and I am very sorry that I shan't be there. A gentleman in an embroidered coat, silk stockings, and a white sash, holding a trowel! There will be a speech, and the ceremony will end with a thousand shouts of 'Long live the King!'

You are going to be very vain at having got me to fill all four pages; but as I have already said, Monsieur, I am bored, and for that reason I give you leave to write to me at great length. Incidentally, I consider it very odd that you have not yet informed me of your safe arrival at Pietranera Castle.

Lydia.

P.S. I beg you to listen to the prefect and to do as he suggests. We are agreed that this is what you should do, and I shall be so pleased if you do it.

Orso read this letter through three or four times, making countless mental comments with each reading. Then he wrote a lengthy reply, which he gave to Saveria to take to a man in the village who was leaving that very night for Ajaccio. Already he had almost abandoned the idea of arguing with his sister about the misdeeds, real or imaginary, of the Barricinis. Miss Lydia's letter had made him see everything through rose-tinted glasses; he no longer felt any suspicion or hatred. He waited for some time for his sister to come downstairs, but as she did not reappear he went to bed, with his heart lighter than it had been for a long time. After Chilina had been dismissed with some secret instructions, Colomba spent the greater part of the night reading through some old papers. Shortly before daybreak, a few pebbles were thrown at her window; at this signal she went down to the garden, opened a secret door, and introduced two villainous-looking men into her house. The first thing she did was to take them to the kitchen and give them a meal. Who these men were, you will learn before long.

CHAPTER FIFTEEN

IN the morning, about six o'clock, one of the prefect's servants knocked at the door of Orso's house. He was received by Colomba, and informed her that the prefect was about to leave and was expecting her brother. Colomba replied without the slightest hesitation that her brother had just fallen down the stairs and sprained his foot; that he was incapable of walking a single step; that he begged the prefect to excuse him; and that he would be extremely grateful if he would take the trouble to call upon him. Shortly after this message had been dispatched, Orso came downstairs and asked his sister whether the prefect had not sent for him.

'He asks you to wait for him here,' she said with complete assurance.

Half an hour went by without any sign of movement in the Barricinis' house. Meanwhile Orso asked Colomba if she had discovered anything of interest; she replied that she would make a statement in the presence of the prefect. She pretended to be completely calm, but her complexion and her eyes revealed a state of feverish excitement.

At last the door of the Barricini house opened. The prefect, dressed in travelling clothes, came out first, followed by the mayor and his two sons. Imagine the astonishment of the inhabitants of Pietranera, who had been on the look-out since sunrise for the departure of the chief magistrate of the department, when they saw him, accompanied by the three Barricinis, walk straight across the square and go into the Della Rebbias' house.

'They are going to make peace!' exclaimed the village politicians.

'I told you so,' added one old man. 'Orso Antonio has

lived too long on the Continent to settle things like a man of honour.'

'All the same,' said a Rebbianist, 'you'll notice that it is the Barricinis who have called on him. They are asking for mercy.'

'It's the prefect who has got round them all,' retorted the old man. 'There's no courage left these days, and young men think no more of their fathers' blood than if they were all bastards.'

The prefect was not a little surprised to find Orso on his feet and walking about without any trouble. Colomba briefly owned up to her lie and asked him to forgive her.

'If you had been staying anywhere else, Monsieur,' she said, 'my brother would have called on you yesterday to pay his respects.'

Orso made fulsome apologies, insisting that he had no part in this ridiculous ruse, about which he was deeply mortified. The prefect and old Barricini appeared to believe in the sincerity of his regret, which indeed was confirmed by his embarrassment and the reproaches he addressed to his sister; but the mayor's sons did not seem to be satisfied.

'They are making fun of us,' said Orlanduccio, loud enough to be heard.

'If my sister played a trick like that on me,' said Vincentello, 'I'd soon cure her of any desire to do it again.'

These words, and the tone in which they were uttered, offended Orso and caused him to lose some of his good will. He and the young Barricinis exchanged glances which were devoid of any hint of benevolence.

Meanwhile, as everybody had sat down except Colomba, who remained standing near the kitchen door, the prefect began to speak. After a few commonplaces about the antiquated ideas of the country, he reminded his listeners that most of the fiercest hatreds were based on nothing but misunderstandings. Then, addressing the mayor, he told him that Monsieur della Rebbia had never believed that the Barricini family had played any part, direct or indirect, in the deplorable event which had deprived him of his father; that he had admittedly entertained a few doubts concerning one feature of the lawsuit between the two families; that these doubts could be explained by Monsieur Orso's long absence and the nature of the information he had received; and that now, enlightened by recent revelations, he felt completely satisfied and wished to establish friendly and neighbourly relations with Monsieur Barricini and his sons.

Orso bowed stiffly; Monsieur Barricini stammered out a few words which nobody could hear; and his two sons stared at the rafters. The prefect was about to go on with his harangue and address to Orso the counterpart of the speech he had just made to Monsieur Barricini when Colomba, taking some papers from underneath her neckerchief, solemnly stepped forward between the two parties.

'It would be a great joy to me,' she said, 'to see an end to the war between our two families, but if the reconciliation is to be sincere, everything must be explained and nothing must be left in doubt. Prefect, I was rightly suspicious of Tomaso Bianchi's declaration, coming as it did from a man with such an evil reputation.... I said that your sons might have seen that man in the prison at Bastia.'

'That's a lie!' interrupted Orlanduccio. 'I didn't see him.'

Colomba threw him a contemptuous glance, and went on with apparent composure:

'If I understood you correctly, you explained the interest Tomaso could have had in threatening Monsieur Barricini in the name of a dangerous bandit by his desire to keep his brother Teodoro in occupation of the mill which my father leased to him at a very low rent?'

'That is correct,' said the prefect.

'With a scoundrel such as Bianchi seems to be, everything becomes quite clear,' said Orso, deceived by his sister's calm appearance.

'The forged letter,' continued Colomba, whose eyes were beginning to shine more brightly, 'is dated the eleventh of July. Tomaso was then staying with his brother at the mill.'

'Yes,' said the mayor, a little uneasily.

'Then what was Tomaso Bianchi's interest?' cried Colomba triumphantly. 'His brother's lease had expired; my father had given him notice to quit on the first of July. Here is my father's ledger, the record of the notice, and the letter from a lawyer in Ajaccio proposing a new miller to us.'

As she spoke she handed the prefect the papers she had been holding in her hand.

There was a moment of general astonishment. The mayor turned visibly pale; Orso, knitting his brows, stepped forward to look at the papers, which the prefect was studying attentively.

'They are making fun of us!' Orlanduccio cried again, standing up angrily. 'Let's go, Father. We ought never to have come here!'

It took Monsieur Barricini only a moment to regain his composure. He asked if he might look at the papers; the prefect handed them to him without a word. Then, pushing his green spectacles up on his forehead, he glanced through them with a fairly casual air, while Colomba watched him with the eyes of a tigress which sees a buck approaching the lair of her cubs.

'But,' said Monsieur Barricini, pulling his spectacles down again and giving the papers back to the prefect, 'knowing the kindness of the late colonel ... Tomaso thought ... he must have thought ... that the colonel would reconsider his decision to give him notice to quit.... And as a matter of fact, he has remained in occupation of the mill, so....'

'It was I,' said Colomba in a disdainful voice, 'who let him stay on. My father was dead, and in my position I had to deal gently with my family's dependents.'

'All the same,' said the prefect, 'this Tomaso admits that he wrote the letter. That much is clear.'

'What is clear to me,' said Orso, interrupting him, 'is that there is something very shady hidden behind this whole affair.'

'I have to contradict another statement made by these gentlemen,' said Colomba.

She opened the kitchen door, and immediately Brandolaccio, the theology student, and the dog Brusco came into the room. The two bandits were unarmed, at least as far as could be seen; each wore a cartridge-pouch at his belt, but not the pistol which is its inevitable complement. As they entered the room they doffed their caps respectfully.

The effect produced by their sudden appearance is easy to imagine. The mayor nearly collapsed; his sons threw themselves bravely in front of him, each reaching for the stiletto in his pocket. The prefect started towards the door, while Orso, seizing Brandolaccio by the collar, shouted at him:

'What are you doing here, you scoundrel?'

'This is a trap!' cried the mayor, trying to open the door; but, as was later discovered, Saveria had double-locked it from outside on the bandits' orders.

'Good people,' said Brandolaccio, 'don't be afraid of me; I'm not as black as I am painted. We mean no harm. Prefect, I am your humble servant.... Gently does it, Lieutenant, you're strangling me.... We have come here as witnesses. Come on, Curé, speak up: you have the gift of the gab.'

'Prefect,' said the theology student, 'I have not the honour of being known to you. My name is Giocanto

Castricóni, but I am better known as the Curé. . . . Ah, I see that you remember me! Mademoiselle, whom I had not the pleasure of knowing either, sent for me to give her some information about a certain Tomaso Bianchi, with whom I was incarcerated three weeks ago in the prison at Bastia. This is what I have to say to you all. . . .'

'Don't bother,' said the prefect; 'I want no information from a man like you. . . . Monsieur della Rebbia, I hope and trust that you had no hand in this odious plot. But are you the master in your own house? Have that door opened. Your sister may have to answer for her strange relations with men who are outside the law.'

'Prefect,' cried Colomba, 'please listen to what this man is going to say. You are here to do justice to everybody, and it is your duty to ascertain the truth. Speak out, Giocanto Castriconi.'

'Don't listen to him!' cried all three Barricinis together.

'If everybody speaks at once,' said the bandit with a smile, 'nobody will hear a word. As I was saying, in prison I had as my companion, though not as my friend, this fellow Tomaso. He had frequent visits from Monsieur Orlanduccio. . . .'

'That's a lie!' the two brothers cried at the same time.

'Two negatives make an affirmative,' said Castriconi coldly. 'Tomaso had money; he ate and drank nothing but the best. I have always liked good fare (that's the least of my failings), and, in spite of my reluctance to rub shoulders with that individual, I went so far as to dine with him on several occasions. Out of gratitude I suggested that he should break out of prison with me. . . . A young girl . . . for whom I had done certain favours . . . had provided me with the means of escaping. . . . I don't want to compromise anybody. Tomaso refused, telling me that he was sure he would be all right, that the lawyer Barricini had interceded for him with all the judges, and that he would leave prison with a character as white as snow and money in his pocket to boot. As for me, I decided that it was time I came out for a breather. *Dixi*.'

'Everything that man has said is a pack of lies,' repeated Orlanduccio resolutely. 'If we were in the open country, and each of us had his gun with him, he wouldn't talk that way.'

'Well, that's a stupid thing to say!' exclaimed Brandolaccio. 'Don't get on the wrong side of the Curé, Orlanduccio.'

'Are you finally going to let me leave, Monsieur della Rebbia?' said the prefect, stamping his foot with impatience.

'Saveria! Saveria!' shouted Orso. 'Open the door, confound you!'

'Just a moment,' said Brandolaccio. 'We have to get away first. Prefect, when people meet at the house of mutual friends, it's customary for them to give each other half-an-hour's truce after separating.'

The prefect threw him a disdainful look.

'Good-bye all,' said Brandolaccio. Then, stretching his arm out horizontally, he said to his dog:

'Come on, Brusco, jump for the prefect!'

The dog jumped, the bandits hurriedly collected their weapons in the kitchen and made off across the garden, and at a shrill whistle the door of the room opened as if by magic.

'Monsieur Barricini,' said Orso, with concentrated fury, 'I regard you as a forger. This very day I intend to bring an action against you for forgery and complicity with Bianchi. I may have another, more serious charge to lay against you.'

'And I, Monsieur della Rebbia,' said the mayor, 'shall bring an action against you for ambush and complicity with bandits. In the meantime, the prefect will order the gendarmes to watch you.'

'The prefect will do his duty,' said the latter sternly. 'He will see to it that the peace is not disturbed at Pietranera, and he will make sure that justice is done. I am speaking to all of you, gentlemen!'

The mayor and Vincentello had already left the room, and Orlanduccio was following them, walking backwards, when Orso said to him in an undertone:

'Your father is an old man whom I could fell with a single blow. It is you and your brother that I intend to deal with.'

In reply, Orlanduccio drew his stiletto and rushed at Orso like a madman; but before he could use his weapon, Colomba seized his arm and twisted it hard while Orso struck him in the face with his fist, causing him to stagger back a few paces and fall heavily against the door-jamb. Orlanduccio's dagger dropped from his hand, but Vincentello had his and was coming back into the room when Colomba, snatching up a gun, convinced him that the odds were against him. At the same time the prefect threw himself between the combatants.

'I'll see you again soon, Ors' Anton',' shouted Orlanduccio; and, slamming the door behind him, he locked it to give himself time to get away.

Orso and the prefect remained for a quarter of an hour at opposite ends of the room without saying a word. Colomba, the pride of victory shining in her eyes, gazed first at one and then at the other, leaning on the gun which had tipped the scales in her favour.

'What a country! What a country!' the prefect finally exclaimed, springing to his feet. 'Monsieur della Rebbia, you have behaved wrongly. I must ask you to give me your word of honour to refrain from all violence and to wait for the law to settle this confounded affair.'

'Yes, Prefect, I did wrong to strike that wretch. But I did strike him, and I can't refuse him the satisfaction he has demanded from me.'

'Oh, no, he doesn't want to fight you!... But if he murders you.... After all, you've done everything you could to bring that upon yourself.'

'We shall be on our guard,' said Colomba.

'Orlanduccio,' said Orso, 'strikes me as a brave fellow, and I have a better opinion of him than you have, Prefect. He was quick to draw his stiletto, but if I had been in his place I might have acted in the same way; and I'm glad that my sister hasn't a delicate lady's wrist.'

'You shall not fight!' cried the prefect. 'I forbid you!'

'Allow me to tell you, Monsieur, that in matters of honour I acknowledge no authority but that of my conscience.'

'I tell you that you shall not fight!'

'You can have me arrested, Monsieur ... that is, if I allow myself to be caught. But if you did that, you would only be postponing an encounter which has now become inevitable. You are a man of honour yourself, Prefect, and you know perfectly well that it cannot be otherwise.'

'If you had my brother arrested,' added Colomba, 'half the village would side with him, and we should see a splendid battle.'

'I warn you, Monsieur,' said Orso, 'and I beg you not to think that this is an idle boast, I warn you that if Monsieur Barricini abuses his authority as mayor to have me arrested, I shall defend myself.'

'From this day forward,' said the prefect, 'Monsieur Barricini is relieved of his duties.... He will vindicate himself, I hope.... Listen, Monsieur, I am concerned about you. What I am asking of you is really very little: just stay quietly at home until I get back from Corte. I shall only be away for three days. I shall come back with the public prosecutor, and then we shall sort out the whole of this wretched affair. Will you promise me to abstain from all violence until then?'

'I cannot promise that, Monsieur, if, as I expect, Orlanduccio challenges me to a duel.'

'What! You, Monsieur della Rebbia, a French officer, you want to fight a man you suspect of forgery!'

'I struck him, Monsieur.'

'But if you struck a convict and he demanded satisfaction from you, would you fight him? Come now, Monsieur Orso! Well, I'll ask even less of you: don't go looking for Orlanduccio.... You have my permission to fight only if he challenges you to a duel.'

'He will: I'm sure of that. But I promise that I won't give him any more slaps to provoke him.'

'What a country!' the prefect said again, striding up and down. 'When shall I get back to France?'

'Prefect,' said Colomba in her sweetest voice, 'it is getting late. Would you do us the honour of breakfasting here?'

The prefect could not help laughing.

'I have stayed here too long already ... it looks like partiality.... And then there's that damned foundation-stone! ... I really must go.... Mademoiselle della Rebbia, how many calamities you may have set in train today!'

'At least, Prefect, you must do my sister the justice of believing her convictions to be sincere, and I feel sure that you yourself now believe them to be well founded.'

'Good-bye, Monsieur,' said the prefect, with a wave of his hand. 'I warn you that I shall give the sergeant of the gendarmes orders to watch your every movement.'

When the prefect had gone, Colomba said:

'Orso, you aren't on the Continent now. Orlanduccio understands nothing about your duels, and besides, that scoundrel mustn't die the death of a brave man.'

'Colomba, my dear, you are a formidable woman. I am greatly indebted to you for having saved me from a good stiletto-thrust. Give me your little hand so that I may kiss it.

But you must let me do as I think fit. There are certain things you don't understand. Give me my breakfast, and, as soon as the prefect has set off, send for little Chilina, who seems to carry out to perfection all the commissions she is given. I shall need her to deliver a letter.'

While Colomba was supervising the preparation of breakfast, Orso went up to his room and wrote the following note:

You must be impatient to meet me; I am no less impatient. Tomorrow morning we can meet at six o'clock in Acquaviva Valley. I am very good with the pistol, and I shall not suggest that weapon to you. I understand that you are a good shot with a gun, so let us each take a double-barrelled gun. I shall come accompanied by a man from this village. If your brother wishes to accompany you, take along another second and let me know beforehand. In that case, but only in that case, I shall bring two seconds.

Orso Antonio della Rebbia.

After spending an hour with the deputy mayor, and then going into the Barricinis' house for a few minutes, the prefect set off for Corte, escorted by a single gendarme. A quarter of an hour later, Chilina delivered the letter you have just read to Orlanduccio in person.

The reply was a long time coming and did not arrive until the evening. It was signed by the elder Barricini and informed Orso that he was passing on to the public prosecutor the threatening letter addressed to his son. 'Strong in my innocence,' he concluded, 'I shall wait for the law to pronounce judgment upon your calumny.'

In the meantime, five or six herdsmen summoned by Colomba arrived to guard the Della Rebbia tower. In spite of Orso's protests, the windows overlooking the square were provided with *archere*, and throughout the evening he received offers of service from different people in the village. A letter even arrived from the bandit-theologian, who promised in his name and Brandolaccio's to intervene if the mayor called in the gendarmes to help him. He concluded with this postscript:

'Dare I ask you what the prefect thinks of the excellent education my friend is giving the dog Brusco? Apart from Chilina, I have never known a more docile or promising pupil.'

CHAPTER SIXTEEN

THE next day went by without any hostilities. Both sides remained on the defensive. Orso did not leave his house, and the Barricinis' door stayed firmly closed. The five gendarmes who had been left to patrol Pietranera could be seen walking around the square or on the outskirts of the village, accompanied by the village constable, the sole representative of the urban militia. The deputy mayor kept his sash on all the time, but, apart from the *archere* in the windows of the two enemy houses, there was nothing to indicate a state of war. Only a Corsican would have noticed that there were only women to be seen around the green oak in the square.

At supper-time, Colomba delightedly showed her brother the following letter she had just received from Miss Nevil:

> My dear Mademoiselle Colomba,
>
> I learn with great pleasure, from a letter from your brother, that your feuding has ended. All my congratulations. My father can no longer stand Ajaccio now that your brother is not here to talk about war and go hunting with him. We are leaving today and we shall sleep at the house of that relative of yours, for whom we have a letter of introduction. The day after tomorrow, about eleven o'clock, I shall come and ask you for some of that mountain *bruccio* which you say is so superior to the town variety.
>
> Farewell, dear Mademoiselle Colomba. Your friend,
>
> *Lydia Nevil.*

'So she hasn't received my second letter?' exclaimed Orso.

'You can see from the date of hers that Mademoiselle Lydia must have been on her way when your letter reached Ajaccio. Why, did you tell her not to come?'

'I told her that we were in a state of siege. It doesn't seem to me that this is a suitable time to receive guests.'

COLOMBA

'Nonsense! These English people are peculiar folk. The last night I spent in her room, she told me that she would be sorry to leave Corsica without having seen a good *vendetta*. If you like, Orso, we could treat her to the sight of an attack on our enemies' house.'

'You know, Colomba,' said Orso, 'Nature was wrong to make you a woman. You would have made an excellent soldier.'

'Possibly. In any case, I'm going to make my *bruccio*.'

'Don't bother. We must send somebody to warn them and stop them before they set off.'

'Really? You want to send a messenger in this weather, to be swept away by a torrent together with your letter? . . . How sorry I feel for the poor bandits in a storm like this! Luckily they have good *piloni** to wear. Do you know what you ought to do, Orso? If the storm passes over, set off very early tomorrow morning, so that you reach our relative's house before your friends have left. That will be easy, as Miss Lydia always gets up late. You will tell them what has happened here; and if they still want to come, we shall be delighted to receive them.'

Orso immediately agreed to this plan, and Colomba, after a few moments' silence, went on:

'Perhaps, Orso, you think that I was joking when I spoke of an attack on the Barricinis' house. Do you realize that we outnumber them, two to one? Now that the prefect has suspended the mayor, all the men here are on our side. We could cut them to pieces. It would be a simple matter to start a fight. If you like, I could go to the fountain and make fun of their women: they would come out. . . . Or perhaps – they are such cowards – they would fire at me through their *archere*; they would miss. Then everything would be settled: they would be the aggressors. So much the worse for the losing side: after a scrap who can tell who killed whom?

* A thick cloth coat with a hood. (P.M.)

You take your sister's word for it, Orso – the lawyers who are going to come here will only dirty a lot of paper and say a lot of useless words. Nothing will come of it. The old fox will find a way of convincing them that black is white. Oh, if the prefect hadn't put himself in front of Vincentello, there'd be one less of them now.'

All this was said as calmly as she had spoken a moment before about her preparations for making the *bruccio*.

An astounded Orso looked at his sister with an admiration mingled with fear.

'My dear Colomba,' he said, getting up from the table, 'you are, I do believe, the Devil incarnate. But don't worry. If I don't manage to have them hanged, I'll find a way to get the better of them in some other fashion. "A hot bullet or cold steel!"* You see, I haven't forgotten my Corsican dialect.'

'The sooner the better,' said Colomba with a sigh. 'What horse will you be riding tomorrow, Ors' Anton'?'

'The black one. Why do you ask?'

'So that he can be given some barley.'

When Orso had gone up to his room, Colomba sent Saveria and the herdsmen off to bed, and remained alone in the kitchen where the *bruccio* was cooking. Now and then she listened intently and seemed to be waiting impatiently for her brother to go to bed. When at last she thought that he had fallen asleep, she took a knife, made sure that it was sharp, slipped her little feet into a pair of heavy shoes, and, without making the slightest noise, stole out into the garden.

The garden, which was walled in, adjoined a fairly large piece of ground, enclosed by hedges, where the horses were kept, for Corsican horses scarcely know what a stable is. They are usually turned loose in a field, and it is left to them to find pasture and shelter from the cold and rain.

* *Palla ealda u farru freddu.* A common Corsican saying. (P.M.)

Colomba opened the garden gate as quietly as she had left the house, went into the paddock, and gave a soft whistle to call the horses, to whom she often gave bread and salt. As soon as the black horse came within reach, she seized him tightly by the mane and slit his ear with her knife. The horse gave a violent start and galloped away, uttering that shrill cry which severe pain sometimes occasions in animals of that kind. Satisfied, Colomba was coming back into the garden when Orso opened his window and called out: 'Who goes there?' At the same time she heard him cock his gun. Fortunately for her, the garden gate was in total darkness, and she was partly hidden by a tall fig tree. Soon, from the intermittent gleams which she saw in her brother's room, she gathered that he was trying to light his lamp. She then hurriedly closed the garden gate, and, stealing along the walls so that her black clothes merged into the dark foliage of the fruit trees, she managed to get back into the kitchen a few moments before Orso appeared.

'What's the matter?' she asked.

'I thought,' said Orso, 'that I heard somebody opening the garden gate.'

'Impossible. The dog would have barked. Anyway, let's go and see.'

Orso walked round the garden, and after making sure that the outside door was locked, he made for the stairs to go back to his room, somewhat ashamed of this false alarm.

'I'm pleased to see, brother,' said Colomba, 'that you are becoming prudent, as you ought to be in your position.'

'You are training me,' replied Orso. 'Good night.'

In the morning Orso was up at the crack of dawn, ready to go. His garb revealed both the pretensions to elegance of a man going to see a woman on whom he wishes to make a favourable impression, and the prudence of a Corsican engaged in a *vendetta*. Over a tight-fitting blue frock-coat he wore a small tin box containing cartridges, slung from a green silk cord; his stiletto was in one of his side-pockets, and he was carrying in his hand the handsome Manton gun, loaded. While he was hastily drinking a cup of coffee Colomba had poured out for him, one of the herdsmen had gone out to saddle and bridle the horse. Orso and his sister followed hard on his heels and went into the paddock. The herdsman had caught the horse, but he had dropped both saddle and bridle, and looked horror-stricken, while the horse, remembering the wound he had received the night before, was rearing, lashing out, neighing, and generally kicking up a tremendous shindy.

'Come on, hurry up!' Orso shouted at him.

'Ha! Ors' Anton'! Ha! Ors' Anton'!' cried the herdsman. 'By the Madonna's blood!'

There followed an endless string of curses, most of which it would be impossible to translate.

'Why, what's happened?' asked Colomba.

Everybody went over to the horse, and when it was seen that he was bleeding and that his ear had been slit, there was a general outburst of surprise and indignation. It should be pointed out that to a Corsican, mutilating an enemy's horse is at once an act of vengeance, a challenge, and a threat of murder. Nothing but a bullet, the Corsicans maintain, can expiate an outrage of this sort. Although Orso, who had lived for so many years on the Continent, was not as sensitive as other Corsicans to the gravity of the insult, none the less, if any Barricinist had appeared before him at that moment, he would probably have made him pay straight away for an outrage which he ascribed to his enemies.

'The cowardly scoundrels!' he cried. 'Avenging themselves on a poor animal, when they daren't meet me face to face!'

'What are we waiting for?' cried Colomba impetuously. 'Are we to stand by and do nothing, when they come and provoke us, and mutilate our horses? Are you men?'

'Vengeance!' replied the herdsmen. 'Let's walk the horse through the village and attack their house.'

'There's a thatched barn adjoining their tower,' said old Polo Griffo. 'I could set that on fire in no time.'

Another man suggested fetching the ladders from the church tower; and a third proposed breaking down the door of the Barricini house with a beam which had been left in the square and which was intended for some building under construction. In the midst of all these angry voices, Colomba could be heard telling her henchmen that before they set to work she was going to give each of them a large glass of anisette.

Unfortunately, or, rather, fortunately, the effect which she had expected to produce by her cruelty to the poor horse was largely lost on Orso. He did not doubt for a moment that this savage mutilation was the work of one of his enemies, and he particularly suspected Orlanduccio; but he did not consider that that young man, whom he had provoked and struck, had wiped out his shame by slitting a horse's ear. On the contrary, this mean and ridiculous act of vengeance had increased Orso's contempt for his adversaries, and he now thought, like the prefect, that such people were unworthy of crossing swords with him. As soon as he could make himself heard, he informed his astonished supporters that they would have to abandon their bellicose plans, and that the law, which was on its way, would amply avenge the injury to his horse's ear.

'I am the master here,' he added sternly, 'and I mean to be obeyed. The first man who takes it into his head to say anything more about killing or burning may find himself burned by me. Come on, saddle my grey horse for me.'

'What, Orso,' said Colomba, taking him aside, 'are you going to allow those people to insult us? When our father was alive, the Barricinis would never have dared to mutilate an animal of ours.'

'I promise you they shall have good reason to regret it; but it is for the gendarmes and the jailers to punish scoundrels who show no courage except against animals. As I've already told you, the law will take vengeance on them for me, and, if not, you will not need to remind me whose son I am....'

'Patience!' said Colomba with a sigh.

'Remember, sister,' Orso went on, 'that if I find on my return that any action has been taken against the Barricinis, I shall never forgive you.' Then, in a gentler voice, he added: 'It is quite possible, indeed extremely probable, that I shall come back here with the colonel and his daughter; see to it that their rooms are ready, that the breakfast is good, and altogether that our guests are as comfortable as possible. It's a very good thing, Colomba, to be brave, but a woman must also know how to manage a house. Come now, kiss me, and be good; here's the grey horse, saddled already.'

'Orso,' said Colomba, 'you must not go alone.'

'I don't need anybody,' said Orso, 'and I promise you I won't let anybody slit my ear.'

'Oh, no, I'll never let you go off alone when there's a feud on. Hey! Polo Griffo! Gian' Francè! Memmo! Get your guns; you are going to accompany my brother.'

After a rather heated discussion, Orso had to resign himself to accepting an escort. From among his most excited herdsmen he chose those who had been loudest in calling for an opening of hostilities; then, after repeating his injunctions to his sister and the herdsmen who were staying behind, he set off, this time making a detour to avoid the Barricini house.

They were already a good way from Pietranera and riding fast when, as they were crossing a little stream which flowed into a marsh, old Polo Griffo noticed several pigs comfortably installed in the mud, enjoying at one and the same time the sunshine and the coolness of the water. Straight away, taking aim at the fattest of them, he fired at its head and killed it on the spot. The dead pig's comrades rose and fled with surprising swiftness; and although the other herdsman fired in his turn, they reached a thicket safe and sound, and vanished.

'Idiots!' cried Orso. 'You've taken pigs for wild boars!'

'No, we haven't, Ors' Anton',' replied Polo Griffo; 'that herd belongs to the lawyer, and that'll teach him to mutilate our horses.'

'What, you blackguards,' cried Orso, beside himself with rage, 'you dare to copy the villainies of our enemies? Leave me, you scoundrels! I don't need you. You're good for nothing but fighting pigs. I swear to God that if you dare to follow me, I'll smash your heads in!'

The two herdsmen looked at each other in bewilderment. Orso spurred his horse and disappeared at a gallop.

'Well!' said Polo Griffo. 'Did you hear that? You like people, and they treat you like that! His father, the colonel, was angry with you because you aimed your gun once at the lawyer.... You were a fool not to have fired.... And now the son.... You saw what I did for him.... And he talks about smashing my head in, like you'd smash a flask that didn't hold the wine any more. That's what you learn on the Continent, Memmo!'

'Yes, and if they find out it was you who killed this pig, they'll sue you, and Ors' Anton' won't speak to the judges for you or pay the lawyer. Luckily nobody saw you, and St Nega's always there to help you out.'

After a short deliberation the two herdsmen decided that the wisest course was to throw the pig into a bog, a plan which they duly carried out, though not of course until each had carved himself a few slices from the innocent victim of the feud between the Della Rebbias and the Barricinis.

CHAPTER SEVENTEEN

Rid of his unruly escort, Orso continued on his way, more preoccupied with the pleasurable thought of seeing Miss Nevil again than with the fear of coming across his enemies.

'The lawsuit which I am going to have with those wretched Barricinis,' he said to himself, 'will oblige me to go to Bastia. Why shouldn't I go there with Miss Nevil? And why shouldn't we travel together from Bastia to the springs at Orezza?'

All of a sudden childhood memories recalled that picturesque spot to his mind. He imagined himself on a green lawn beneath some ancient chestnut trees. On the shining grass, strewn with blue flowers like eyes smiling at him, he saw Miss Lydia sitting beside him. She had taken off her hat, and her fair hair, finer and softer than silk, shone like gold in the sunlight filtering through the foliage. Her eyes, which were of the purest blue, seemed to him to be bluer than the sky. With her cheek resting on one hand, she was listening thoughtfully to the faltering words of love he was addressing to her. She was wearing the muslin dress she had worn on the last day he had seen her in Ajaccio. From under the folds of this dress a tiny foot in a black satin slipper peeped out. Orso told himself that he would be happy to kiss this foot; but one of Miss Lydia's hands was bare and it was holding a daisy. Orso took this daisy, and Lydia's hand pressed his; and he kissed the daisy, and then the hand, and she was not angry with him. . . . And all these thoughts prevented him from watching the road as he rode along at a trot. In his imagination he was about to kiss Miss Nevil's white hand for the second time when in actual fact he very nearly kissed the head of his horse, which halted in its tracks. Little Chilina was barring his way and had seized his bridle.

'Where are you going, Ors' Anton'?' she asked. 'Don't you know that your enemy is somewhere in these parts?'

'My enemy?' cried Orso, furious at being interrupted at such an interesting moment. 'Where is he?'

'Orlanduccio is near here. He's waiting for you. Go back! Go back!'

'Oh, he's waiting for me, is he? Have you seen him?'

'Yes, Ors' Anton'. I was lying in the bracken when he went by. He was looking all around with his field glass.'

'Which way was he going?'

'He went down there, the same way that you are going.'

'Thank you.'

'Ors' Anton', wouldn't you do better to wait for my uncle? He won't be long, and you'd be safe with him.'

'Have no fear, Chili, I don't need your uncle.'

'If you like, I could go ahead of you.'

'No, thank you.'

And, spurring his horse, Orso rode swiftly away in the direction the little girl had indicated.

His first reaction had been a feeling of blind fury, and he had told himself that fate was offering him a splendid opportunity to punish the coward who had mutilated a horse to avenge a blow. But then, as he galloped along, the half-promise he had made to the prefect, and above all the fear of missing Miss Nevil's visit altered his feelings and made him almost hope that he might not come across Orlanduccio. Before long, however, the memory of his father, the outrage inflicted on his horse, and the threats of the Barricinis rekindled his anger and incited him to look for his enemy in order to provoke him and force him to fight. Thus stirred by contrary resolutions, he continued on his way, but cautiously now, examining the bushes and hedges, and sometimes even stopping to listen to the vague sounds one hears in the countryside. Ten minutes after leaving little Chilina (it was then about nine o'clock in the morning), he found himself at the top of an extremely steep slope. The road, or rather the ill-defined path which he was following crossed a heath which had recently been burnt. The ground was covered with whitish ashes, and here and there some shrubs and a few big trees, blackened by fire and completely stripped of their leaves, still stood erect, although they were dead. Anybody seeing a burnt heath is likely to fancy that he has been transported to some northern clime in midwinter, and the contrast between the barrenness of the ground over which the flames have passed and the luxuriant vegetation all around makes the scene appear even more sad and desolate. But at this particular moment, Orso noticed only one thing about this landscape, though an important thing in his position: the bare ground could offer no concealment to an ambush – and a man who has reason to be afraid that at any moment he may see a gun-barrel aimed at his chest poke out of a thicket regards a stretch of bare ground, with nothing on it to interrupt the view, as a sort of oasis. The burnt heath was followed by several cultivated fields, enclosed, according to the local practice, by breast-high dry-stone walls. The path ran between these fields, where huge chestnut trees, growing here and there, produced from a distance the impression of a thick wood.

Forced by the steepness of the slope to dismount, Orso, leaving the bridle reins on the horse's neck, slid and scrambled down the ash-covered hill. He was barely twenty-five paces from one of these stone walls to the right of the path when he noticed, straight in front of him, first a gun-barrel, and then a head poking over the top of the wall. The gun was lowered, and he recognized Orlanduccio, ready to fire. Orso quickly took up a defensive position, and the two men, taking aim, gazed at each other for a few seconds with that poignant emotion which the bravest man feels when the time comes to kill or be killed.

'You wretched coward!' cried Orso.

While he was still speaking, he saw the flash from Orlanduccio's gun, and almost at the same time a second shot came from the left, from the other side of the path, fired by a man whom he had not noticed, and who had aimed at him from the cover of another wall. Both bullets hit him: one, Orlanduccio's, went through his left arm, which Orso had exposed to him while taking aim; the other struck him in the chest, ripping his coat, but fortunately met the blade of his stiletto, flattened itself against it, and made only a slight bruise. Orso's left arm fell limply to his thigh, and the barrel of his gun dropped for a moment; but he raised it again straight away, and, aiming his weapon with his right hand only, he fired at Orlanduccio. His enemy's head, which he could see only down to the eyes, disappeared behind the wall. Turning to his left, Orso fired his second barrel at a man whom he could barely make out in a cloud of smoke. This man likewise disappeared. The four shots had followed one another at incredible speed; no trained soldiers ever fired in quicker succession. After Orso's last shot silence descended once more. The smoke from his gun rose slowly into the air; there was no movement behind the wall, or even the slightest sound. If it had not been for the pain he could feel in his arm, he might have thought that the men he had just fired at were figments of his imagination.

Expecting a second volley, Orso took a few steps to place himself behind one of the burnt trees which had remained standing on the heath. Behind this cover, he put his gun between his knees and hurriedly reloaded. Meanwhile his left arm was causing him excruciating pain, and he felt as if he were carrying a tremendous weight. What had become of his enemies? He could not understand what had happened. If they had fled, if they had been wounded, he would certainly have heard some noise, some movement in the foliage. Were they dead then, or were they – as seemed more likely – just waiting behind the cover of their walls for another chance to fire at him? In this uncertainty, and feeling his strength ebbing, he put his right knee on the ground, rested his wounded arm on the other, and used a branch which protruded from the trunk of the burnt tree to support his gun. With his finger on the trigger, his gaze fixed on the walls, and his ears straining to catch the slightest sound, he remained motionless for several minutes, which seemed to him an eternity. At last, a long way behind him, he heard a shout, and soon a dog sped like an arrow down the hillside and came to a stop beside him, wagging his tail. It was Brusco, the bandits' disciple and companion, doubtless heralding his master's arrival; and never was a good man more impatiently awaited. With his muzzle in the air, pointing in the direction of the nearest field, the dog sniffed uneasily. All of a sudden, he gave a low growl and cleared the wall with a single bound, reappearing almost immediately on the top of it, from which vantage point he gazed fixedly at Orso, expressing surprise with his eyes as clearly as a dog can. Then he sniffed the air again, this time in the direction of the other field, before jumping over that wall like the first. A second later he reappeared on the top, revealing the same expression of astonishment and uneasiness. Then he jumped down on to the heath, his tail between his legs, and moved slowly away from Orso, walking sideways and watching him all the time, until he was some way off. Then, starting off again at a run, he rushed up the hill as fast as he had come down, to meet a man who was moving quickly in spite of the steepness of the slope.

'Help, Brando!' cried Orso as soon as he thought that the other was within earshot.

'Ho! Ors' Anton'! Are you wounded?' asked Brandolaccio, running up, all out of breath. 'In the body or in the limbs?'

'In the arm.'

'The arm? That's nothing. And the other man?'

'I think I hit him.'

Brandolaccio ran after his dog to the nearest wall and leaned over to look on the other side. Then, taking off his cap, he said:

'God speed, Orlanduccio,' he said. Then, turning to Orso, he bowed gravely to him too and said:

'That's what I call settling a man's hash.'

'Is he still alive?' asked Orso, who was breathing with difficulty.

'Oh, he wouldn't want to go on living; he's too upset about the bullet you've put through his eye. By the Madonna's Blood, what a hole! Upon my word, that's a fine gun. What a calibre! Blows a man's brains out very neatly! You know, Ors' Anton', when I first heard piff, piff, I said to myself: "Dammit all, they're killing my lieutenant." Then I heard bang, bang. "Ah," I said, "that's the English gun answering back...." Hey, Brusco, what do you want?'

The dog led him to the other field.

'Well, I'm blessed!' exclaimed Brandolaccio in amazement. 'A double hit! That's all! Dammit, you can see that powder's dear, because you don't use much of it!'

'What is it, for God's sake?' asked Orso.

'Come now, don't try pulling my leg, Lieutenant. You bring down the game, and you want somebody else to pick it up for you.... Well, there's one man who's not going to enjoy his supper tonight, and that's the lawyer Barricini. There's plenty of butcher's meat here, and no mistake. But now who the devil is the old man's heir?'

'What! Vincentello dead too?'

COLOMBA

'Dead as a doornail. Good health to the rest of us!*
What I like about you is that you don't let them suffer.
Just come and look at Vincentello: he's still on his knees,
with his head against the wall. He looks as if he's asleep.
That's what I call sleeping soundly, poor devil!'

Orso turned his head away in horror.

'Are you sure he's dead?'

'You're like Sampiero Corso, who never fired more than
one shot. There, you see... in the chest, on the left – where
Vincileone was hit at Waterloo. I'm willing to bet the
bullet isn't far from the heart. A double hit! Oh, I'll never
talk about shooting again. Two hits with two shots!...
And with ball cartridges!... Both brothers!... If he'd had
a third shot, he'd have killed their papa too.... Better luck
next time.... What a morning's shooting, Ors' Anton'!...
And to think that a good fellow like me will never have the
chance to score a double hit against the gendarmes!'

As he spoke, the bandit was examining Orso's arm and
slitting his sleeve with his stiletto.

'It's nothing,' he said. 'But this frock-coat will give
Mademoiselle Colomba something to do.... Ah, what's
this I see? This tear over the chest – did anything go in
there? No, of course not, you wouldn't be so perky. Look,
try to move your fingers.... Can you feel my teeth when I
bite your little finger?... Not much?... Never mind, it
won't come to anything. Let me take your handkerchief and
your cravat.... Well, your frock-coat is ruined.... Why
the devil did you get yourself up so smartly? Were you
going to a wedding?... There, have a drop of wine....
Why don't you carry a flask? Have you ever seen a Corsican
go out without one?'

Then, in the midst of dressing the wound, he broke off to
exclaim:

* *Salute a noi!* This is an exclamation generally made after the word 'death', and which is intended as a safeguard. (P.M.)

'A double hit! Both of them stone dead! . . . This is going to make the Curé laugh. . . . A double hit! Ah, here's that little dawdler Chilina at last.'

Orso made no reply. He was as pale as death and was trembling all over.

'Chili,' shouted Brandolaccio, 'go and have a look behind that wall. What do you think about that?'

Using both hands and feet, the child scrambled up on to the wall, and as soon as she saw Orlanduccio's corpse she made the sign of the Cross.

'That's nothing,' the bandit went on; 'go and look farther on, over there.'

The child made another sign of the Cross.

'Was it you, Uncle?' she asked timidly.

'Me? Don't you know that I've become an old good-for-nothing? No, Chili, this is Monsieur's work. Give him your congratulations.'

'Mademoiselle will be delighted,' said Chilina, 'and she'll be very upset to know that you are wounded, Ors' Anton'.'

'Come now, Ors' Anton',' said the bandit, when he had finished dressing the wound, 'Chilina's caught your horse. Mount and come along with me to the Stazzona *maquis*. It'll be a clever fellow who finds you there. We'll look after you as well as we can. When we come to the Cross of St Christine, you'll have to dismount. You'll give your horse to Chilina, who will go and tell Mademoiselle. On the way, you can give the little girl any messages you want to send. You can tell her anything you like, Ors' Anton': she would let herself be hacked to pieces rather than betray her friends.' And in an affectionate voice he said to the little girl: 'Get along with you, you little hussy, be excommunicated and accursed!'

Brandolaccio, who was superstitious like many bandits, was afraid of casting a spell over children by blessing them or praising them, for it is well known that the mysterious powers which govern the *Annocchiatura** have an unfortunate habit of doing the very opposite of what we wish for.

'Where do you expect me to go, Brando?' Orso asked in a faint voice.

'Dammit, the choice is up to you: either to prison or to the *maquis*. But no Della Rebbia knows the road to prison. To the *maquis*, Ors' Anton'!'

'Good-bye, then, to all my hopes!' the wounded man exclaimed sadly.

'Your hopes? Good God, did you hope to do any better with a double-barrelled gun? . . . But how the devil did they manage to hit you? Those scoundrels must have been as hard to kill as a couple of cats!'

'They fired first,' said Orso.

'That's true. I was forgetting. . . . Piff, piff. Bang, bang. . . . A double hit with one hand!† . . . If anybody ever does better than that, I'll go and hang myself! There, now you're mounted. . . . Before we go, have a look at your handiwork. It isn't polite to leave people like that without saying good-bye.'

Orso put his spurs to his horse; not for anything in the world would he have looked at the wretches he had just killed.

'You know, Ors' Anton',' said the bandit, taking hold of the horse's bridle, 'do you want me to be frank? Well, without meaning any offence, I feel sorry for those two poor fellows. I hope you'll excuse me. . . . So handsome, so strong, so young! . . . Many's the time I've hunted with

* An involuntary spell cast either by the eyes, or by speech. (P.M.)

† If any incredulous sportsman were to cast doubt on the possibility of Monsieur della Rebbia's double hit, I would urge him to go to Sartène and learn how one of the most distinguished and likeable inhabitants of that town extricated himself, alone and with his left arm broken, from a no less dangerous situation. (P.M.)

Orlanduccio. . . . Four days ago he gave me a packet of cigars. . . . And Vincentello was always so cheerful. . . . It's true that you only did what you had to do . . . and besides, the shooting was too good for anybody to regret it. . . . But I hadn't anything to do with your vengeance. . . . I know you were right: when you have an enemy, you have to get rid of him. But the Barricinis were an old family. Now they're finished, like so many others . . . and the curious thing about it is that it's a double hit that has put paid to them.'

As he pronounced this funeral oration on the Barricinis, Brandolaccio was hurriedly leading Orso, Chilina, and the dog Brusco towards the Stazzona *maquis*.

CHAPTER EIGHTEEN

In the meantime, shortly after Orso's departure, Colomba had learnt from her spies that the Barricinis were on the warpath, and since then she had been a prey to the keenest anxiety. She was to be seen wandering all over the house, going from the kitchen to the bedrooms which had been prepared for her guests, doing nothing but perpetually busy, constantly stopping to look out of the window to see whether there was any unusual movement in the village. About eleven o'clock, a fairly large cavalcade rode into Pietranera; it was the colonel, his daughter, their servants, and the guide. Colomba's first words as she welcomed them were: 'Have you seen my brother?' Then she asked the guide by which road they had come and at what time they had set out; and, judging by his replies, she could not understand why they had not met Orso.

'Perhaps your brother took the upper road,' said the guide. 'We came by the lower road.'

But Colomba shook her head and asked more questions. Despite her natural composure, which was reinforced by her proud insistence on concealing any sign of weakness from strangers, it was impossible for her to disguise her anxiety. Soon she had communicated it to the colonel and above all to Miss Nevil, once she had informed them of the ill-fated attempt at reconciliation. Miss Nevil was thoroughly alarmed and wanted messengers to be sent off in all directions, while her father offered to remount and go off with the guide in search of Orso. Her guests' fears reminded Colomba of her duties as mistress of the house. She made an effort to smile, urged the colonel to sit down at table, and found a score of plausible reasons why her brother should have been delayed, which she herself destroyed a moment later. Believing that it was his duty as a man to reassure womenfolk, the colonel produced his own explanation.

'I'm willing to wager,' he said, 'that Della Rebbia came across some game; he couldn't resist the temptation, and we'll see him come home with his game-bag full to overflowing. Why, now I come to think of it,' he added, 'we heard four shots on the way here. Two of them were louder than the others, and I said to my daughter: "I bet that's Della Rebbia hunting. My gun is the only one that would make so much noise".'

Colomba turned pale, and Lydia, who was watching her closely, guessed straight away what suspicions the colonel's conjecture had just suggested to her. After a few minutes' silence, Colomba anxiously asked whether the two loud shots had preceded or followed the others. But neither the colonel nor his daughter nor the guide had paid much attention to this all-important detail.

About one o'clock, since none of the messengers sent out by Colomba had yet returned, she summoned up all her courage and insisted on her guests' sitting down at table; but, apart from the colonel, nobody could manage to eat anything. At the slightest noise in the square, Colomba would run to the window, only to return sadly to her seat and, even more sadly, try to resume an insignificant conversation to which nobody paid the slightest attention and which was broken by long intervals of silence.

All of a sudden, they heard the sound of a galloping horse.

'Ah, this time it's my brother,' said Colomba, getting up from the table.

But when she saw Chilina sitting astride Orso's horse, she cried in a piercing voice:

'My brother is dead!'

The colonel dropped his glass, Miss Nevil uttered a cry, and all three ran to the outside door. Before Chilina had time to jump from her mount, she was lifted off like a feather by Colomba, who squeezed her fit to suffocate her. The child understood the terrible look in her eyes, and her first words were those of the chorus in *Otello*: 'He is alive!' Colomba released her grip, and Chilina dropped to the ground as nimbly as a kitten.

'What about the others?' Colomba asked in a hoarse voice.

Chilina made the sign of the Cross with her index and middle fingers. Colomba's face promptly changed from deathly pale to bright red. She darted a fierce glance at the Barricinis' house, and said with a smile to her guests:

'Let's go in and drink our coffee.'

The Iris of the bandits had a long story to tell. Her tale, translated straight from dialect into Italian by Colomba, and then into English by Miss Nevil, drew more than one oath from the colonel, more than one sigh from Miss Lydia. Colomba listened with apparent impassivity, but she twisted her damask napkin in her hands until it was almost in shreds. She interrupted the child five or six times to make her repeat that Brandolaccio had said that the wound was not dangerous and that he had seen many far more serious injuries. In conclusion, Chilina reported that Orso particularly asked for some writing paper, and that he instructed his sister to beg a lady who might be at his house not to leave before she had received a letter from him.

'That,' added the child, 'was what worried him most. I had already set off when he called me back to remind me not to forget this message. That was the third time he repeated it to me.'

When she heard this request of her brother's, Colomba smiled faintly and squeezed the English girl's hand. Miss Lydia burst into tears, and decided that it would be inappropriate to translate this part of the story for her father.

'Yes, my dear, you shall stay with me,' cried Colomba, embracing Miss Nevil, 'and you shall help us.'

Then, taking a bundle of old linen out of a cupboard, she started cutting it up to make bandages and lint. Anybody seeing her sparkling eyes, her flushed complexion, and her alternation between anxiety and composure, would have been hard put to it to say whether she was more concerned about her brother's wound or delighted at the death of her enemies. At one moment she was pouring out some coffee for the colonel and boasting of her skill at making it; the next, she was distributing tasks to Miss Nevil and Chilina, exhorting them to sew bandages and roll them up. For the twentieth time she would ask whether Orso's wound was causing him much pain; and she kept interrupting what she was doing to say to the colonel:

'Two cunning, dangerous men like that! . . . And him all alone, wounded, with only one good arm. . . . He killed both of them. What courage, eh, Colonel? Isn't he a hero? Ah, Miss Nevil, how wonderful it must be to live in a peaceful country like yours! . . . I am sure that you didn't know what my brother was like till now. . . . I said that the sparrow-hawk would spread his wings! . . . You were deceived by his gentle manner. . . . That's because when he was with you, Miss Nevil. . . . Ah, if he could see you working for him. . . . Poor Orso!'

Miss Lydia was doing scarcely any work and could not find a word to say. Her father kept asking why a complaint had not been lodged straight away with a magistrate. He talked about a coroner's inquest and a great many other things equally unknown in Corsica. Finally he wanted to know if the country house of that worthy Monsieur Brandolaccio, who had given succour to the wounded man, was a long way from Pietranera, and if he could not go there himself to see his friend.

And Colomba replied with her usual calm that Orso was in the *maquis*; that a bandit was looking after him; that it would be extremely risky for him to show himself before he was sure what attitude the prefect and the judges were going to adopt; and finally that she would arrange for a skilled surgeon to go secretly to see him.

'Above all, Colonel,' she said, 'remember that you heard the four shots, and that you told me Orso fired second.'

The colonel was unable to make head or tail of the affair, and his daughter could do nothing but sigh and wipe her eyes.

It was already late in the day when a melancholy procession entered the village. They were bringing the lawyer Barricini the corpses of his sons, each body slung across a mule led by a peasant. A crowd of dependents and idlers followed the sad cortege. With them could be seen the gendarmes, who always come too late, and the deputy mayor, who kept raising his hands to heaven and repeating: 'What will the prefect say?' A few women, among them Orlanduccio's old nurse, were tearing their hair and giving wild screams. But their noisy grief was less impressive than the mute despair of a man on whom all eyes were fixed. This was the unhappy father, who, going from one corpse to the other, lifted their earth-stained heads, kissed their purple lips, and supported their already stiffened limbs, as if to protect them from the jolts of the road. Now and then he was seen to open his mouth to say something, but not a word, not a cry came from his lips. With his eyes constantly fixed on the corpses, he tripped over stones, bumped into trees, and stumbled over every obstacle he encountered.

The wailing of the women and the curses of the men increased when they came in sight of Orso's house. When some of the Rebbianist herdsmen went so far as to raise a shout of triumph, their adversaries' indignation could not be contained. 'Vengeance! Vengeance!' shouted a few voices. Stones were thrown, and two shots fired at the windows of the room in which Colomba was with her guests pierced the shutters and sent splinters of wood flying on to the table at which the two women were sitting. Miss Lydia uttered some terrible screams, the colonel grabbed a gun, and Colomba, before he could stop her, rushed to the door of the house and flung it open. There, standing on the lofty threshold, with both hands outstretched to curse her enemies, she cried:

'Cowards, to fire at women and strangers! Are you Corsicans? Are you men? Wretches who can only kill a man from behind, come nearer if you dare! I am alone; my brother is far away. Kill me, kill my guests; that would be just like you. . . . But you daren't, cowards that you are! You know that we avenge ourselves in this family. Go on, go and weep like women, and be thankful that we don't ask you for more blood!'

There was something impressive and awe-inspiring in Colomba's voice and attitude; at the sight of her, the crowd drew back in terror, as if she had been one of those evil fairies about which so many frightening stories are told during the long winter evenings in Corsica. The deputy mayor, the gendarmes, and a few women seized the opportunity provided by this movement to throw themselves between the two factions; for the Rebbianist herdsmen were already cocking their guns, and for a moment it looked as if a regular battle was going to take place in the square. But the two parties were without their leaders, and Corsicans, who are disciplined in their rages, rarely come to blows in the absence of the principal figures in their internal wars. Besides, Colomba, rendered cautious by success, restrained her little garrison.

'Let the poor wretches weep,' she said. 'Let the old man carry his flesh and blood home. Why kill that old fox now that he has no more teeth to bite with? . . . Giudice Barricini! Remember the second of August! Remember the bloodstained notebook in which you wrote with your forger's hand! My father had entered your debt in that notebook; your sons have paid it. We are all square now, old Barricini!'

With her arms folded and a contemptuous smile playing about her lips, Colomba watched the corpses being carried into her enemies' house and the crowd slowly breaking up. She closed her door and, coming back into the dining-room, said to the colonel:

'I humbly apologize, Monsieur, for my fellow countrymen. I would never have believed that Corsicans would fire on a house which contained strangers, and I feel ashamed of my country.'

That evening, after Miss Lydia had retired to her room, the colonel followed her and asked her whether they ought not to leave the very next day a village in which they were liable to have a bullet in their heads at any moment, and depart as soon as possible from a country where one saw nothing but murder and treachery.

Miss Nevil took some time to answer, and it was obvious that her father's proposal was causing her no little embarrassment. Finally she said:

'How can we leave this poor girl just when she is so badly in need of consolation? Don't you think that would be cruel of us, Father?'

'I was thinking of you, my dear,' said the colonel; 'and I must admit that if I knew that you were safe in the hotel in Ajaccio, I should be sorry to leave this confounded island without shaking hands with that good fellow Della Rebbia.'

'Well, Father, let us wait a little longer, and, before we go, see if we cannot do something to help him.'

'You have a kind heart,' said the colonel, kissing his daughter on the forehead. 'I like to see you sacrificing yourself like that to help other people in their misfortune. Let's stay; nobody ever regrets doing a good deed.'

Miss Lydia tossed about in her bed without managing to get to sleep. Sometimes the vague sounds she could hear struck her as the preparations for an attack on the house; sometimes, reassured as to her own safety, she thought of the poor wounded man, who was probably stretched out at that very moment on the cold ground, with no other help than he could expect from a bandit's charity. She imagined him covered with blood and writhing in terrible pain; and the strange thing was that every time she pictured Orso to herself, he appeared to her as she had seen him when he had set off from Ajaccio, pressing to his lips the talisman she had given him.... Then she thought of his courage. She told herself that, if he had exposed himself to the terrible danger from which he had just escaped, it had been on her account, in order to see her a little sooner. She all but persuaded herself that it had been in her defence that Orso had had his arm broken. She reproached herself for his wound, but she admired him all the more for it; and if the remarkable double hit did not have as much merit in her eyes as in Brandolaccio's and Colomba's, she none the less considered that few heroes of romance would have behaved with such courage and sang-froid in so dangerous a situation.

The room she occupied was Colomba's. Above a sort of oak *prie-Dieu*, and next to a consecrated palm, a miniature portrait of Orso, in the uniform of a second lieutenant, hung on the wall. Miss Nevil took this portrait down, gazed at it for a long time, and finally placed it beside her bed, instead of putting it back in its place.

She did not fall asleep until dawn, and the sun was already high above the horizon when she awoke. At the foot of the bed she saw Colomba, motionless, waiting for her to open her eyes.

'Well, Mademoiselle, you appear to be very uncomfortable in our poor house. I fear that you have scarcely slept at all.'

'Have you any news of him, my dear friend?' asked Miss Nevil, sitting up in bed.

She noticed Orso's portrait, and hastily threw a handkerchief over it to hide it.

COLOMBA

'Yes, I have some news,' said Colomba with a smile.

Then, picking up the portrait, she asked:

'Do you think this is a good likeness? He looks better than that.'

'Heaven!' said Miss Nevil, in considerable embarrassment. 'I took that portrait down ... absentmindedly.... I have a dreadful habit of touching everything ... and never putting things back.... How is your brother?'

'Fairly well. Giocanto came here this morning before four o'clock. He brought me a letter ... for you, Miss Lydia; Orso hasn't written to me. True, the letter is addressed: "To Colomba", but further down he has added: "For Miss N—". But sisters are not jealous. Giocanto says that it cost him a great effort to write. Giocanto, who writes beautifully, offered to write it at his dictation. He refused, and wrote it himself in pencil, lying on his back. Brandolaccio held the paper for him. My brother kept trying to sit up, but the slightest movement would produce an excruciating pain in his arm. Giacanto said it was a pitiful sight. Here is his letter.'

Miss Nevil read the letter, which, doubtless as an additional precaution, was written in English. It read as follows:

Mademoiselle,

An unhappy fate has pursued me. I do not know what my enemies will say nor what calumnies they will invent. It matters little to me provided that you, Mademoiselle, do not believe them. Since I last saw you I had deluded myself with mad dreams. It needed this catastrophe to show me my folly; now I have come to my senses. I know the future that lies before me, and I am resigned to it. This ring which you gave me, and which I believed would bring me good fortune, I dare not keep. I am afraid, Miss Nevil, that you may regret having bestowed your gift so unfortunately, or rather, I am afraid that it might remind me of the time when I was mad. Colomba will return it to you.... Farewell, Mademoiselle. You will leave Corsica, and I shall never see you again; but tell my sister that I still enjoy your esteem, and, I say this confidently, I still deserve it.

O.D.R.

Miss Lydia had turned aside to read this letter, and Colomba, who was watching her closely, handed her the Egyptian ring with an inquiring look which asked what all this meant. But Miss Lydia did not dare to raise her head, and she gazed sadly at the ring, alternately putting it on and taking it off her finger.

'Dear Miss Nevil,' said Colomba, 'may I not know what my brother says to you? Does he mention his condition?'

'Why,' said Miss Lydia, turning red, 'he doesn't say anything about it.... His letter is in English.... He asks me to tell my father.... He hopes that the prefect can arrange....'

With a mischievous smile, Colomba sat down on the bed, took Miss Nevil's hands, and, gazing intently at her, said:

'Will you be kind? You will answer my brother's letter, won't you? That will do him so much good! For a moment I thought of waking you when his letter arrived, but then I didn't dare.'

'You were wrong,' said Miss Nevil. 'If a word from me could....'

'I can't send him any letters now. The prefect has arrived, and Pietranera is full of his henchmen. Later on, we'll see. Oh, if you only knew my brother, Miss Nevil, you would love him as I do.... He's so good, so brave! Just think what he did! One man against two, and wounded at that!'

The prefect had come back. Informed of what had happened by a messenger sent by the deputy mayor, he had arrived with gendarmes and riflemen, together with the public prosecutor, his clerk, and other officials, to investigate the new and terrible catastrophe which had just complicated, or rather put an end to the feud between the two Pietranera families. Shortly after his arrival, he saw Colonel Nevil and his daughter, and he did not conceal from them his fear that the whole affair was going to take a turn for the worse.

'You know,' he said, 'that there were no witnesses of the fight, and the reputation of those two unfortunate young men for skill and courage was so well established that everybody refuses to believe that Monsieur della Rebbia could have killed them without the assistance of the bandits with whom he is said to have taken refuge.'

'That's impossible,' exclaimed the colonel. 'Orso della Rebbia is the soul of honour; I can vouch for him.'

'So I believe,' said the prefect. 'But the public prosecutor (these officials are always suspicious) doesn't seem to me to be very favourably disposed towards him. He has a piece of incriminating evidence against your friend. This is a threatening letter addressed to Orlanduccio, in which he arranged a meeting ... and the public prosecutor believes that this meeting was a trap.'

'That fellow Orlanduccio,' said the colonel, 'refused to fight like a gentleman.'

'That isn't the custom here. In this country they lay ambushes and kill men from behind. Admittedly there is one piece of testimony in his favour: a little girl states that she heard four reports, of which the last two were louder than the first, and came from a large-calibre gun like Monsieur della Rebbia's. Unfortunately this child is the niece of one of the bandits suspected of complicity, and she has probably learnt her piece off by heart.'

'Monsieur,' Miss Lydia broke in, blushing to the roots of her hair, 'we were on the road when those shots were fired, and we heard the same thing.'

'Really? Now that's very important. And I suppose that you noticed the same thing, Colonel?'

'Yes,' Miss Nevil went on hurriedly. 'It was my father, who knows all about firearms, who said: "That's Monsieur della Rebbia shooting with my gun."'

'And are you sure that those shots which you recognized were the last to be fired?'

'The last two, weren't they, Father?'

The colonel did not have a very good memory, but he took care never to contradict his daughter.

'I must report this to the public prosecutor straight away, Colonel. Besides, we are expecting a surgeon to arrive tonight who will examine the corpses and determine whether the wounds were caused by the gun in question.'

'It was I who gave it to Orso,' said the colonel, 'and I wish it were at the bottom of the sea. . . . I mean, I'm glad the good fellow had it with him; for, if it hadn't been for my Manton, I don't know how he would have got out of that situation.'

CHAPTER NINETEEN

THE surgeon arrived rather late. He had had his own little adventure on the road to Pietranera. Waylaid by Giocanto Castriconi, he had been invited with exemplary politeness to come and attend a wounded man. He had been taken to where Orso was hiding and had dressed his wound. Then the bandit had accompanied him some distance on his way, and had greatly edified him by talking about the most famous professors in Pisa, who, so he said, were close friends of his.

'Doctor,' said the theologian as he took leave of him, 'you have inspired me with such a feeling of esteem for you that I consider it unnecessary to remind you that a physician should be as discreet as a confessor.' And he worked the lock of his gun. 'You have forgotten the spot where we had the honour of making each other's acquaintance. Good-bye. Delighted to have met you.'

Colomba begged the colonel to attend the post-mortem examination of the bodies.

'You know my brother's gun better than anybody else,' she said; 'and your testimony will be extremely useful. Besides, there are so many wicked people here that we would be in serious danger if we had nobody to defend our interests.'

Left alone with Miss Lydia, she complained of a terrible headache, and suggested that they should go for a stroll outside the village.

'The fresh air will do me good,' she said. 'I haven't been out for such a long time.'

As they walked along she talked about her brother; and Miss Lydia, who was deeply interested in this subject, failed to notice that she was leaving Pietranera far behind. The sun was setting when she became aware of the fact and urged Colomba to turn back. Colomba said that she knew a short cut; and, leaving the path she was following, she took another which appeared to be much less used. Soon she started climbing a slope so steep that she was continually obliged to hang on to the branches of trees with one hand while she pulled her companion up after her with the other. After a good quarter of an hour of this laborious climb, they found themselves on a small plateau covered with myrtle and arbutus, in the midst of huge granite crags which jutted out of the ground on all sides. Miss Lydia was very tired, there was no sign of the village, and it was almost dark.

'You know, my dear Colomba,' she said, 'I do believe that we are lost.'

'Have no fear,' replied Colomba. 'Let's go on. Follow me.'

'But I'm sure you are going the wrong way; the village can't be in this direction. I could swear that it is behind us. Look there, at those lights we can see in the distance; Pietranera must lie over there.'

'My dear friend,' said Colomba, looking rather agitated, 'you are right; but two hundred paces from here . . . in this *maquis*. . . .'

'Well?'

'My brother is hiding. If you were willing, I could see him and embrace him.'

Miss Nevil gave a start of surprise.

'I left Pietranera without being noticed,' Colomba went on, 'because I was with you . . . otherwise I would have been followed. . . . It would be dreadful to be so close to him and not see him! Why shouldn't you come with me to see my poor brother? It would give him so much pleasure!'

'But, Colomba . . . that wouldn't be at all seemly on my part.'

'I see. You city women always worry about what is

seemly; we village women only think of what is good.'

'But it is so late! . . . And what will your brother think of me?'

'He'll think that he hasn't been forsaken by his friends, and that will give him courage to bear his suffering.'

'And my father will be so worried. . . .'

'He knows that you are with me. . . . Well, make up your mind. . . . You were looking at his portrait this morning,' she added with a mischievous smile.

'No, really . . . Colomba, I daren't. . . . Those bandits who are there. . . .'

'Well, those bandits don't know you, so what does it matter? And you wanted to see some. . . .'

'Good gracious!'

'Come, Mademoiselle, make up your mind. I can't leave you here by yourself; there's no telling what might happen. Let's go to see Orso, or else let's go back to the village together. I shall see my brother . . . heaven knows when . . . never, perhaps.'

'What are you saying, Colomba? . . . All right, let's go! But just for a minute, and we'll go back straight away.'

Colomba squeezed her hand, and without making any reply she started walking so fast that Miss Lydia found it hard to keep up with her. Fortunately Colomba stopped before long and said to her companion:

'Let's not go any farther without giving them some warning; otherwise we might be fired at.'

She then started whistling between her fingers; soon afterwards they heard a dog barking, and it was not long before the bandits' advance sentry appeared on the scene. It was our old acquaintance, Brusco, who promptly recognized Colomba and took it upon himself to act as her guide. After a great many turnings in the narrow paths of the *maquis*, they were met by two men armed to the teeth.

'Is that you, Brandolaccio?' asked Colomba. 'Where is my brother?'

'Over there,' replied the bandit. 'But walk softly: he's asleep, and it's the first time that has happened since his accident. Good God, this shows that where the devil finds a way, a woman does too!'

The two women approached quietly, and, beside a fire whose glow had been prudently concealed by a little stone wall built around it, they saw Orso lying on a pile of bracken and covered with a *pilone*. He was extremely pale and they could hear that he was breathing with difficulty. Colomba sat down beside him and gazed at him in silence with her hands joined, as if she were praying wordlessly. Miss Lydia, hiding her face with her handkerchief, pressed close to her; but now and then she raised her head to look at the wounded man over Colomba's shoulder. A quarter of an hour went by without anybody speaking. At a sign from the theologian, Brandolaccio had disappeared into the *maquis* with him, much to the relief of Miss Lydia, who for the first time in her life felt that there was too much local colour about bandits' weapons and bushy beards.

At last Orso stirred. Immediately Colomba bent over him and kissed him several times, plying him with questions about his wound, his sufferings, and his needs. After replying that he was as well as could be expected, Orso asked her in his turn whether Miss Nevil was still at Pietranera and whether she had written to him. Bending as she was over her brother, Colomba completely hid her companion from sight, and in any case the darkness would have made recognition difficult. She was holding one of Miss Nevil's hands, and with her other hand she raised the wounded man's head slightly.

'No, brother, she gave me no letter for you. . . . But you are always thinking about Miss Lydia. Does that mean you are fond of her?'

'Need you ask, Colomba?... But she ... perhaps she despises me now!'

At that moment, Miss Nevil tried to withdraw her hand; but it was far from easy to loosen Colomba's grip. Small and shapely though it was, her hand possessed a strength of which you have already seen some proof.

'Despise you?' cried Colomba. 'After what you have done?... On the contrary, she has nothing but praise for you.... Oh, Orso, I could tell you so many things about her!'

The hand kept trying to escape, but Colomba drew it even closer to Orso.

'But then,' said the wounded man, 'why didn't she answer my letter?... Just one line would have made me so happy.'

By dint of pulling Miss Nevil's hand, Colomba finally managed to place it in her brother's. Then, moving suddenly to one side, she burst out laughing.

'Orso,' she cried, 'be careful not to speak ill of Miss Lydia, for she understands Corsican very well.'

Miss Lydia promptly drew back her hand and stammered out a few unintelligible words. Orso thought that he was dreaming.

'You here, Miss Nevil! Good Lord, how did you dare? Oh, how happy you have made me!'

And, raising himself with difficulty, he tried to approach her.

'I came with your sister,' said Miss Lydia, 'so that nobody would suspect where she was going.... And besides, I wanted also ... to make sure.... Oh, how uncomfortable you must be here!'

Colomba had sat down behind Orso. She lifted him carefully so that his head rested in her lap. She put her arm round his neck and beckoned to Miss Lydia to come nearer.

'Closer! Closer!' she said. 'A sick man mustn't speak too loudly.' And, when Miss Lydia hesitated, she took her hand and forced her to sit down so close that her dress touched Orso, and her hand, which she kept hold of, rested on the wounded man's shoulder.

'He's comfortable like that,' said Colomba gaily. 'Isn't it pleasant, Orso, camping in the *maquis* on a beautiful night like this?'

'Oh, yes! It's a wonderful night!' said Orso. 'I shall never forget it.'

'How you must be suffering!' said Miss Nevil.

'I am not suffering any more,' said Orso, 'and I should like to die here.'

And his right hand stole towards Miss Lydia's, which Colomba still held prisoner.

'You really must be moved somewhere where you can be properly cared for, Monsieur della Rebbia,' said Miss Nevil. 'I shan't be able to sleep any more now that I have seen you lying so uncomfortably in the open. . . .'

'If I hadn't been afraid of meeting you, Miss Nevil, I would have tried to return to Pietranera and given myself up.'

'And why were you afraid of meeting her, Orso?' asked Colomba.

'I had disobeyed you, Miss Nevil . . . and I wouldn't have dared to see you just then.'

'Do you realize, Miss Lydia, that you can make my brother do anything you wish?' said Colomba with a laugh. 'I'm going to prevent you from seeing him.'

'I hope that this unfortunate affair will soon be cleared up,' said Miss Nevil, 'and that you will have nothing more to fear. . . . I shall be happy if, when we leave, I know that justice has been done and that your loyalty and courage have been recognized.'

'You are leaving, Miss Nevil? Don't say that yet.'

'What would you have us do? . . . My father cannot hunt for ever. . . . He wants to go.'

Orso dropped his hand, which had been touching Miss Lydia's, and there was a moment's silence.

'Nonsense!' said Colomba. 'We won't let you go so soon. There are still a lot of things we have to show you at Pietranera. . . . Besides, you promised to do a portrait of me, and you haven't even begun it yet. . . . And then I promised to compose a *serenata* for you in seventy-five couplets. . . . And then. . . . But what's Brusco growling for? . . . There's Brandolaccio running after him. . . . Let's see what's happening.'

She got up straight away, simply laid Orso's head in Miss Nevil's lap, and ran after the bandits.

Somewhat astonished to find herself supporting a handsome young man, alone with him in the middle of a *maquis*, Miss Nevil did not know quite what to do, for she was afraid that if she drew away suddenly she might hurt the wounded man. But Orso himself abandoned the delightful pillow his sister had just given him, and, raising himself on his right arm, he said:

'So you are going to leave soon, are you, Miss Lydia? I never imagined that you would stay for long in this wretched country . . . and yet . . . now that you have come here it hurts me a hundred times more to think that I must bid you good-bye. . . . I am a poor lieutenant . . . with no future . . . and now an outlaw. . . . What a time, Miss Lydia, to tell you that I love you . . . but this is probably the only time I shall be able to tell you, and it seems to me that I feel less unhappy now that I have unburdened my heart.'

Miss Lydia turned her head away, as if the darkness were not enough to hide her blushes.

'Monsieur della Rebbia,' she said in a trembling voice, 'would I have come here if. . . .' And as she spoke she slipped the Egyptian talisman into Orso's hand. Then, making a determined effort to regain her usual bantering tone, she went on:

'It's most unfair of you, Monsieur Orso, to say such things.... Here in the middle of the *maquis*, surrounded by your bandits, you know perfectly well that I would never dare to be cross with you.'

Orso bent forward to kiss the hand which was giving back the talisman; and as Miss Lydia drew it back rather quickly, he lost his balance and fell on his wounded arm. He could not restrain a groan of pain.

'Have you hurt yourself?' she cried, lifting him up. 'It's my fault! Forgive me....'

They went on talking for some time in low voices, very close together. Colomba, running up to them, found them in exactly the same position in which she had left them.

'The riflemen!' she cried. 'Orso, try to get up and walk! I'll help you.'

'Leave me,' said Orso. 'Tell the bandits to run for it.... If they capture me, I don't care, but take Miss Lydia away. For God's sake don't let them see her here.'

'I won't leave you,' said Brandolaccio, who had come after Colomba. 'The sergeant of the riflemen is a godson of the lawyer's; instead of arresting you, he'll kill you, and then he'll say it was an accident.'

Orso tried to get up, and even took a few steps; but then he suddenly stopped.

'I can't walk,' he said. 'Flee, all of you. Farewell, Miss Nevil. Give me your hand, and then farewell!'

'We won't leave you!' cried the two women.

'If you can't walk,' said Brandolaccio, 'I'll have to carry you. Come now, Lieutenant, show a little courage. We'll have time to get away by the ravine, there behind you. The Curé will keep them busy in the meantime.'

'No, leave me,' said Orso, lying down on the ground. 'For God's sake, Colomba, take Miss Nevil away!'

'You are strong, Mademoiselle Colomba,' said Brandolaccio. 'Take him by the shoulders and I'll hold his feet. Good! Now, forward, march!'

They started carrying him along quickly, in spite of his protests. Miss Lydia was following them, terribly frightened, when a shot was heard, which was promptly answered by five or six others. Miss Lydia screamed and Brandolaccio cursed, but he quickened his pace, and Colomba, followed his example, ran on across the *maquis*, paying no attention to the branches lashing her face and tearing her dress.

'Bend down! Bend down, my dear!' she said to her companion. 'Or you'll be hit by a bullet.'

They had walked or rather run about five hundred yards like this when Brandolaccio declared that he could go no farther, and he dropped on to the ground, in spite of Colomba's entreaties and reproaches.

'Where is Miss Nevil?' asked Orso.

Frightened by the shots, and continually impeded by the density of the undergrowth, Miss Nevil had soon lost all trace of the fugitives and had been left all alone in a state of utter terror.

'She has stayed behind,' said Brandolaccio; 'but she isn't lost, for women always find their way. Just listen, Ors' Anton', to the din the Curé is making with your gun. Unfortunately it's pitch dark, and you can't do much damage with a gun in the dark.'

'Hush!' cried Colomba. 'I can hear a horse. We're saved!'

Sure enough, frightened by the shooting, a horse which had been grazing in the *maquis* was coming towards them.

'We're saved!' repeated Brandolaccio.

In no time at all, with Colomba's help, the bandit had run up to the horse, seized him by the mane, and slipped a knotted rope through his mouth to act as a bridle.

'Now let's warn the Curé,' he said.

He whistled twice; a distant whistle answered this signal,

and the loud voice of the Manton fell silent. Then Brandolaccio leapt on to the horse. Colomba hoisted her brother up in front of the bandit, who held him tight with one hand while he guided his mount with the other. In spite of his double load, the horse, encouraged by two hearty kicks in the belly, started off briskly and galloped down a steep slope on which any but a Corsican horse would have broken his neck.

Colomba then retraced her steps, calling to Miss Nevil at the top of her voice, but nobody answered her. After walking about at random for some time, trying to find the path she had taken earlier, she came upon two riflemen who shouted: 'Who goes there?'

'Well, gentlemen,' said Colomba mockingly, 'what a noise! How many dead?'

'You were with the bandits,' said one of the soldiers. 'You're coming with us.'

'With pleasure!' she replied. 'But there's a friend of mine somewhere around, and we have to find her first.'

'Your friend has already been caught, and the two of you are going to spend the night in prison.'

'In prison? We'll see about that! But, in the meantime, take me to her.'

The riflemen then took her to the bandit's camp, where they had gathered together the spoils of their raid, namely the blankets which had covered Orso, an old cooking-pot, and a pitcher of water. Miss Nevil was there too; found, half dead with fear, by the soldiers, she was replying with nothing but tears to all their questions about the number of bandits and the direction in which they had gone.

Colomba threw herself into her arms and whispered in her ear: 'They are safe.'

Then, turning to the sergeant, she said:

'Monsieur, you can see that Mademoiselle knows nothing about what you are asking her. Allow us to go back to the village, where we are impatiently awaited.'

COLOMBA

'You'll be taken there, and sooner than you want, my pet,' said the sergeant; 'and you'll have to explain what you were doing in the *maquis* at this time of night with the brigands who have just made their escape. I don't know what spells those scoundrels use, but they must cast a spell over women, because wherever there are bandits, you're sure to find some pretty girls.'

'You are very flattering, Sergeant,' said Colomba; 'but you would be well advised to watch your tongue. This young lady is a relative of the prefect's, and you had better not trifle with her.'

'A relative of the prefect's!' one of the riflemen whispered to his leader. 'It's true she's wearing a bonnet.'

'A bonnet means nothing,' said the sergeant. 'They were both with the Curé, the smoothest-tongued rascal in the country, and my duty is to run them in. Besides, there's nothing more for us to do here. If it hadn't been for that confounded Corporal Taupin – that drunken Frenchman turned up before I could surround the *maquis* – we'd have caught them like fish in a net.'

'Are there only seven of you?' asked Colomba. 'You know, gentlemen, if by any chance the three Poli brothers – Gambini, Sarocchi, and Teodoro – were at the Cross of St Christine with Brandolaccio and the Curé, they could give you a lot of trouble. If you must have a conversation with the Commandante della Campagna,* I'd rather not be there. Bullets are no respecters of persons at night.'

The possibility of running into the redoubtable bandits whom Colomba had just mentioned seemed to have its effect on the riflemen. Still cursing Corporal Taupin, 'that dog of a Frenchman', the sergeant gave orders for a retreat, and his little band set off for Pietranera, taking the blanket and the cooking-pot with them. As for the pitcher, it was disposed of with a kick. One of the riflemen tried to take

* This was the title Teodoro Poli assumed. (P.M.)

Miss Lydia by the arm; but Colomba promptly pushed him away.

'Don't anybody touch her!' she said. 'Do you think we want to run away? Come, now, Lydia, my dear, lean on me and stop crying like a baby. We're having an adventure, but it will all turn out all right; half an hour from now we shall be having supper. For my part, I can hardly wait.'

'What will people think of me?' whispered Miss Nevil.

'They'll think you lost your way in the *maquis*, that's all.'

'What will the prefect say? .... Above all, what will my father say?'

'The prefect? You can tell him to mind his own business. Your father? Judging by the way you were talking to Orso, I should have thought you had something to say to your father.'

Miss Nevil squeezed her arm, but made no reply.

'Doesn't my brother deserve to be loved?' Colomba whispered in her ear. 'Don't you love him a little?'

'Oh, Colomba,' replied Miss Nevil, smiling in spite of her embarrassment, 'you've betrayed me. And I trusted you so!'

Colomba slipped an arm round her waist and kissed her on the forehead.

'Little sister,' she said in a very low voice, 'will you forgive me?'

'I shall have to, my terrible sister,' replied Lydia, returning her kiss.

The prefect and the public prosecutor were staying with the deputy mayor of Pietranera. The colonel, who was very worried about his daughter, had come for the twentieth time to ask them if there was any news when a rifleman sent on ahead by the sergeant arrived and told them of the terrible fight with the bandits which had taken place – a fight in which, admittedly, nobody had been killed or wounded, but which had resulted in the capture of a cooking pot, a blanket, and two girls who, he said, were the bandits' mistresses or spies. Thus announced, the two prisoners appeared in the midst of their armed escort. You can imagine Colomba's radiant expression, the prefect's surprise, the colonel's joy and astonishment. The public prosecutor permitted himself the mischievous pleasure of submitting poor Lydia to a sort of interrogation which did not end until he had put her completely out of countenance.

'It seems to me,' said the prefect, 'that we can set everybody free. These young ladies went for a walk: nothing could be more natural in fine weather. They happened to meet a charming young man, who was wounded: again, nothing could be more natural.'

Then, taking Colomba aside, he said to her:

'Mademoiselle, you can send word to your brother that his case is turning out better than I had expected. The post-mortem examination and the colonel's testimony show that all he did was defend himself and that he was alone when the fight took place. Everything will work out all right, but he must leave the *maquis* as soon as possible and give himself up.'

It was almost eleven o'clock when the colonel, his daughter, and Colomba sat down to a supper which had gone cold. Colomba ate heartily, poking fun at the prefect, the public prosecutor, and the riflemen. The colonel ate too, but said nothing. He kept looking at his daughter, who never raised her eyes from her plate. At last, in a gentle but serious voice, he said to her in English:

'Lydia, are you engaged to Della Rebbia?'

'Yes, Father, as from today,' she replied, blushing but speaking without hesitation.

Then she looked up, and, seeing no sign of anger in her father's face, she threw herself into his arms and kissed him, as all well-bred young ladies do on such occasions.

'All right,' said the colonel. 'He's a good fellow, but by God, we aren't staying in this confounded country of his, or else I'll refuse my consent.'

'I don't know any English,' said Colomba, who was watching them with considerable curiosity; 'but I'm willing to bet that I can guess what you have been saying.'

'We were saying,' said the colonel, 'that we are going to take you for a trip to Ireland.'

'Oh, I should like that. And I shall be the *surella* Colomba. Is it settled, Colonel? Shall we shake hands on it?'

'On these occasions,' said the colonel, 'the correct thing is to kiss.'

CHAPTER TWENTY

A FEW months after the double killing which, as the newspapers put it, 'plunged the village of Pietranera into consternation', a young man with his left arm in a sling rode out of Bastia one afternoon in the direction of the village of Cardo, a place famous for its spring, which in summer provides the delicate inhabitants of the town with delicious water. A tall young lady of exceptional beauty accompanied him, riding on a small black horse whose strength and elegance any connoisseur would have admired, but which had unfortunately had one of his ears lacerated in some strange accident. When they reached the village, the young woman leapt nimbly to the ground, and, after helping her companion to dismount, she unstrapped some fairly heavy bags fastened to his saddlebow. The horses were left in the charge of a peasant, and the couple set off towards the mountains, taking a steep path which did not seem to lead to any dwelling, the girl carrying the bags concealed under her *mezzaro*, and the young man a double-barrelled gun. When they had reached one of the higher ledges of Mount Quercio, they stopped, and the two of them sat down on the grass. They seemed to be waiting for somebody, for they kept looking towards the mountain, and the young woman frequently consulted a pretty gold watch, possibly as much to admire a trinket which she did not appear to have had for very long as to find out whether the time fixed for a rendezvous had arrived. They did not have long to wait. A dog emerged from the *maquis*, and when the young woman called out: 'Brusco!' he ran up to them to lick their hands. Soon afterwards two bearded men appeared with guns under their arms, cartridge-pouches hanging from their belts, and pistols at their sides. Their torn and patched clothes contrasted with their gleaming weapons, which were of a famous continental make. In spite of the apparent inequality of their positions, the four actors in this scene greeted one another familiarly like old friends.

'Well, Ors' Anton',' said the older of the two bandits to the young man, 'so it's all over. No ground for prosecution. My congratulations. I'm only sorry that the lawyer has left the island, because I'd have liked to see him fume. And how's your arm?'

'They tell me I'll be able to get rid of my sling in another fortnight,' replied the young man. 'Brando, old fellow, I'm leaving for Italy tomorrow, and I wanted to say good-bye to you and the Curé. That's why I asked you to come here.'

'You're in rather a hurry, aren't you?' said Brandolaccio. 'You were acquitted only yesterday and you're off tomorrow?'

'We have some business to attend to,' said the young woman gaily. 'Gentlemen, I have brought you some supper: eat up, and don't forget my friend Brusco.'

'You spoil Brusco, Mademoiselle Colomba, but he's very grateful. You'll see. Come on, Brusco,' he said, holding out his gun horizontally, 'jump for the Barricinis.'

The dog remained motionless, licking his chops and looking at his master.

'Jump for the Della Rebbias!'

And he jumped two feet higher than was necessary.

'Listen, my good friends,' said Orso, 'you're in an ugly trade; and even if you don't end your careers in that square we can see down there,* the best you can look forward to is to die by some gendarme's bullet in the *maquis*.'

'Well,' said Castriconi, 'it's as good a death as any other, and it's better than dying in bed of a fever, with your heirs standing round you weeping more or less sincerely. When

* The square in Bastia where executions take place. (P.M.)

you're used to the open air, like us, there's nothing like "dying with your boots on", as our villagers put it.'

'I should like to see you leave this country,' Orso went on, 'and lead a more peaceful life. Why, for instance, shouldn't you go to Sardinia and settle down there, as several of your comrades have done? I could arrange it all for you.'

'To Sardinia?' exclaimed Brandolaccio. '*Istos Sardos!* The devil take them and their lingo! They're not fit company for us.'

'There's no scope for us in Sardinia,' added the theologian. 'Speaking for myself, I despise the Sardinians. They use mounted militiamen to hunt their bandits: that says all there is to say about both the bandits and the country.* To hell with Sardinia. What surprises me, Monsieur della Rebbia, is that you, a man of taste and learning, should not have adopted our life in the *maquis* after seeing at first hand what it was like.'

'But,' said Orso with a smile, 'when I had the good fortune to be your companion, I wasn't really in a condition to appreciate the charms of your situation, and my ribs still ache when I remember the ride I had one fine night, slung like a bundle over a saddleless horse led by my friend Brandolaccio.'

'And the pleasure of escaping from your pursuers,' Castriconi went on, 'doesn't that count for anything with you? How can you remain insensible to the delights of absolute freedom in such a beautiful climate as ours? With this persuader,' (he held up his gun), 'we are kings everywhere, as far as it can shoot. We give orders, we redress

---

* I am indebted for this criticism of Sardinia to a friend of mine who is a former bandit, and he alone must bear the responsibility for it. He means that bandits who allow themselves to be caught by cavalrymen are idiots, and that militiamen who look for bandits on horseback have very little chance of finding any. (P.M.)

wrongs. . . . That's a highly moral and extremely pleasant pastime, Monsieur, and one which we don't deny ourselves. What life could be finer than that of a knight errant, when he has better weapons and more common sense than Don Quixote? Listen, the other day I learned that little Lilla Luigi's uncle, old miser that he is, didn't want to give her a dowry. I wrote to him, without any threats – that isn't my way – and believe it or not, he saw my point of view at once. He married off his niece, and I had made two people happy. Take my word for it, Monsieur Orso, there's nothing like a bandit's life. Bah, perhaps you'd become one of us it it weren't for a certain English lady of whom I've caught only a glimpse but about whom everybody in Bastia speaks admiringly.'

'My future sister-in-law doesn't like the *maquis*,' said Colomba with a laugh. 'She had too much of a fright here.'

'Well,' said Orso, 'are you going to stay here? So be it. Tell me if I can do anything for you.'

'Nothing,' said Brandolaccio, 'except remember us a little. You have already done so much for us. There's Chilina who has a dowry, and who can now find a good match without my friend the Curé having to write any of his letters without any threats. We know that your tenant farmer will give us bread and powder whenever we need them. So, good-bye. I hope we shall see you again in Corsica one of these days.'

'In times of pressing need,' said Orso, 'a few pieces of gold don't come amiss. Now that we are old acquaintances, you won't refuse this little *cartouche* which can help you to obtain cartridges of a different kind.'

'No money between us, Lieutenant,' Brandolaccio said firmly.

'Money can buy anything in the world,' said Castriconi; 'but in the *maquis* all that matters is a stout heart and a gun that doesn't misfire.'

'I wouldn't like to leave you,' Orso went on, 'without giving you something to remember me by. Come, Brando, what can I leave you?'

The bandit scratched his head and cast a sidelong glance at Orso's gun.

'Dammit, Lieutenant ... if I dared ... but no, you're too fond of it.'

'What do you want?'

'Nothing. ... The thing itself is nothing. ... What matters is the way you handle it. I keep thinking about that splendid double hit of yours – and with one hand too. ... Oh, a thing like that couldn't happen twice!'

'Is it this gun you want? I had brought it along for you; but don't use it more than you have to.'

'Oh, I won't promise that I'll use it as well as you did. But have no fear: when another man has it, you will know that Brando Savelli has gone to his last resting-place.'

'And you, Castriconi, what can I give you?'

'Since you insist on leaving me some tangible souvenir, I'll ask you straight out to send me the smallest edition of Horace you can find. That will keep me amused and prevent me from forgetting my Latin. There's a little girl who sells cigars by the harbour in Bastia. Give it to her, and she'll see that I get it.'

'You shall have an Elzevir, my learned friend; it so happens that I have one among the books I was going to take with me. ... Well, my friends, the time has come for us to part. Give me your hands. If you ever change your minds about Sardinia, write to me; the lawyer N—— will give you my address on the Continent.'

'Lieutenant,' said Brando, 'tomorrow when you've left the harbour, look up at this spot on the mountains. We shall be here, and we'll wave to you with our neckerchiefs.'

Then they parted, Orso and his sister taking the road to Cardo, and the bandits heading up the mountain.

CHAPTER TWENTY-ONE

ONE fine April morning, Sir Thomas Nevil, his daughter and Orso, who had been married only a few days before, and Colomba drove out from Pisa to visit a recently discovered Etruscan hypogeum which all the foreigners were going to see. Orso and his wife went down into the monument, took out their pencils, and set about drawing the wall-paintings; but the colonel and Colomba, neither of whom was particularly interested in archaeology, left them to themselves and went for a stroll in the vicinity.

'My dear Colomba,' said the colonel, 'we shall never get back to Pisa in time for our luncheon. Aren't you hungry? Now Orso and his wife are in the midst of their antiquities, and once they start sketching together, they never stop.'

'Yes,' said Colomba, 'and yet they never bring home so much as a single drawing.'

'In my opinion,' the colonel went on, 'we ought to go to that little farm over there. We shall find some bread there, and perhaps some *aleatico* – who knows? – or even some strawberries and cream. We can wait there patiently for our artists.'

'You are right, Colonel. You and I, who are the sensible members of the family, would be foolish to make martyrs of ourselves for those lovers, who live on nothing but poetry. Give me your arm. Don't you think I am making progress? I take a gentleman's arm; I wear hats and fashionable dresses; I have jewels to put on; and I'm learning all manner of wonderful things. In short, I'm not a little savage any more. Just look how gracefully I wear this shawl. ... That fair-haired young officer from your regiment who came to the wedding – good heavens, I can't remember his name – a tall, curly-headed fellow whom I could knock down with one blow. . . .'

'Chatsworth?' said the colonel.

'That's right . . . though I shall never be able to pronounce his name. Well, he's madly in love with me.'

'Oh, Colomba, you are becoming a dreadful coquette. We shall be having another wedding before long.'

'What, me marry? And then who would bring up my nephew – when Orso gives me one? Who would teach him to speak Corsican? Yes, he shall speak Corsican, and I shall make him a pointed cap just to annoy you.'

'Let's wait first until you have a nephew, and then you can teach him how to use a stiletto if you think fit.'

'No, good-bye to stilettos,' said Colomba gaily. 'I have a fan now, to rap you on the knuckles when you speak ill of my country.'

Chatting thus, they went into the farm, where they found wine, strawberries, and cream. Colomba helped the farmer's wife to pick some strawberries while the colonel drank his *aleatico*. At a bend in a path Colomba noticed an old man sitting in the sun on a straw-bottomed chair. He looked ill, for his cheeks were hollow and his eyes sunken; he was extremely thin, and his stillness, his pallor, and his fixed gaze made him look more like a corpse than a living creature. For several minutes Colomba gazed at him with such curiosity that she attracted the attention of the farmer's wife.

'That poor old man,' she said, 'is a fellow-countryman of yours, for I can tell from the way you talk that you come from Corsica, Mademoiselle. He suffered a dreadful misfortune over there; his children died a terrible death. They do say – begging your pardon, Mademoiselle – that your fellow-countrymen don't show one another much mercy when they have a feud. Well, this poor gentleman, left all alone, came over to Pisa to stay with a distant relative, the lady who owns this farm. The poor fellow is a bit cracked, on account of his grief and unhappiness. It was rather awkward for the lady, who entertains a great deal; so she sent him here. He's very quiet and no trouble at all; he doesn't say three words a day. The doctor comes every week, and he says he hasn't very long to live.'

'Ah, so there's no hope for him?' said Colomba. 'In his case, death will be a release.'

'You ought to speak a little Corsican to him, Mademoiselle. It might cheer him up to hear his own language.'

'We must see if it does,' said Colomba with an ironic smile.

And she walked towards the old man until her shadow took the sunshine away from him. Then the poor idiot raised his head and stared at Colomba, who stared back at him, smiling all the time. After a moment the old man passed his hand over his forehead and shut his eyes, as if to avoid Colomba's gaze. Then he opened them again, but this time with a look of horror; his lips started trembling; he wanted to stretch out his hands, but, hypnotized by Colomba, he remained glued to his chair, incapable of speaking or of moving a muscle. At last great tears rolled down his cheeks and a few sobs escaped his lips.

'This is the first time I've seen him like this,' said the farmer's wife. 'This young lady is from your country,' she told the old man, 'and she has come to see you.'

'Mercy!' he cried in a hoarse voice. 'Mercy! Aren't you satisfied? That page ... which I burned ... how did you manage to read it? ... But why both of them? ... You can't have read anything about Orlanduccio. ... You should have left me one of them ... just one ... Orlanduccio. ... You didn't read his name. ...'

'I had to have them both,' whispered Colomba, speaking in the Corsican dialect. 'The branches have been cut off; and if the stump had not been rotten, I would have torn it out of the ground. Come, now, don't complain; you haven't long to suffer. I suffered for two years!'

The old man uttered a cry, and his head dropped on to his chest. Colomba turned her back on him and walked slowly back towards the house, singing in a low voice a few incomprehensible words from a *ballata*:

'I must have the hand that fired, the eye that aimed, the heart that thought. . . .'

While the farmer's wife was trying to revive the old man, Colomba, her eyes blazing and her face flushed, sat down at table opposite the colonel.

'What's the matter with you?' he asked. 'You look exactly as you did at Pietranera, that day they fired at us while we were having dinner.'

'It's some memories of Corsica which came back to me. But it's all over now. I shall be the boy's godmother, shan't I? Oh, what beautiful names I shall give him! Ghilfuccio-Tomaso-Orso-Leone!'

Just then the farmer's wife came back into the house.

'Well,' said Colomba with perfect composure, 'is he dead or did he just faint?'

'It was nothing, Mademoiselle; but it's strange what an effect you had on him.'

'And the doctor says he hasn't long to live?'

'Less than two months, perhaps.'

'He won't be any great loss,' observed Colomba.

'Who the devil are you talking about?' asked the colonel.

'A senile creature from my country who is boarding here,' said Colomba with a casual air. 'I shall send for news of him from time to time. Why, Colonel Nevil, do leave a few strawberries for my brother and Lydia!'

When Colomba left the farmhouse to get into the carriage, the farmer's wife gazed after her for a little while.

'You see that pretty lady?' she said to her daughter. 'Well, I'm sure she has the evil eye.'

1840

MORE ABOUT PENGUINS

If you have enjoyed reading this book you may wish to know that *Penguin Book News* appears every month. It is an attractively illustrated magazine containing a complete list of books published by Penguins and still in print, together with details of the month's new books. A specimen copy will be sent free on request.

Penguin Book News is obtainable from most bookshops; but you may prefer to become a regular subscriber at 3s. for twelve issues. Just write to Dept EP, Penguin Books Ltd, Harmondsworth, Middlesex, enclosing a cheque or postal order, and you will be put on the mailing list.

Some other books published by Penguins are described on the following pages.

Note: *Penguin Book News* is not
available in the U.S.A.

A SHORT HISTORY OF FRENCH LITERATURE

Geoffrey Brereton

This compact history deals in outline with the whole of French literature, from the *chansons de geste* to the theatre today. Over eight hundred years of rich and varied writing are treated on a scale which makes clear the great general movements of thought and taste without neglecting the characteristic qualities of individual authors and their works. These are approached primarily as literature, to be read as the personal expressions of particularly interesting minds but they are related to the social history of their time and on occasion to the literatures of countries other than France.

'Likely to remain the standard manual in English for many years to come' – *Spectator*

THE PENGUIN CLASSICS

The Most Recent Volumes

MAUPASSANT
A Woman's Life   *H. N. P. Sloman*

CLASSICAL LITERARY CRITICISM
T. S. Dorsch

PLAUTUS
The Pot of Gold and Other Plays   *E. F. Watling*

TERENCE
The Brothers and Other Plays   *Betty Radice*

PLUTARCH
Makers of Rome   *Ian Scott-Kilvert*

POEMS OF THE LATE T'ANG
A. C. Graham

PETRONIUS
The Satyricon and Fragments   *J. P. Sullivan*

THE UPANISHADS
Juan Mascaró

PLATO
Timaeus   *H. D. P. Lee*

MORE
Utopia   *Paul Turner*